Death and the

Phillip Strang

Copyright Page

ISBN: 9781973510598

Dedication

For Elli and Tais who both had the perseverance to make me sit down and write.

Chapter 1

Someone had once told Detective Inspector Keith Tremayne that some people were lucky and some weren't. Tremayne knew only one thing: the man lying dead in a pool of blood had qualified on the lucky after winning sixty-eight million pounds on a lottery ticket, but now his luck had run out.

Tremayne knew the victim, Alan Winters; even knew his family.

The man with all his new wealth had not hidden behind closed doors, fending off the scrounging relatives, the newly-found friends. That wasn't Winters' style. He had been out and about, driving expensive cars, living well.

It had been big news at the time in Salisbury, a small city to the south-west of London with its imposing cathedral, the spire at four hundred and four feet the highest in the United Kingdom. Tremayne remembered the day Winters had won his prize: the front page of the local newspaper, interviewed on the radio and the television. He recalled the next week when Winters, drunk after treating all of the patrons of his local pub to copious rounds of drink, wrapped a Ferrari that he had purchased the previous day around a lamppost. The car had been written off, yet the alcohol-sodden multi-millionaire had staggered away with no more than a scratch. He had lost his driving licence as a result of the escapade, not that it stopped him from driving, often with a chauffeur, one of his numerous relatives.

Tremayne knew how many relatives he had, no more than could be counted on one hand, but Winters had hundreds. He was going through the money at a rapid rate, but still had plenty to go, and the man, not the most attractive in that he was in his forties, balding and overweight, had plenty of friends as well, plenty of female companions.

And now he was dead. Tremayne knew the questions would start to roll. And why was he lying on the Altar Stone at Stonehenge, naked, with his throat cut? Clare Yarwood had seen the body as well, turned away initially at the sight of it, but had taken a deep breath and stood alongside Tremayne. 'Nasty one, guv,' she said.

Time had moved on since Harry Holchester, her fiancé, had died the night he had saved her from the pagan worshippers in Cuthbert's Wood, not more than five miles from where they were now standing.

'It can't be the Druids,' Tremayne said. 'They're into communing with nature, smelling the flowers and whatever.'

Clare Yarwood knew that her DI would, as usual, affect ignorance, yet she knew the man well enough. They had been working together almost two years; she, the young officer in her late twenties, he, the curmudgeon going on sixty. Apart from the few months that she had been on compassionate leave after the death of her fiancé, she had stayed in the Homicide department at Bemerton Road Police Station in Salisbury.

Tremayne knew that the national media would soon be on the scene and the gossip mill would be working overtime in Salisbury and the surrounding area: local boy makes good, comes to a sticky end. Not that Tremayne was surprised about the man's demise, having seen his behaviour in the time since he had been feted locally and nationally as the man who had beaten the odds. How he had been struggling to make ends meet, how his mother, ailing and infirm, was going to have that long-overdue holiday in Europe, and so on.

Tremayne had heard it all before, read about it enough times, and he knew the problem with Alan Winters' life before he had bought that one ticket in a newsagent on the way home from the pub of a Saturday lunchtime. The man, a labourer for Salisbury City Council, was bone idle, did nothing much as far as Tremayne could see except for getting drunk once too often.

And as for Winters' mother, ailing and infirm, Tremayne knew her story well enough. The Winters, Tremayne knew, were not battlers, struggling to make ends meet; they were the flotsam of society who drifted along from one disaster to another, one fractious relationship to the next. The ailing and infirm mother had seven children, including the lucky man. Two were in prison, one was selling herself around the area, another was married and living in Southampton, and as for the other children, Tremayne knew their stories as well.

At Stonehenge on a cold morning, the wind rattling across Salisbury Plain, he realised that it was not going to be a straightforward murder investigation. There was a story here, he could see that, as could his sergeant, Clare Yarwood.

Tremayne knew that he could not bring himself to call her Clare; it was always Yarwood, although he had relented when he had gone with her to Avon Hill to visit the grave of her fiancé, who had been publican of his favourite pub. She had proved herself to be resilient on her return to Salisbury after compassionate leave, even attempting to enter the dating scene again: disastrous, according to her. All they wanted was a few drinks, a decent meal, and then back to the man's place. These were facts that Tremayne did not want to hear, but for whatever reason, he had become the one person that she could open up with.

Tremayne remembered the visit to Harry's grave, the almost pleasant look of the village as they passed through it. After the paganists had been dealt with, the church authorities had been quick to re-consecrate the old church and had soon installed a new vicar. He had hovered around the two of them in the graveyard until Tremayne had taken him to one side to allow his sergeant time to reflect over the man who was buried there.

'I shouldn't have come,' Clare had said.

Tremayne had understood and had put his arm around her. He had watched her standing next to the grave, cleaning the weeds growing around the edge, touching the headstone, even seeing her name as the beloved – she had to thank Harry's relatives in Salisbury for that. Clare knew that if he had lived, he would not have been free. The evidence against him was overwhelming, and he had been party to multiple murders, including the deaths of two police officers, who had attempted to leave Avon Hill that night to bring help.

Tremayne remembered the only words she had spoken when they had driven back to Salisbury: 'Now's my time to get on with my life,' she had said.

Not that he believed her. He knew that she was an emotional woman, and it would be a long time before she detached from Harry, a long time before she was emotionally stable. One thing he knew above all else: he'd always be there for her.

For once, Stonehenge was closed to the general public, not that the visitors were allowed to get too close anymore, and the tourist couches were lined up in the park across the road. Tremayne realised that if they enclosed the crime scene, the tourists would have something else to send home on their smartphones – an actual murder at the ancient moment. And Stonehenge had never been a place of death, although even after thousands of years the history of the site, the people who had built it, what they had worshipped, even its significance, were still hotly debated by academics, and the archaeologists were conducting another dig not more than three hundred yards away.

Jim Hughes, the crime scene examiner, and his team were at the scene, busy as usual, impervious to the dead body, conducting their investigation. 'His throat's been slit,' he said.

'Stating the obvious,' Tremayne replied.

'Is this a sacrificial slaying?'

'I hope not. Did you know the man?'

'I've seen him around the city, showing off, flashing his money. I was not impressed by what I saw.'

'I knew him even before he won all that money. If there was anyone less deserving, it was Alan Winters. I can't say I liked him. Some of the villains, ne'er do wells, and the plain useless can be charming, but he wasn't.'

'It didn't stop him having plenty of friends.'

'That wouldn't have lasted long the way he was burning money. He would have been back in a council house before long, pleading for a handout.'

'Instead of that place he bought.'

'Instead of that. It hasn't pleased the police too much. Every weekend the parties, the drunkenness, the abuse of the neighbours if they dare to complain.'

'Any ideas as to who might have killed him?' Hughes asked as he continued with his investigation, oblivious of the tourists in the distance.

'There's no shortage of suspects this time.'

'Relatives?'

'More than you and I ever had, but that's not surprising the way the Winters spread their seed around the area.'

'And Winters didn't care that some were bleeding him.'

'With over sixty million pounds, what do you think?'

'I'd certainly care,' Hughes said. 'Mind you, I'd not agree with any publicity.'

'That's because you've had money, know how to handle yourself. Alan Winters never had any, just enough to get drunk and cause trouble. I'm surprised he lasted long enough to be murdered.'

'Regardless, he was, but what's the significance? I'd say there were at least two people up here, possibly three.'

'That many?'

'Whoever brought him up here, even if he were unconscious, would have had to carry or drag him. We'll try to be more specific, but two to three people.'

'Any chance of fingerprints?'

'We'll try, but don't hold out too much hope. The murderers, are they likely to have a criminal record?'

'Judging by the company the man kept, a few suspects would. We'll work our way through his known associates. It may take some time. It'll keep Yarwood busy. She's been taking it easy lately, decorating her cottage, wanting to decorate my house as well.'

'I've given up on yours,' Clare said.

***

On Tremayne and Clare's return to Bemerton Road Police Station, the welcoming presence of Detective Superintendent Moulton, the last man that Tremayne wanted to see. They had been at a freezing murder site, and now the one man who never gave up on trying to retire the detective inspector was in his office.

'What's the situation?' Moulton asked. Tremayne knew it was the opening salvo leading up to the inevitable.

'Alan Winters, forty-eight, a council worker, or he was until he won the lottery.'

'The fancy cars, the raucous parties?'

'That's the one. He's been murdered up at Stonehenge, spread-eagled across the Altar Stone, his throat cut.'

'Is there a religious significance?'

'Not that we know, and besides, although the Altar Stone is the name given to it, there's no history that it was ever used for any religious purpose, pagan or Christian.'

Tremayne could see the superintendent was lingering, waiting for an opportunity to offer a comment. He did not intend to give him a chance. 'If you've got no more questions, Yarwood and myself have got a busy day ahead.'

'Are you sure you're up to it?' Moulton asked.

'I've still a few more years in me if that's what you mean,' Tremayne said with a brusqueness verging on insubordination. He'd already received a rap over the knuckles for talking disrespectfully to his senior. 'Apologies, sir, but this case has legs, and plenty wanted the man alive, not so many who would want him dead.' Tremayne hoped his last sentence had defused the tension that was building between the two men, and if it hadn't, then the man could go to hell. He had a murder to deal with, and even after so many years, so many deaths, the freshness of a new one always excited him.

'Don't be reluctant to take on help. You and Yarwood make a good team, but this man had a lot of acquaintances. It may take you some time to get around to them all.'

'I may be on this case until my retirement, is that it?'

'I hope not. Tremayne, you're a fine detective, but I've got a job to do, you know that.'

'So have I, sir.'

'You're a hard man, Tremayne, I'll grant you that.'

'You know what happens with one murder.'

'At least with yours.'

'The man died for a reason. He was likely to kill himself within the next year with his drunken driving, not to mention his alcoholism, the greasy food that he consumed, and the women he went around with.'

'Okay, I relent. I'm off, but don't take too long with this case. A prompt conviction always looks good.'

'The man never gives up,' Tremayne said to Clare after Moulton had left.

'You two were almost friendly there.'

'Never,' Tremayne said, not wanting to be seen as anything other than difficult to deal with.

'Regardless of your new-found friend,' Clare said, aiming to rustle Tremayne's feathers, 'Alan Winters must have a lot of relatives. Where do we start on this?'

'His wife, has she been notified?'

'Probably, but we should go there first. I didn't know he had a wife, or one that was still with him.'

'She's the first person we'll talk to. When we get back, start compiling a dossier of all his relatives, all of his friends, where he drank and ate, who he gave money to.'

'We've got a department of people who can do that.'

'Then delegate. Regardless, before anyone goes home tonight, we need a board up on the wall with a list of all the salient facts.'

'It'll be there. Let's go and see the grieving widow,' Clare said.

'Grieving? The Winters? I doubt it.'

Chapter 2

Alan Winters, it was known, had, before his big win, lived with his wife in an area to the west of the city, in an enclave populated by the least motivated, the least educated, the most likely to be in trouble with the forces of law and order.

'I've spent too much time up there,' Tremayne said.

Clare, who had only driven through the area on the occasional basis, could not see what he was referring to. Sure, the old cars jacked up on wooden blocks in some of the driveways, the abundance of graffiti, the children aimlessly wandering around the streets were all a little disconcerting, but at least the weather was pleasant, and even the worst day always looked the better for the sun's rays. 'Have there been many murders up here?' she said.

'It's normally wanton violence, the husband beating the wife, that sort of thing, or the local hooligans vandalising the toilet block in the park.'

'So why were you up here?'

'It's where I first lived when I came to Salisbury. A group of us from the police station clubbed together to pay the rent. Back then vacant accommodation was hard to come by. Alan Winters was in his teens then, but he was starting to become a nuisance.'

'Did he cause you any trouble?'

'A houseful of four junior police officers? I don't think so. Everyone gave us a wide berth, and we were all fit back then, not averse to giving anyone a smack if they played up.'

The Winters had moved on from the small terraced house that Tremayne had shown Clare, and after his win, Alan Winters had purchased a substantial six-bedroom home in Quidhampton, a small village between Salisbury and Wilton.

Tremayne and Clare drew up at the entrance to the house. Two men were standing in front of the secured gate. 'Who are you?' Tremayne asked as he flashed his ID.

'Security.'

'Is that necessary?'

'With the money here, what do you think?' the tougher-looking of the two said.

'We've come to see Mavis Winters,' Tremayne said.

'She's already been told. You're not welcome here.'

'Don't give me any of your nonsense. I know you well enough.'

'And we know you, Tremayne. Unless you've got a warrant, you're not going in.'

'Now look here, Gerry, your brother's been murdered, and I'm in charge of the case. Unless you want to put yourself down as a suspect, or I haul your sorry arse into the police station, in handcuffs if you resist, you'll open that gate and let us through.'

Gerry Winters moved away and made a phone call.

'You know this man?' Clare asked.

'The man's vermin, but don't let Superintendent Moulton know that was how I referred to his villains.'

'Okay, you're free to progress,' Gerry Winters said. 'And don't go upsetting Mavis. Her husband has just died. You know what will happen if she's upset?'

'And what's that? You'll be making a complaint down at Bemerton Road, is that it?'

'Not me, but I'll come into the house and deal with the situation.'

'Lay one hand on either my sergeant or me, and you'll be in the cells.'

'Don't threaten me, Tremayne. You've got nothing on me.'

'Petty crime verging on stupidity is not my area of responsibility.'

'I'm not involved in any crime.'

Clare could see the heavily-tattooed man getting agitated. She could also see that Tremayne was doing nothing to calm the situation. The gate swung open, and she drove in, parking behind a Bentley.

'Why did you bait the man?' Clare asked.

'Gerry Winters, the prime suspect.'

'Is he?'

'Alan Winters was a braggart, argumentative, drunk, worthless. So's his brother, except with Gerry, he can be violent,' Tremayne said.

'Mrs Winter's husband has just been murdered, she's hardly likely to be in a mood to talk to us.'

'She'll be interested in the money.'

'It would belong to the wife surely?'

'That's what we would assume, but they were independent most of the time; she'd go her way, he'd go his. The money has to be the motive, but who has first claim to it? It's important, you know that.'

'If he was killed for his money, then those who killed him must be certain of not being caught.'

'That's what doesn't make sense. Why kill the man at Stonehenge? Maybe it's nothing to do with his money? Maybe it's something to do with the belief that the man's luck is transferred by his death, not that I'd believe in such nonsense. Anyway, there's another problem up ahead,' Tremayne said.

Clare could see what Tremayne was on about. From out the front door of the house, a woman was approaching and fast. 'You bastard, Tremayne. In my hour of sorrow, and you're here raking over the coals. Can't a woman mourn in peace?'

'If I believed in your sadness for one minute, I'd leave you alone, but I don't, so don't try to get me on the sympathy vote. This is Sergeant Yarwood, by the way.'

'She's just a child. What are you doing? Training them young or is she there to look pretty, make you feel important?'

'You've got a foul mouth, Mavis, so let's just cut out this nonsense. Your husband's been murdered. I don't believe that you

11

did it, but someone did, and if it was for his money, then you could be next on the list.'

'Okay, Tremayne, come on into the house and bring your sergeant. If you drink a beer with me, then we can talk. However, it doesn't stop you being a bastard.'

'Thanks, Mavis.'

Clare leant over to Tremayne. 'You were rough there, guv,' she said.

'If you want respect from these kind of people, you've got to talk in a language they understand. Your fancy educated Norfolk accent, your polite manners, are not going to cut much mustard with this these people. I've known them long enough, and I can tell you one thing about Mavis Winters, she isn't grieving.'

'Involved in the murder of her husband?'

'It's possible, but I'd discount it for now, and besides, we need her cooperation. She's the key to the motive for her husband's death, and remember, the woman can be coarse, so you'll need to be.'

***

To Clare, the house was staggering in its beauty, although the interior, no doubt initially resplendent when the current occupants had moved in, was showing the signs of wear and tear. In the first room to the left, apparently the main room of the house, a stereo blasted gangster rap and a couple of drunken men gyrated to the music, a female lying sprawled across the couch. 'That's Bertie and some of his friends,' Mavis Winters said.

'Aren't they upset that your husband is dead?' Clare said.

'Why should they be? With him gone, Bertie believes he's in for a share of his money.'

'Even so, it seems sad that your husband has died.'

'Why? The man was going to kill himself anyway, and he was burning through the money. Whoever killed him has saved us all a lot of aggravation.'

Tremayne looked over at Clare with an 'I told you' look.

At the rear of the house, the kitchen had marble-tiled work areas, an air of opulence. An older woman slaved over the hot stove. 'That's his mother,' Mavis Winters said.

Clare could see that the woman had been crying.

'How long before our lunch is ready?' Mavis shouted to the woman. Clare was upset by the scene; Tremayne remained impassive.

'Soon, very soon. I was just upset by Alan's death, that's all,' the older woman said.

'Why? You bred the mongrel. What did you expect to happen to him, that he'd live into his nineties? He was going to go soon anyway, and as far as I'm concerned, good riddance to bad rubbish.'

Clare found the situation intolerable. Tremayne glanced her way, nodded his head, a sign to keep calm; it was a murder investigation, not a social outing. Clare could only imagine the hell the neighbours were going through. She considered herself blessed that her neighbours in Stratford sub Castle were caring people, and if she were working late, one or the other of them would ensure that her cats were fed. And they were always quiet, not like the house she was in now. If this was what sixty-eight million pounds did to a family, then she was glad that she was struggling with a police sergeant's salary. Not that it had been enough to buy her cottage and furnish it entirely. The inevitable result of the five-thousand-pound temporary loan from her parents was a visit for four days by her mother, and the constant redecorating that she wanted to force on her daughter. Clare had put up with the negativity of the woman, and once she was gone, cancelled all of her ideas and bought what she wanted. One thing she knew, that five thousand had to be paid back as soon as possible.

'Mavis, what can you tell us about your husband's death?'

'Tremayne, I'll be honest with you,' the woman said. She was holding a can of beer, as was Tremayne. Clare, to be agreeable, had consented to a glass of wine, cheap and nasty though it turned out to be. 'Alan was a bastard, but somehow we'd stuck together through good and bad for over twenty years.'

'You don't seem upset,' Clare said.

'You look like a gentle soul, not like your boss,' Mavis said to Clare. 'Tremayne knows where I'm coming from. Alan, for once in his miserable life, struck it lucky. He'd go his way, I'd go mine. I didn't ask about what mischief he got up to.'

'Did you get up to mischief?'

'A lot less than Alan.'

'And your husband said nothing?'

'What could he say? And now that he's Lord of the Manor, he expects to bring them around here.'

'And you agreed?'

'He had made it clear that if I left the house, then I wouldn't receive any money, and I'd be out on the street.'

'Would he have done that?' Tremayne said.

'Alan was easy to handle when he had no money, and I'd be out cleaning houses to help out with the bills, but now, there he is, driving around in a fancy car, screwing fancy women, buying them expensive gifts. I could control him back then, but now he's receiving bedroom advice from these tarts. Of course he'd follow through and cut me off with nothing.'

'You would have been legally entitled,' Clare said.

'Legally, yes, but he could afford the best legal advice. I've checked, and he could tie up my money for years.'

'It's not much of a relationship if after twenty years he's willing to do that,' Clare said.

'Alan was a weak man. In some ways I loved him once, but since the lottery I've grown to loathe him. Maybe when it's quiet, and I reflect back to when we first married, then maybe I'll be sad, but for now, I'm not.'

'Do you know who killed him, Mavis?' Tremayne asked.

'Not me, but I've told you the truth from my side. No doubt we'll have a get-together after the funeral, say lovely words about what a good man he was and how he had looked after the relatives.'

'Had he?' Clare asked.

'If they came asking, he'd help.'

'Did they come?'

'How long have you been in Salisbury? Haven't you heard about the Winters?'

'Nearly two years, but apart from being aware that your husband had won a lot of money, I hadn't.'

'Tremayne has; he'll tell you how many have been around. You tell her,' Mavis said, looking over at Tremayne.

'Everyone of them, plus a few more.'

'Tremayne's right. There was a queue halfway around the block the day the news of his win became public. How we celebrated that night.'

'The queues?' Clare reminded the woman.

'Not only that. The bags of begging letters, the onslaught of Facebook messages once they knew our eldest's name. In the end, we moved here and made sure there was security. Not that it hasn't stopped people trying to get in, but Gerry, he deals with them.'

'How?'

'He scares them, and gives them a good belting.'

'He's got a bad reputation around Salisbury. Do you trust him?'

'I'm the next of kin, and I'm not stupid with money.'

'You've given us the motive for your husband's murder, Mrs Winters,' Clare said.

'I didn't kill him; I wished him dead. Why do you think I'm telling you all this?'

'To pre-empt our suspicions.'

'There are those who wanted him dead because he was a bastard; there are others, the women, the parasites, those where he frittered away our fortune, who wanted him very much alive.'

'And what about those who had benefited by his generosity?'

'The women, Gerry has already dealt with them, nothing violent.'

'What did he do?'

'Whatever Alan gave them, he's taken back.'

'Such as?'

'Cars, clothing, accommodation.'

'They've been thrown out on the street?'

'That's up to them. I'm not supporting them.'

'Your children, his relatives?'

'It depends, but I'll support those that deserve assistance; the others can go to hell.'

Tremayne took another beer from the woman who was now friendly after her earlier outburst. Clare was not sure who the real Mavis Winters was, although she was sure that she did not like either. The woman looked tired for someone in her late forties, the effects of a lifetime of smoking reflected in her voice, the sagginess in the body indicative of a fast food diet, the discarded KFC and Big Mac containers still visible in a rubbish bin in the kitchen. The old woman, the mother of the dead man, continued to slave away. Clare could tell that she had led a hard life.

In the other room, the stereo played loudly, the singing of the occupants all too clear. Clare did not like the house and its occupants; Tremayne took no notice and continued with his questioning.

'Now that your husband's dead, what are your plans for the future?'

'We'll bury him first, give him a good send-off, Winters' style.'

'A lot of drinking?' Tremayne said.

'Of course.'

'And then?' Clare said.

'I've already started. Those who deserve help will receive it, the others won't. It's as simple as that.'

'Then whoever killed your husband will target you,' Tremayne said.

'Alan was weak, I'm not.'

'Are you strong enough to have dragged him up to Stonehenge and killed him, Mavis?'

'Tremayne, don't try your tricks with me. I remember when you lived two doors down from us. You weren't so high and mighty then, always trying to look up my skirt, mentally undressing me.'

'A long time ago.'

'That didn't stop you grabbing me at that Christmas party and dragging me off into the other room, did it?'

'We were both over the age of consent.'

'Am I shocking your sergeant?'

'Nothing shocks me, Mrs Winters,' Clare said.

'You're prim and proper. I'm surprised you can put up with Tremayne.'

'He's a good man, but that doesn't alter the fact that your husband has been murdered, and you act as if it's not important.'

'Sergeant, Alan was going to kill himself anyway. The man continued to drive when he was drunk, even though he had no licence, the women he fooled around with would have given him a heart attack, and his friends, if you could call them friends, were determined to fleece him. He put two hundred thousand pounds into the lame-brained idea of a friend to open a used car dealership not far from your police station, and what did the man do?'

'It's your story, Mrs Winters.'

'I'll tell you what he did. The bastard took off to the South of France with the money. Gerry found him shacked up in a fancy hotel with a couple of tarts.'

'He took the money back?'

'What was left off it.'

'And the man who took the money?'

'He's not shown his face in Salisbury since.'

'Does he still have a face?'

'Gerry didn't kill him, if that's what you're asking. He just won't be so pretty now, that's all.'

'I'll need to conduct interviews with all those close to Alan,' Tremayne said.

'Start with my family first.'

'Are you confident that they're all innocent.'

'Of killing Alan? I'd say so. Some of them are villains, not averse to violence, but none are that stupid to kill the golden goose.'

'You're the golden goose now,' Clare said.

'Maybe I am, and if anyone thinks otherwise, they'll find my foot in their arse.'

'Who's living in this house?'

'I am, plus our two children – Rachel, she's the eldest at twenty-four, and then there's Bertie, he's twenty-two – and Alan's mother.'

'Good children?' Clare asked.

'Rachel's sensible, takes after me, although it didn't stop her getting pregnant at sixteen, and landing me with her son to look after.'

'And where is the child now?'

'He died. He was a nice boy, but that's how it is.'

'And your daughter, how did she take it?'

'She was upset for a while, but now she's fine. Even with all our money, she still goes to work every day. According to her, she likes her job, although I made sure that she had a decent car to drive.'

'Bertie?'

'That's him next door, celebrating. He's as useless as his father. He thinks I'm going to be a soft touch, the same as his father, although his father wouldn't let him have an expensive car, just gave him a Toyota to drive.'

'Could he handle an expensive, no doubt powerful, car?' Tremayne asked.

'He's the same as his father. He'll be dead in a week.'

'And you intend to indulge him?' Clare said, appalled by the wife's callousness towards her dead husband, uncaring that her son was likely to commit involuntary suicide due to her generosity.

'Not a chance, Sergeant. He's still my son. He'll be lucky to keep the Toyota, and as for lying around the house snorting cocaine with his so-called friends, that'll stop once I've secured legal control of all of the money.'

'Any dispute over that?'

'None that I can see. It was Alan who bought the ticket in the first place, and he only spent two pounds. Not a bad return on his investment, don't you think? Although he must have spent plenty over the years on lottery tickets. It was about time for our luck to change.'

'Any idea how much money is left?' Tremayne asked.

'Of the sixty-eight million. I reckon there's still thirty, maybe thirty-two. Not bad for two years, is it? Between us, we've spent over thirty million pounds, or mainly squandered it.'

'Have you, Mavis?'

'Not me. I have always worked. I know the value of money. This house is in my name, for one thing, and there are a few other properties that I've bought. Regardless of how much is left, there's still money. Alan never had a clue with money. What he brought home from his council job, half was gone at the end of payday on alcohol and gambling. Financially, we're sound.'

'Who would want him dead?'

'I would, but then you know that. As for others, I've no idea. There were some he refused to help: relatives, friends. They won't be sad that he has died.'

'Will they receive any assistance from you now?'

'Some will, but I'll want security. I've no intention of handing out vast sums of money with no surety, that's for sure.'

'Would they know that?'

'Probably not.'

'We'll need their names.'

'I'll help you,' Mavis Winters said.

'Why?' Clare asked.

'I want you to find his murderer as soon as possible. No doubt the transfer of full financial control will be delayed until the murder investigation is concluded, and I don't want any doubts over my involvement remaining.'

'And Alan's mother?'

'She'll be looked after. I can't say I like her, but she'll have a place to stay.'

'She works hard.'

'She can go and sit in her room for all I care, but if she wants to look after the place, I'll not stop her.'

'And your son?'

'His day of reckoning is coming.'

'He has a motive,' Tremayne said.

'Bertie? Too bone idle to commit murder. He can find his way to the fridge for a beer, but Stonehenge, I don't think so.'

'Why the change of attitude? You were belligerent when we arrived.'

'Tremayne, we go back a long way. I'm still angry with you from that party all those years ago.'

'Why?' Clare asked.

'A woman doesn't forget her first man, and there he is, the next day, pretending that nothing happened. Mind you, he'd have been in trouble. I'd only just turned sixteen, and he was a police officer. No doubt seducing the neighbour's daughter after she had drunk a few too many would not have looked good up at Bemerton Road. Sergeant Yarwood, your DI is not the saint he pretends to be.'

'Saint Tremayne, I don't think so,' Clare said. The two women looked over at Tremayne. He shrugged his shoulders and turned away. 'Come on, Yarwood, we've got work to do,' he said.

Chapter 3

Back at the station, Tremayne focussed on the board set up in the Homicide department. He had purposely avoided talking to Clare on the drive back from Mavis Winters' house, knowing full well that she'd attempt to wind him up. Not that he had anything to regret, he knew that, and back then Mavis has been a pretty young thing, mature for her age, and he'd been in his twenties, starting to make his mark at Bemerton Road. The most that he would have received, if it had become known, would have been a rap on the knuckles from his senior and a pat on the back with a 'we're only young once' comment.

And now Yarwood wanting to make a sarcastic comment was not what he needed. It also brought in another complication, Tremayne knew, that he had some involvement with one of the suspects, even though it was almost thirty years ago. Superintendent Moulton may have some issues with it, but Tremayne didn't.

'Yarwood.' Tremayne decided to speak to her in the office. 'Mavis and me, it was a long time ago. Do you have any issue with it?'

'Not me, guv.'

'But it amuses you.'

'I might remind you occasionally.'

'A joke at my expense, is that it?'

'You've got to admit it's not what an innocent young sergeant expects to hear.'

'What? That her senior was young and foolish once.'

'It must have been a hell of a party.'

'It was. Now drop the subject. Where do we go from here?' Tremayne said, noticing the smile on Yarwood's face.

'We need Jim Hughes's report, see if he can give us the number of persons up at Stonehenge.'

'And why Stonehenge? That just doesn't tie in. If we accept that he was murdered for his money, then why up there, and why was his throat cut?'

'Mavis Winters, could she be involved?'

'She has the strongest motive, but it's unlikely that she murdered him.'

'Why? She's the one who'd gain most from it.'

'We'll check of course, but you've met the woman. What do you think of her?'

'She's not stupid.'

'Exactly, and she knows that we'll find the murderer eventually.'

'Involved?'

'If she is, she'll have covered her tracks well. We'll not find a link back to her, or, at least, not easily. For now, she's our best means of uncovering the truth. You'll need to go back to the house and interview her again, get a list of all known relatives, all friends, all the women that Alan Winters was messing around with.'

'And Mavis?'

'Check on who she was involved with. She seems to place a lot of reliance on her brother-in-law, Gerry. Check him out and see if they were up to something.'

'A bit close to home,' Clare said.

'It's a big home, and if Alan was bringing his women there, then Mavis could have been fooling around with Gerry.'

'Does she have a history of other men?'

'Not that I know of. Apart from running into Alan and Mavis on an occasional basis, I've not seen much of them for more than twenty years. I know that she latched on to Alan when she was eighteen, going on nineteen, but apart from that, I can't help much.'

'Was she attractive?' Clare asked.

'As a teenager.'

'What do you know about Alan Winters?'

'I never really knew him. I remember him as a skinny kid, always getting into trouble, but I'm not sure if I spoke to him more than once or twice as a youth. I arrested him a few times when he became older, but we didn't dwell on his childhood, and Mavis was never mentioned.'

'Did he know about you and Mavis?'

'It's unlikely, and besides, it was just the one time at a party. After that, I'd see her on the street with her friends, but we never went out together. It was our secret, that's all. And even if he knew, what did it matter? It was the start of the age of sexual freedom; nobody, not even Alan, would have been concerned. And besides, my private life is past history.'

'It's a murder investigation, and you know two of the main players. I don't think it is. What about Gerry, Alan Winter's brother?'

'He was a few years younger. I knew him vaguely.'

'Capable of murder?'

'It's possible.'

'Any other brothers?'

'Alan Winters was one of seven; I knew Stan and Fred, the older brothers.'

'What about them?'

'They were closer to my age. Back then they were starting down the slippery slope. They're both in jail now: one for extortion, the other for attempting to pull out an ATM from a bank building with a truck and chain.'

'What happened to the ATM?'

'It didn't budge, ripped off the back of the truck. Fred Winters is serving time courtesy of Her Majesty. The other brother, Stan, attempted to heavy the boss of a construction company in Salisbury.'

'What happened?'

'He offered to protect the man's equipment on site, to ensure that no damage occurred to any of his construction projects. The only problem was that Stan had failed to do his homework.'

'What do you mean?'

'The boss of the construction company had wrestled professionally a few years earlier. One night, after the man had refused Stan's generous offer, Stan and some of his colleagues decided to visit one of the construction sites.'

'And?'

'They found the boss there with three of his former wrestling friends. They beat the hell out of Stan and his people, put one in hospital.'

'Did anything happen after that?'

'Stan and his friends were arrested; there was verifiable proof.'

'The other siblings?'

'Cyril, waste of space, Dean made good and left the area, no idea what he's doing now, and then there's Margie.'

'What about her?'

'She's the worst of the lot: heroin addiction, pretty as a child, but now she's in her early forties. I see her occasionally late at night as I leave the pub. She's attempting to feed an addiction, and there's only one way to get sufficient money.'

'What about Alan? He had money.'

'You'll need to ask Mavis, but Margie's still out there selling herself.'

'And the children?'

'Not much I can tell you there. Neither has been in trouble with the law, although the son looks as though he's heading that way. That's about it for now. It's up to you, Yarwood, to find out more.'

'The women who he wanted to move into the house?'

'Mavis may not know who they are, not totally, and if they're not there now, we need to find them. I'll make some enquiries. I know where Alan Winters liked to drink. As for you, there's the less immediate family, and what about Mavis's siblings? I can't say I knew if there were any, although I think she was an only child. It's worth checking, anyway.'

Tremayne picked up his phone and called Jim Hughes. 'Any updates?'

'We've moved the body to Pathology. What I can tell you is the following: one, the man was unconscious when he was laid out on the Altar Stone.'

'Drugged, drunk, bashed?'

'Bashed. There's a clear sign that he had been hit on the back of the head with a blunt instrument.'

'Any idea what type.'

'Not at the present moment. Pathology may be able to help.'

'What else?'

'Two sets of footprints, slightly off-centre to the direction they were walking.'

'What does that mean?'

'They were carrying something between them.'

'Alan Winters?'

'Almost certainly. It would have required two men of sufficient strength.'

'What else?'

'Apart from his throat being cut, there's not much more I can tell you.'

'How would they have got the body to the site unseen?'

'You're the detective. I would have thought it would have been difficult. Even at night, there's always cars driving by, and no doubt everyone takes a look. It's hard to ignore. The death seems symbolic, although there were no signs of a ceremony, just the man's body and a slit throat.'

'Weapon?'

'We never found one. It's probably just a sharp knife, but we can't be sure.'

'Okay, thanks. Send me the full report when it's ready. In the meantime, we'll continue our investigation.'

'Tremayne, how do you do it? Every time you become involved, the deaths multiply.'

'Just lucky, I suppose,' Tremayne said, which to him seemed a flippant comment, seeing that the luckiest man in

England at the time of his win was dead and about to be carved up by the pathologist.

***

Tremayne left the office soon after. It was six in the evening, and whereas there was plenty to do, paperwork included, they still needed to find out about any friends, as well as the women that Winters had wasted his money on. Clare had an appointment to meet up with Winters' widow again.

The Old Mill Hotel in Harnham, twelfth century originally, although modernised since then, had been one of Winters' favourites. The publican knew Tremayne on sight, pulled a pint of beer for him as he entered the pub. 'What'll it be, Tremayne? We've salad or sirloin steak.'

'Are you joking?'

'The steak then.'

'Correct, well done, not half cooked as you normally serve it up to the trendies.'

'The trendies are into the salads. What is the reason for you gracing our premises so early?'

'Alan Winters.'

'Salisbury's richest inhabitant.'

'I never thought about that,' Tremayne said, 'although he must have been.'

'Couldn't have happened to a more deserving person.'

'Mike, you may serve the best beer in Salisbury, but you're full of hot air. What's your genuine opinion on Alan Winters?'

The publican drew a pint for himself and sat on his side of the bar, Tremayne on the other. An open fire burnt in one corner. It was still early, and apart from Tremayne, there was only a couple in one corner snuggled up close to each other, which caused the detective inspector to reflect back to his recent trip to Spain with Jean, his former wife.

He had to admit the trip had been a success, in that they had both enjoyed it, but both were set in their ways, although they were meeting up again next month, which seemed an ideal relationship to both of them. The occasional getting together, the romantic weekends, and then back to their regular lives.

'Winters, quite frankly, was a pain in the rear end. All that money and he's still an ignoramus,' the publican, a red-faced man, said. He downed his pint, drew another for himself and Tremayne. 'On the house,' he said.

'We need to know who he was friendly with, the people bleeding him for money, the ones who didn't get close, the women.'

'The who's who of the city's ratbags, is that it?'

'Are they?'

'I'd say so. He used to bring me plenty of business, but I've tried to go upmarket here. Anyone not into drunkenness and whores wouldn't stay in the bar for very long when Winters was here.'

'Were the women whores?'

'They weren't here for Winters' charm, were they?'

'I suppose not. What else can you tell me about his friends?'

Another pint appeared in front of Tremayne, along with his steak. As he commenced to eat his meal, the publican continued to talk. The Old Mill had not been his favourite pub, Tremayne knew that, but since the Deer's Head had lost his patronage, he'd been looking for somewhere to visit on a regular basis, although he assumed the pints on the house would not occur every time he visited.

'Three to four nights a week, Winters would breeze into here, his retinue in hot pursuit.'

'Describe them,' Tremayne said between mouthfuls of food.

'His brother, Gerry, as well as Cyril.'

'Any sign of the sister?'

'Margie?'

'The only one that I know of.'

'No. I've never seen her in here.'

'You know her?'

'Professionally, yes.'

'Is she still heavily into heroin?'

'She's still injecting herself. I hope I haven't shocked you.'

'You'd be surprised what people will tell a police officer. If I were charging for confessions, I'd be a rich man by now. And besides, I'm interested in solving a murder before there's another.'

'Will there be?'

'More often than not, although this case is unique.'

'The Altar Stone?'

'That's it. Does it mean anything to you?'

'Not really. It's odd though. People always want to attach significance to Stonehenge that's not there.'

'Tell me about the men who came in with Winters?'

'Apart from the brothers, there were a few others from where he lived before he won the money. I don't know their names, although they looked as though they were bad news, and then there's a loose group of drunks looking to con Winters out of a drink.'

'Did they?'

'Not always. He could be a moody bugger. Some days he'd only buy for his inner group, other days he'd buy for everyone. He splashed the money around like there was no tomorrow, which in the case of last night, there wasn't.'

'What does that mean?'

'He was in here. In a good mood as well. He must have spent a thousand pounds in here, fed everyone as well. I had to call in extra staff at short notice, cost me plenty due to penalty rates. Not that I'm complaining as it was profitable.'

'Any reason for the good mood?'

'Not that I could see. I know he was shouting off at one stage that he had dealt with a major problem.'

'Any idea what he was talking about?'

'With the workload behind the bar? You've got to be joking. I was exhausted, glad when he left.'

'What time did he leave?'

'About ten in the evening. The man had had a few drinks by then, hardly seemed up to the task.'

'What do you mean?'

'He had a couple of women draped around him. They got into the back seat of the Bentley, the three of them. His brother Gerry was driving. I assumed his idea of a celebration was a threesome with the two women, not that I can blame him.'

'Why?'

'Both of them were very tasty.'

'Do you know who they are?'

'Neither of them is on the game, I know that.'

'How?'

'If they were, I would have found them and treated myself.'

'Who were they? They're important. We believe that Winters died between the hours of three and four this morning. It may be that they were the last two people to see him alive.'

'Or passed out on a bed.'

'As you say, but I need to find these women.'

'They're not the only women I've seen him with. Bees round a honeypot, they were. Mind you, he looked after them well.'

'Let's focus on these two women. Who were they?'

'The blonde, she goes by the name of Polly Bennett. You'll find her working during the day at a furniture store out on Devizes Road.'

'I know it. If they're not on the game, then what were they doing cheapening themselves with Winters?' Tremayne asked, realising that he was on his fifth pint.

'As I said, bees round a honeypot, hoping he'd spend it on them.'

'Would he?'

'The man had won sixty-eight million pounds. There were plenty more women ready and willing after he had tired of Polly and her friend.'

'The friend's name?'

'Liz worked at the same place, a double act.'

'What do you mean?'

'Both of them were attractive. One was blonde, the other brunette. Winters wouldn't know what had hit him.'

'And you never will.'

'Not unless I win the lottery,' the publican said. 'Mind you, I'm not complaining, but it's always good to dream.'

'Winters had the dream, and now he's dead and on a slab.'

Tremayne phoned Clare on leaving the pub, the fresh air making him realise that he had drunk more than he should: six pints eventually, a good steak, and it was nine thirty in the evening. It was a murder investigation, and he should have continued, but he knew it would have to wait for tomorrow, early.

'Where are you, Yarwood?'

'I'm just wrapping up in the office. I've been to see Mavis Winters again. She was friendly, tried to set me up with her brother.'

'Gerry?'

'Not a chance.'

'You can do better, Yarwood.'

'Another compliment. You'll have to watch yourself, guv.'

'None of your lip. I've just had to spend a tough three hours in the pub at Harnham interviewing the publican.'

'What did he have to say?'

'We've got to meet a couple of Winters' women in the morning. Meet me in the office at six, and we'll go over what we've got.'

'At 6 a.m. I'll be there bright and breezy. And you, guv?'

'I'll be neither. How I suffer for the police force,' Tremayne said.

Clare knew his kind of suffering.

Chapter 4

Polly Bennett was not pleased to see two police officers at the door of the furniture store.

'Detective Inspector Tremayne and this is Sergeant Yarwood,' Tremayne said to her, the first of the women to arrive. Clare couldn't see what Winters would have found attractive in her, as the woman was showing dark roots in her hair and her fashion sense was woeful in that her skirt rode too high, her blouse was too tight.

'What can I do for you?' Polly said as she grabbed herself a cup of coffee. 'Do you want one?' she said.

'White, two sugars,' Tremayne said.

'I'll pass,' Clare said, noticing the dirty cups in the sink.

'Alan Winters,' Clare said after the other two were settled. Tremayne, she could see, liked the look of the woman. A man thing, Clare thought.

'When was the last time you saw him?'

'Yesterday morning, early.'

'What time?'

'He gave us a lift home. Just after midnight.'

'Us?'

'Liz and I.'

'Did he often do that?'

'Sometimes. It's nice to be driven home in a Bentley.'

'And after he dropped you home?'

'I went to bed.'

'Where is Liz Maybury?'

'She'll be here soon. She's not an early morning person.'

'Alan Winters was found dead. Are you aware of this?'

'He was alright when I last saw him.'

'You don't seem concerned,' Clare said.

'He was a generous man, plenty of money.'

'You and Liz Maybury spent a lot of time with the man. If he was so generous, why are you working here? And what time did you last see him? The truth this time. We are well aware that you and Liz were involved with Winters.'

'Okay, what if we were? He had plenty of money; we had what he wanted. There's nothing wrong with what we were doing.'

'We're not your mother. We're police officers, we only want the truth,' Clare said. Tremayne could tell that she did not like the woman, did not approve of her behaviour.

Polly Bennett shifted in her seat and went and made herself another cup of coffee. She returned and sat facing Clare, giving a sideways smile to Tremayne. 'Sometimes Alan likes to come in.'

'And?'

'You know.'

'No, I don't,' Clare said. 'He comes in for what? To play games, watch the television?'

'Games – I suppose you could call it that. Liz and I, we've got an agreement with him. He pays for our accommodation, and we look after him.'

'Sex, is that it?'

'We're not prostitutes. It's just an agreement we have with him.'

'This place?' Tremayne asked.

'Alan owns the business. He promised to put it in our names.'

'We were not aware that the man had any business sense.'

'Alan, not a clue, but Liz and I have. We dealt with the purchase; he supplied the money.'

'But not as a gift to you?'

'If he's dead, I suppose it won't happen. That cow will see us out on the street soon enough.'

Clare thought that was where Polly Bennett belonged anyway but said nothing.

The door to the store's kitchen burst open. 'I slept in again,' a woman said. The two police officers had just had an abrupt introduction to Liz Maybury. 'Oh, sorry. I thought Polly was here on her own.'

'I'm DI Tremayne, this is Sergeant Yarwood,' Tremayne said, eying the woman who had barged in.

'Oh, okay.'

'Alan's died,' Polly said to her friend.

'Not Alan. I don't believe it,' Liz said. Clare took stock of the woman: early thirties, shoulder length hair, brunette, seemed natural, firm figure, medium height, attractive even if the makeup was laid on too thick. She judged the woman to be the more attractive of the two.

'Why don't you believe it?' Clare asked.

'He was very much alive the last time we saw him.'

'When you two had a threesome with him, is that it?'

'What's with you two? Are you here to judge us? The man looked after us; we looked after him,' Polly Bennett said.

'What you ladies did with Alan Winters does not concern us. What we are interested in is when you last saw him.'

'He left at one o'clock in the morning.'

'Was there anyone waiting for him outside?'

'Only Gerry.'

'He doesn't come in.'

'Alan's the one with the money. And besides, Gerry's rough with his women,' Liz said.

'How would you know?'

'Before Alan struck it rich, when we were younger, we'd sometimes mess around with him.'

'Are you upset that Alan Winters is dead?'

'Should I be?'

'We're asking the questions. Are you sad that Alan is dead?'

'His bitch wife will want everything back.'

'Alan's wife has instructed Gerry to deal with it.'

'We've not seen him.'

Tremayne took note. According to Mavis Winters, Gerry Winters, her brother-in-law, was dealing with the reclaiming of all assets from Alan Winters' mistresses, yet he had not got around to Polly Bennett and Liz Maybury. If that was the case, then there were other women, or he was intending to maintain the relationship with the two women, substituting himself in their affections.

'When did Alan die?' Polly asked.

'You've taken a long time getting around to asking,' Clare said.

'We believe that Alan Winters died between the hours of two and four on the morning that you last saw him. Are you certain of the time he left you?'

'One o'clock. Gerry was waiting for him.'

'Can you confirm it was Gerry?'

'It was the Bentley. I assume it was.'

'And you've not heard about the death at Stonehenge?'

'Why? Did he die there?'

'Are you telling us that since the news of the death at Stonehenge, you've heard nothing?'

'We don't listen to the news,' Liz said. 'And we were at home last night, drank a few too many bottles of wine.'

'Yet you are smart enough to run this place?'

'That's as maybe, but we don't concern ourselves with local gossip.'

'The murder of a man is hardly gossip.'

'Alan was murdered?'

'His throat was cut. It took two people to carry him up to the site, two people with a reason to want him dead. Had he told you that he was not going to sign over the deeds to this business? Is his wife taking control? Did Gerry pick him up, or have you hatched a deal with him once he transfers Alan's wife's affections to him? It seems that you women had a strong motive for his death, and this nonsense about not knowing he was dead, I can't believe you,' Clare said.

Tremayne sat back, taking in how his sergeant was dealing with the women. He had to admit that his mentoring was paying off.

The two women sat still, not sure what to say. Polly was the first to speak. 'We did not kill him. A person has got to use whatever to get ahead. Alan, maybe we're sad to some extent, but our arrangement with him was business, not emotional. The thought of someone slitting his throat sounds gruesome, but it wasn't us.'

'Mavis Winters?' Tremayne asked.

'The woman hated us.'

'Have you been to the Winters' house?'

'Sometimes.'

'When Mavis was there?'

'Yes.'

'And what did she say?'

'Not a lot. She called us tarts, hit Alan once, but we took no notice, and besides, she had someone there.'

'Who?'

'No idea, but Alan said she had another man.'

'And you believed him?'

'Believe, not believe, what did it matter?'

'As long as you two were fine, is that it? What about the children, Rachel and Bertie? Were they there?'

'Bertie's a space cadet, and Rachel, we never saw her.'

***

Tremayne was a man who did not judge people, not even Polly Bennett and Liz Maybury, and if the two women wanted to screw Alan Winters, he had no issues either way.

Yarwood, Tremayne knew, was more uptight, a believer in common decency, the distinction between right and wrong, and she had not approved of the two women. Tremayne thought it was her upbringing, her parents, especially her mother, whom he had met when she was fussing over Yarwood's cottage. He had to admit he had not warmed to the woman, even if she was ingratiatingly pleasant. He understood why Yarwood preferred to be in Salisbury with him. Even so, the mother had subjected him

35

to the third degree: how is Clare coming along? What are her promotion prospects? Is she cut out to be a police officer, so much unpleasantness, so much crime?

He had left the woman feeling as though he was Yarwood's school teacher giving an end of year evaluation at a parent's evening instead of a work colleague. Clare had apologised for her mother afterwards, although it wasn't important.

'What do you reckon?' Tremayne said as the two officers drove to Pathology.

'They'd do anything if it was to their advantage.'

'Most people will, but we're looking for two people who committed a murder. Would they have been capable?'

'Liz Maybury, maybe,' Clare said.

'Polly Bennett?'

'I'm not so sure about her. She seems more responsible, although she didn't care that the man was dead.'

'As if they already knew. But why pretend to us? It can't be a great secret in Salisbury. Even customers in their business must have been talking about it. It's been on the television, another case of the downfall of an average man who strikes it lucky.'

'They knew,' Clare said. 'As to why they said they didn't needs to be added to the board in the office, and why's Gerry sitting in the car while Alan's with the women?'

'The man must not have liked that, and Gerry Winters would be capable of murder.'

The two officers arrived at Pathology and entered the depressingly cold and austere premises. They found Stuart Collins, the pathologist, washing up after completing his investigation. He was pleased to see Clare, not as much to see Tremayne standing next to her.

'Alan Winters, I assume?' Collins said.

'What can you tell us?' Tremayne asked.

'Considering that I've just concluded my examination, you're a little premature.'

'You've had the body for a day.'

'We're not here for you. We have other responsibilities. And besides, I needed to send some samples away for analysis.'

Clare, sensing the tension, entered the conversation. 'What can you tell us before you file your report?' she said.

Collins mellowed. 'As you know, a male aged forty-eight, in reasonable health considering.'

'Considering what?' Tremayne said.

'Tremayne, just hang on and let me speak. Winters was carrying about twenty pounds too much weight, his liver was showing the early signs of cirrhosis.'

'The heavy drinking?' Clare said.

'As you say, but it wasn't advanced; he probably hadn't noticed any of the signs such as fatigue, fluid build-up in the legs, yellowing of the skin, itching. There are other symptoms; I'll not go into them now.'

'You'd sent off some samples?'

'The man was taking high dosages of Viagra.'

'He needed it,' Tremayne said.

'He also had pancreatic cancer, although it was in the early stages. Yet again, he would not have known about it until it was too late. The man was a smoker, tending to obesity. Over time, it would have claimed his life.'

'If he had known?' Clare asked.

'Assuming he did, then moderating his lifestyle: no smoking, healthy weight, salads, low red meat diet.'

'That would have been anathema to Alan Winters,' Tremayne said.

'Then the man would not have made fifty-five years of age.'

'What can you tell us about the wound to the back of the head?'

'It was probably inflicted with a metal object, flat, and used with a degree of force.'

'Could a woman have inflicted the wound?'

'I don't see why not,' Collins said. 'Also, his throat had been cut with a sharp knife. A kitchen knife would have sufficed.'

'Type, brand?'

'I'm a pathologist, not a clairvoyant. It's a kitchen knife, approximately six inches long, small serrations, and very sharp.'

***

Clare left Tremayne at Bemerton Road; he had some paperwork to deal with, a few phone calls to make.

Mavis Winters was welcoming on Clare's arrival, a pre-arranged meeting. The front room where the son had wasted his time on the previous visit was empty. 'Bertie?' Clare asked.

'He's in a clinic. He's not coming back until they've sorted him out.'

Outside in the driveway were two vans belonging to a professional cleaning company. Inside, a team of workers in overalls, the sound of vacuum cleaners pervading the house. 'I couldn't stand the mess anymore,' Mavis said.

'You could have done it when your husband was alive.'

'Maybe I could, but it wasn't my house then, not with him and his women, and then Bertie making a nuisance of himself.'

'We've interviewed the women.'

'Which ones?'

Clare did not feel it was wise to mention their names. 'Are there many?'

'Two that I've seen here. He set them up in a furniture store.'

'That's who were interviewed.'

'That Polly's sharp. The other one, Liz, she's not so much.'

'You knew them from before?'

'Polly, she's the youngest daughter of one of my mother's friends. Liz, she's the extra. That Polly would have had me out of here in an instant if she could.'

'She'll not be able to do it now.'

'Not a chance, and I've sent Gerry up there to deal with them.'

'When?'

'Today. He was taking his time, probably anxious to grab them for himself, or maybe they laid on the charm, bedded the man.'

'He'd disobey you?'

'For a chance to get his leg over? What man wouldn't? They're all the same, you must know that.'

'I suppose I do,' Clare said, although she was sure that was not a suitable analogy to apply to all men.

Once the cleaner had moved out of the room, the two women sat down. Clare looked around her. 'We paid for an interior decorator to furnish the house. I couldn't have done it, nor could Alan, although as soon as it was finished he was spoiling it,' Mavis said.

'Was he?'

'It's his mother. She never brought him up correctly, neglected him. Out every night on the town, bringing home stray men, even when he was a child. You can't blame Alan for turning out the way he did.'

'And you?'

'My father was strong on discipline, and my mother was always at home. I had a good childhood, Alan didn't.'

'You still don't seem upset that he's dead.'

'Stoic, a family tradition. I'm sorry that he's dead, although I don't miss him, never will. I had tried to make something of him, but he wouldn't bend, and besides, I wasn't much of a role model.'

'What do you mean?'

'You saw how I treated Tremayne, what I said about him and me.'

'It came as a bit of a surprise.'

'Why? He was a good-looking man back then, fit and strong. It was me who grabbed him, and he'd had a few beers by then. After that, he didn't come back for seconds. He's a decent man, better than Alan was. I should have taken your detective inspector instead, but then he went and met someone else.'

'Jean.'

'That's her. I used to see her sometimes, occasionally have a chat.'

'Did she know about you and Tremayne?'

'Not from me.'

'You said that you weren't much of a role model before.'

'I'm common. Don't say anything or try to deny it. You went to the best schools, elocution lessons probably. Me, I had the local secondary school, always in trouble. Not boy trouble, just a general disinterest in school really. I regret it now, but it's too late.'

'It's never too late.'

'I suppose you're right, but my father was a strict disciplinarian, easy to anger. School and outside of the house was my chance to rebel. It's a wonder I stayed a virgin until Tremayne.'

'Why did you?'

'I don't know. I always think that I wanted my own place, my own house, the loving husband, the ideal children.'

'And now?'

'Rachel's turned out fine. Bertie will once I've dealt with him. Alan was a major disappointment, and now I've got this house.'

'Another man?'

'In time, maybe. Who knows?'

'Your mother-in-law?'

'She took off upstairs to her room when the cleaners came in.'

'What will you do about her?'

'I'll do the right thing. I'll buy her a flat in town, make sure she's got money. Apart from that, I don't want to see her.'

'Do you have access to all the money now?' Clare asked.

'Sufficient. Until you solve Alan's death, the full amount will probably be held up.'

'But you know where it is?'

'I know exactly where it is and how much is remaining. I'll need a death certificate before I can access all of it.'

'There'll be no death certificate yet.'

'It doesn't matter. I still have access to a few million, and no one's going to get any of it unless I agree.'

'Gerry, Alan's brother?'

'He's an employee, would like to be more.'

'Is that possible?'

'After he took advantage of those two women, and them not kicking him out of their house? He's tarred with the same brush as Alan, and he's violent.'

'Your claim on the money, is it indisputable?'

'It should be. Apart from some money for Rachel and Bertie, then the rest is mine, and besides, I intend to contest Bertie's share. He'll only fall into bad company again.'

'Let us come back to who would have benefited from your husband's death?' Clare said, her initial negative impressions of Mavis Winters moderated.

A woman came in with tea and biscuits. Mavis said, 'I've hired some help for the house. I'm not much of a cook, chicken and rice is about my limit, and I eat too much fast food. I intend to get myself into shape now.'

'You look fine,' Clare said.

'Next to you with your perfect body? You're too kind. Anyway, who would benefit from his death? I'm the only one. No one else has a clear claim. I know a few have their noses out of joint because Alan wouldn't give them anything.'

'Names?'

'Cyril, his useless brother, but the man's too lazy to tie his own shoelaces. He'd not be capable. There's his brother, Dean. The only one of the brothers who's amounted to anything. I've seen him once since Alan bought that ticket, but he's never asked for a handout. There are the two brothers, Stan and Fred, but they're both in jail. No doubt they'd appreciate some money, no doubt they'll be a nuisance when they're released.'

'What will you do when that time comes?'

'I'll give them a cash settlement, legally tied up on the condition that they ask for no more.'

'Bad men?'

'Not really, just weak. Fred concerns me; Stan doesn't.'

'What about your side of the family?'

'I'm an only child. I've a few cousins, but I've not seen them in years. Nothing there.'

'You realise that if there are no more suspects, then the suspicion will fall on you and Gerry. There were two people at Stonehenge, and the link will be made.'

'But no proof.'

'No proof, but guilt by association will remain. It may delay your inheritance.'

'Where was he the night he died? After the pub, I mean,' Mavis asked.

'Is it important?'

'If he was with his two women, then I'd be looking to them. What does Gerry say? He's normally the driver.'

'We've not spoken to him about that night yet.'

'Why not? He's more integral to the investigation than I am. I'm just the wronged woman sitting at home waiting for her man to come back.'

'You don't qualify for that description.'

'You mean the bitch with the rolling pin, ready to bash him over the head for his misbehaving.'

'That's more like it,' Clare said.

'I've already told you that I'm useless in the kitchen. I wouldn't know one end of a rolling pin from the other.'

'They're the same,' Clare said.

'As you say, but I didn't kill Alan. Whoever it was did me a favour. I know that sounds callous, but that's how I feel.'

'Did you know that his health was suffering?'

'He was putting on weight, but apart from that, no.'

'There was Viagra in his system,' Clare said.

'Not because of me,' Mavis said. 'We were sleeping in separate beds, almost from the day we moved in here. No doubt Polly and her friend reaped the benefit, not that I envy them.'

'Why's that?'

'Alan was not one of the world's great romantics. I can't say I miss that side of our marriage.'

'With someone else?'

'Once I'm fit. Give me three months, and I'll be giving you a run for your money.'

'More of a saunter,' Clare said.

'A pretty woman like you? You must have plenty of men.'

Clare did not respond, only smiled.

Chapter 5

'The golden boy,' was Dean Winter's reply after Tremayne and Clare had introduced themselves at the man's house in Southampton.

Tremayne had noticed a late-model car in the driveway, the neat and tidy house, the same as all the others in the street. It was middle-class, middle management territory, mow the lawn on a Saturday, trip to the sea on a Sunday with their two or three children, and it did not excite him.

'We've a few questions about your brother.'

'What do you want me to tell you? That he had spent a lifetime on his backside, and the most he had ever done was to walk into the pub or the local newsagent to buy a lottery ticket.'

'You're bitter about his good fortune?' Clare asked. The two police officers and Dean Winters were sitting in the front room of the house.

'Bitter, not really, but it's ironic, isn't it? I get out of that awful area, educate myself, put myself through university, and put in the hours, and there he is or was, sitting on sixty-eight million pounds.'

'It was fairly won,' Tremayne said.

'I'm not saying it wasn't, but there wasn't a more undeserving person.'

'Have you been up to his house since he died?'

'I've phoned Mavis. That'll do.'

'Will it?' Clare said.

'It will for me. I'm not about to profess friendship and brotherly love now, not for you or anyone.'

A woman busied herself in the kitchen. 'Your wife?' Clare asked.

'Tell us about your childhood,' Tremayne said.

'Our father was a bastard, never there, and by the time I was seven, he'd disappeared.'

'Where to?'

'I've no idea, none of us does.'

'Your mother?'

'She didn't care. You've met her?'

'We have,' Clare said.

'What did you think?'

'She seemed sad that your brother had died.'

'She probably was, but it's too little, too late for her to care.'

'What do you mean?'

'She was always out and about. There was a succession of men pretending to be our father, some hitting us, one abusing Margie. That's why she's on drugs and prostituting herself. Did anyone tell you that?'

'No. What happened to him?'

'I've no idea. When Stan and Fred found out about it, they took him out of the house. He never came back.'

'How old was Margie?'

'Twelve, going on thirteen.'

'What did Margie say?'

'Nothing. She'd sit quietly after that, barely said a word to anyone. She could have done with some professional help, but we had no money, no idea where to go, and our mother just brushed it away as a foolish child's make-believe.'

'Was it?'

'Hell, no. I was two years older. I tried to pull him off of her, but he punched me in the face, broke two of my teeth. By the time I came around, the man was out of the house and down the pub. That's when I phoned Stan. When the man returned, Stan and Fred confronted him; Stan had an old car, and they bundled him into the back seat and took off.'

'You have your suspicions as to what happened to him?'

'I was fourteen at the time. I hoped that they had killed him.'

'But they never said.'

'I never asked, but to them, I was just a kid. And now, they're both in jail.'

'Do you go to see them?'

'Sometimes, more for Margie than for me. I like Stan, not so much Fred, but both of them were violent, and they'd been in trouble with the law in their youth. We're not a good family, mongrel DNA, probably some inbreeding in the past. I don't want to associate with any of them, only I feel guilt over Margie.'

'Do you ever see her?'

'Not for a long time. I know where she is, or which part of Salisbury she hangs out, but it's painful to see what has become of her. Pretty when she was young, but now? I suppose she's still pretty, but the years must have taken their toll on her, and there's our bitch mother living with Alan. Do you think they did anything to help her? Nothing, I'll tell you, nothing.'

'You're an angry man, Mr Winters,' Clare said.

'That's why I keep away. I'd prefer Alan to be alive and well, and then you wouldn't be here making me revisit the past.'

'Angry enough to wish your brother dead?'

'Angry, yes. But I didn't kill him. Stan and Fred are violent, I'm not. If they weren't in jail, I wouldn't put it past them.'

'After what they did to the man who'd raped your sister?'

'I don't know about him. And besides, it a long time ago. Don't go raking up the past. It's only Margie who will suffer.'

'Why did you tell us?' Clare asked.

'Outside of the family, no one knows. You're bound to want to question Margie at some time. I told you in the hope that you'll be sensitive to her past, not too judgemental.'

'We'll not mention it to her, but, yes, you're right. We will speak to her in the next day or so.'

Outside Dean Winter's house, Clare made a phone call. 'Mavis, what do you know about Margie?'

'We offered her help, even paid for a month in the same place that Bertie is.'

'What happened?'

'She walked out after two days. There's no hope for her. The offer of a place to live, treatment for her addiction, is always there. She's a strange one.'

Clare ended the phone call and turned to Tremayne who had lit a cigarette. 'Someone's not telling the truth. We'd better talk to Margie Winters as soon as possible,' she said.

***

Mavis Winters' description of her sister-in-law, Margie, that she was a strange one, was correct. Clare could see that on meeting the woman. This time she had left Tremayne back in the office, knowing full well he wouldn't be there long before he was out interviewing someone else. And in this case, there wasn't a shortage of people to interview. Apart from the immediate family, there was a group who attempted to stay close to the money, as well as those who had begged: former work colleagues of Alan's, childhood friends, the usual types that hang around money – the reason that Alan Winters, as well as Mavis, always had security.

As Clare sat in the small room at the top of a terraced house in Wyndham Road, she could see someone who definitely needed help. Surrounded by cats, a woman bizarrely dressed in leopard-patterned stretch pants and a white blouse sat leaning back, a cigarette in a holder hanging out of her mouth.

Clare knew her to be forty years of age, although she looked older.

'You're aware of what's happened?'

'Dead, up at Stonehenge, is that it?'

'You don't seem concerned,' Clare said. To her, the woman seemed out of it, and if she was on the game, then she was a poor representative of her profession. Apart from the cats which smelt, the room was in a general state of disarray. Over to one side of the room there was a double bed, its sheets pulled back and clearly unchanged for some time.

Clare prided herself that in the short time she had been in her new cottage, the restricted hours that she had to devote to such matters, it was always clean, and the bed was changed regularly, not that anyone else saw it apart from her two cats.

'Mavis tried to get me to leave here and go and live with them.'

'Why didn't you?'

'I've got my gentlemen friends, they'd not want to go there. And what about my cats? Mavis would only let me take one of them, and I can't part with any of them, not now, not after what we've been through.'

'And what have you been through?'

'You'd not understand,' Margie said. As she spoke, she drank from a small glass, constantly stopping to top it up from a bottle of gin. 'Do you want one?' she asked.

'Not for me,' Clare said.

'They wanted to put me in a home first to clean me up.'

'Mavis told me that. What happened?'

'They wouldn't let me take my cats.'

'So you left?'

'I'm comfortable the way I am. And they wanted me to wear their clothes. I've got plenty of my own.'

At least that was true, Clare realised, as she looked inside a wardrobe to one side of the bed. It was full of clothing equally odd to what the woman was wearing, some on hangers, some just stuffed in the bottom, a cat sleeping on the pile.

'Your brother has died. Were you close?'

'Alan, when we were younger, but not now, not since he left home and left me on my own.'

'He won a lot of money, you do know that?'

'I know it, but what's it to me? I've got all that I want.'

'Tell me about yourself,' Clare said. 'What do you do for a living.'

'A whore, is that what they tell you?'

'Yes.'

'They're right. I'm nothing but a dirty whore.'

'You don't seem concerned.'

'Why should I be? Men, they're all bastards, only after one thing. At least I make them pay these days.'

'You've had a lifetime of abuse?'

'Abuse? Men pawing me, sleeping with me, forcing their tongues down my throat.'

'According to Mavis, one of your mother's boyfriends raped you.'

'Him and others.'

Clare could tell that the woman was embittered, psychologically disturbed. She knew that may have been the alcohol and the drugs, although there was no sign of a syringe or the tell-tale signs of shooting up.

'Is there anyone who would want Alan dead?'

'Dead, Alan?'

'I thought you understood.'

'Maybe I did, maybe I didn't. Sometimes I'm not sure…'

'Of what?'

'Not sure of what's real or what's not. Mavis wanted to lock me up, did I tell you that?'

Clare realised that Margie Winters was not capable of murder, not even capable of looking after herself. The woman may not want to take advantage of her brother's good fortune, but she needed help, voluntary or otherwise.

'Alan, your brother? Anyone who'd want to kill him?' Clare repeated the question.

'Not him. He was everyone's friend.'

'And you?'

'He looked after me once, a long time ago, but now he doesn't care.'

Clare left the woman to her cats and her bottle of gin.

***

Tremayne, as Clare had suspected, had been unable to stay in his office for more than forty-five minutes. He knew where the Winters had grown up, a council house identical to the one he had shared all those years before. He drove past the old place, smiled as he remembered Mavis and that night.

Tremayne pulled up outside Cyril Winters' house. A car in the driveway, a late-model BMW, a clear sign that the man had gained something from his brother's wealth. Tremayne walked up the driveway, knocked on the door twice before there was any movement from inside. 'What do you want?' a voice shouted upstairs.

'Detective Inspector Tremayne. I've got a few questions.'

'Okay, hang on while I put on my trousers.'

Five minutes later the door opened. In front of Tremayne stood a slovenly man dressed in a pair of navy tracksuit bottoms and a string vest. 'I was having a nap,' he said.

'Cyril Winters?'

'That's me. You're here about Alan?'

'If you've got thirty minutes.'

'Me? I've got all the time in the world.'

'Why's that?'

'I've retired.'

'At forty-nine?'

'Why not? No law that says a man has got to work until he keels over.'

'I suppose not. Alan's money?'

'He gave me some, enough to live on.'

'Enough to live here?'

'Tremayne, I remember you from when you lived here. I was only young, but you were a snob then, thought you were better than us, and there's your sucking up to Mavis.'

'Mavis?'

'She fancied you. You could have had her, and then she'd have not married Alan.'

'Are you saying she's not been a good wife to him?'

'Alan was tired of her. He wanted fresh meat.'

'Polly Bennett and Liz Maybury?'

'Them and others.'

'Who were the others?'

'Whoever he wanted. There's plenty out there wanting a man with money.'

'How about you?'

'I've got no money.'

'But you were close to it. Attraction by association.'

'I took advantage, sometimes I told them that I could get them close to Alan, get them a car, a holiday in the sun.'

'And did you?'

'Sometimes.'

Tremayne had recognised the man when he opened the door, having seen him with Alan Winters a few times. The similarities between the two men had been striking. Both men were unambitious, in poor condition, and less than ideal specimens of manhood. If the situation had been reversed, and it had been Cyril who had purchased that lottery ticket, it would be Alan living in the council house, Cyril in the mansion with the fancy cars. Tremayne realised that if he had struck lucky, unlikely given his poor record of picking the winning horses, he'd be content, although he couldn't imagine a future without the police station on Bemerton Road. Sometimes, late at night while lying in bed, he regretted that no one was there beside him. He considered whether he and Jean should attempt to move in together again, instead of the occasional weekend, although he realised that would be doomed to failure. He was, he knew, a solitary man, comfortable in his own skin, content with his life.

'Cyril, your wife?'

'Don't you remember? I married Mavis's friend, the pretty one.'

Tremayne cast his mind back. He recollected Mavis and a friend: the same age, dark hair, thin with a pleasant face. 'Vaguely,' he said.

'She took off a few years back.'

'Sorry about that. Any children?'

'Not us. I wasn't keen, and she wasn't able. After growing up in a family of seven children, the last thing you want is to bring any more into the world.'

'A tough childhood?'

'You know it was. You know about Margie?'

'My sergeant's gone to see her. What's the relationship with your mother?'

'Alan was easier with her, more on account of Mavis.'

'What do you mean?'

'Alan hated her. He'd have thrown her out on the street, but Mavis wouldn't hear of it. Kept telling him that she's his mother, and regardless of what has happened in the past, she still deserves respect.'

'She didn't look happy in his house.'

'No more than a drudge, there to serve them hand and foot. Still, it's no more than she deserves.'

'Your enmity, is it as intense as your brother's?'

'If you mean that I hated her, then yes. She'd come back here, but I'll not take her, not after what she subjected us to.'

'Apart from Margie?'

'Some of the men she brought home were perverts; some wanted to hit us, make us squeal, some wanted to touch us.'

'Sexual abuse?'

'A fancy police term, but yes.'

'And what happened to these men?'

'When Stan and Fred were not in jail, we'd tell them, and they'd sort it out.'

'The same as the man who abused Margie?'

'We never saw them again.'

'Murdered?'

'We were only young, but I don't think so. Not that I cared.'

'Cyril, you're not an ambitious man, are you? Why is that?'

'It's not a crime.'

'I never said it was. You've retired to do what? And what about Mavis? Is she going to support you? She could even send your mother back here.'

'I'll not let her in the door. And Mavis, she'll look after me.'

'Are you sure? She's not a stupid woman. The car in your driveway, she could take it back.'

'She wouldn't dare.'

'Why not?'

'I'll stop her.'

'How? You can barely get out of bed, yet you think you can hold off a woman with that much money? Did you kill Alan? Was he starting to tighten up on you? Thought you'd have a better chance with Mavis, maybe take her out, get her drunk, get her into your bed, and then you could move into her house, is that it?' Tremayne knew he was pushing the man to see if there was any emotion in him.

'Tremayne, you're a bastard. You were back then when you screwed Mavis in your house.'

'How do you know about that?'

'Mavis told my wife; she told me. You're lucky Stan and Fred didn't know about it. They'd have sorted you out.'

'The same as the other men?'

'Maybe.'

'What do you know? Are Stan and Fred capable of murder? What will happen when they're released? Will they want their share of Alan's money?'

'They're bad men, especially Fred, I'll grant you that. None of us is looking forward to the day when he is released.'

'How long before they're out?'

'Stan's out in thirteen, maybe fourteen months; Fred's got another three years. Alan wasn't concerned.'

'Alan's dead, Mavis is alive, the same as you. Will they be around here looking for accommodation, looking for you to help them?'

'With Stan, I've no idea.'

Tremayne could see that Cyril was typical Winters stock in that he contributed little to society. The man seemed incapable of anything other than a general apathy, and if the mother were foisted on him, his complaints would be muted. He could not see the man as a murderer. Stan and Fred were possible, although

their dealings with the mother's previous lovers were in the past;
if there was a case to be answered, it was for others to investigate,
a cold case, but Tremayne assumed it wouldn't be. The men who
had died, if that had indeed happened, were possibly low
achievers, probably criminals, and their disappearances would not
have registered significantly in any database.

'And you're worried?'

'I'll deal with it when it happens.'

'Your philosophy on life?'

'You'll be the one dying of an ulcer, not me,' Cyril
Winters said. Tremayne thought the man's comments banal as he,
DI Keith Tremayne, was still active and motivated.

Tremayne left the man to his rest and walked down the
driveway. As he closed the gate, he could see Cyril Winters turn
on the television, a reality show, set on a tropical island. In the
man's hand, a can of beer. Tremayne knew that later that night
he'd have a few beers himself in the pub, and woe betide anyone
who flicked the channel on the television high in one corner of
the room from horseracing to a reality show or a quiz with insipid
contestants answering insipid questions, revelling in their
stupidity. He'd had enough of that with one of the Winters
brothers. He still had three more to see. Although two could not
have committed the murder, the third was a distinct possibility.

Chapter 6

'I'm giving you two whores thirty minutes to vacate this shop and to hand over the keys to that fancy place Alan rented for you, and no showing your assets, the same as you did to Gerry. I'm not interested,' Mavis Winters said as she stood in the furniture store. On one side of her stood Gerry Winters, on the other a couple of customers with a young child.

The customers moved away and quickly left the shop, Gerry bolting the door after them, turning the sign to closed.

'You've no right to come in here demanding anything,' Polly Bennett said. Liz Maybury, the third member of Alan's threesome, also Gerry's the first time he had tried to evict them, stood slightly behind Polly.

'I've every right. I put up with you when Alan was alive, had no option, but now you're out, and if that means you're back on the street, letting any drunk screw you, that's up to you.'

'We were running this place for Alan, making a good job of it as well, turning a profit. Don't you want us to continue?'

'A lousy thousand pounds a week. Do you think I care about that?'

'Just because you married money, what makes you think you can order us around?'

'It's ours,' Liz Maybury said.

'Gerry, grab hold of them and kick them out. You know where they live?'

'I do.'

'I want the keys now. You've organised some men to deal with their belongings?'

'Are you sure you want to do this?'

'Gerry, watch what you're saying. I've got control of the money. Any trouble with you and you'll be on the street with these women, or keeping Cyril company in that hovel he calls home.'

'For your information,' Mavis said, addressing Polly Bennett, 'I didn't marry money. I married a weak and lazy man who happened to buy a lottery ticket and was rapidly throwing it away on whores like you. You've got thirty-five minutes now before I call the police.'

'We've not broken the law. Alan gave us this place, the cars, the flat.'

'Legally, or just when you and your friend were screwing him?'

'Legally,' Polly said.

'Where's the proof?'

'It's with my solicitor.'

'Where is he?'

'He's out of town.'

'Gerry, grab hold of these women and their bags. I want the keys.'

'Did you kill Alan?' Liz Maybury blurted out.

'You bitch,' Mavis said as she lunged at the woman, grabbing her by the hair, forcing her to the ground. Polly joined in, pushing Mavis's head to the floor. Gerry stood back, not sure what to do. If it had been three men, he would have grabbed the first one, hit him across the head, before starting on the second, but three women? Gerry had to admit that he was enjoying the spectacle: two women that he had slept with, another one that he wanted to if he played his cards right, although if he helped Polly and Liz out of their current predicament, they'd see him right later that day. If he helped Mavis, she'd see that his current employment lasted, and he'd be able to drive the Bentley, an ideal machine for picking up women.

He chose Mavis as the more in need of his attention. He leant down, took hold of Polly's arm and yanked her up. 'You bastard, we screwed you, not that we enjoyed it, and now you're taking her side,' she said.

'Gerry, take hold of this other tart. I don't pay you to screw the women.' Mavis said. 'I pay you to do your job, to

56

protect me from the parasites with their bleeding-heart letters, their lives that have gone wrong, and the first time there's something for you to do, you stand there gawping.'

Mavis pulled herself up from the ground, steadying herself on Gerry's spare arm. In the other Polly Bennett wrestled, trying to free herself from his grip. 'I'll have the law on you,' she said. 'This is assault. There are laws in this country.'

'What chance do you think you'll have? The only money you'll have is from spreading your legs, and not much judging from what I've seen here today. I don't know what Alan saw in you two, both skinny with barely an arse between you. Your breasts, a bicycle pump every night, is that it?'

'You'd know his taste in women,' Liz said, standing at some distance away. 'A worn-out old prune for a wife.'

Mavis took her hand from the table she'd been using for support and launched herself at the woman again, almost a flying leap. Both of them hit the wall behind, Liz collapsing to the ground unconscious.

'You've killed her. It's murder. I'm a witness,' Polly screamed. Gerry, stunned by what had happened, released the woman.

'Check her out,' Mavis said.

Polly had hold of Liz's head. 'Can you hear me?' A weak murmur from the woman on the floor.

'She's alright,' Mavis said.

'It's assault. We'll sue.'

'Join the queue. You'll not be the first, not the last either.'

'She'll need a doctor,' Gerry said.

'Rubbish. The woman's feigning injury, hoping that I'll relent, give them some money.'

'I don't think so. She's genuinely hurt.'

'Okay, take her to the hospital, get her fixed up.'

'In the Bentley?'

'Not a chance. Take one of their cars. And when you've finished, bring both of the cars to the house.'

'You'll pay for this,' Polly said, her friend slowly coming around.

'Pay? I've paid enough for you two already, screwing my husband, disturbing my life. Once she's better, you're out of your flat, two days maximum. At least she's gained some experience of being flat on her back. All she needs is a man on top of her, and she's got it made.'

'It wasn't like that, us and Alan,' Polly said.

'Rubbish. You thought he was an easy touch, plenty of money. How you two got past the other tarts is beyond me, but you did. You've had your fun, but now it's over. Forty-eight hours and you're out, and next time I'll send someone other than Gerry. If he comes, he's more likely to screw you than do his job. And let me be clear, if he stuffs up one more time, brother-in-law or no brother-in-law, he's out on the street with you two. Maybe he can pimp for you.'

Gerry said nothing, realising that his chances of getting into Mavis's bed were looking very remote indeed.

***

After dealing with Margie, Clare found Rachel Winters, the eldest child of Alan Winters, to be a breath of fresh air. She was hard at work at Salisbury Hospital on Odstock Road. 'I'm interested in hospital administration,' she said. Clare could see the resemblance to the mother, although the young woman looked after herself, the mother did not.

The two women sat in the cafeteria; Clare bought herself a latte, another one for Rachel. 'You seem to be handling the situation well enough,' Clare said.

'Not really. I just need to keep busy.'

'What can you tell me about your father?'

'He was a weak man, I suppose you know that.'

'We do. What about his behaviour after the lottery win?'

'It destroyed him, Mum as well.'

'All that money?'

'Before, my dad didn't do much, but he'd go to work, come home, get drunk, and my mother was there for him. The pair didn't have the greatest of marriages, not many do, but at least they were together, and most times they were content.'

'And you?'

'I had a child when I was young, but you know that.'

'An accident?'

'Young and silly, I thought it was love. Never considered that I'd end up pregnant. Anyway, he died.'

'Sad about that?'

'What do you think?'

'Devastated.'

'At the time, but I'm okay now. I'm still young, there's still time to find another man, have a few children.'

'You're not like your parents,' Clare said.

'Bertie's like my dad; I'm the spitting image of my mother.'

'I can't see it.'

'Mum never had the opportunities or the education. She's a hard worker, always there for Bertie and me, and then with Dad, well, he was another child as well, even before we had money, and then after the win.'

'You'd prefer that it hadn't happened?'

'I suppose so, but how can anyone resist that much money? It would drive anyone mad. The fact that you never have to worry again about paying the bills, the ability to indulge every obsession, every fantasy.'

'The women?'

'Dad never looked at another woman before, except in his mind, but then, there they were, so many.'

'He had two specials.'

'Polly and Liz.'

'You knew them?

'Vaguely, before they latched on to Dad. Polly, I liked, not so much Liz, but they were decent enough, but then the money and the clothes, and being squired around in a Bentley. Any woman would be seduced.'

'I wouldn't,' Clare said. 'You weren't.'

'Don't get me wrong. I love the money, the fact that I can drive a nice car, live well, but I need the mental satisfaction that I'm contributing, not just hanging like a leech on the fortune. It's good to know that I can attend all the courses, buy all the books I want, but I refuse to let the money dictate my life.'

'The people here? Do they hassle you?'

'Not the people I work with, although if someone in one of the wards finds out, they can sometimes be a nuisance.'

'Your brother?'

'Same as Dad, but with money. My father could only drink so much with no money, Bertie has no such restraint.'

'Your father could have stopped him having the money to buy drugs.'

'My mother will deal with Bertie.'

'Will she?'

'As long as she controls the money.'

'And now, will you stay at the house?'

'I'm not sure. I've got a boyfriend, or I think he's my boyfriend.'

'You're not sure?'

'There's been a few who've fancied their chances, but I've never been sure if it's the money or me.'

'You're an attractive woman,' Clare said.

'Maybe I am, but I can't be sure if it's me they want. You won't tell Mum, will you?'

'Your secret is safe with me.'

***

Clare was preparing to leave the hospital and to drive back to Bemerton Road Police Station when her phone rang. 'Stay where you are,' Tremayne said.

'What's up?'

'Liz Maybury. She's in the Intensive Care Unit.'

'How? Why?'

'I've just had a phone call from Polly Bennett. Apparently, there was an altercation with Mavis Winters. It'd be best if you get over to her as soon as possible, find out what's going on.'

Clare locked her car and walked the hundred yards from Administration to the Intensive Care Unit. She found Gerry Winters soon enough. 'What's going on?'

'Liz, she hit her head hard on a wall. There's internal bleeding in the brain.'

'Polly Bennett?'

'She's nearby. It was an accident.'

'After we've found out her condition, we need to talk.'

'Mavis blew it, took her anger out on the women.'

'Where?'

'At the furniture store. Mavis wanted them out, the cars back, and then to evict them from the flat Alan had set them up with.'

'She's within her rights.'

'I know, but Mavis is acting unreasonably. Alan was the one with the money. Polly and Liz were just taking advantage, trying to survive.'

'Are you defending their behaviour?'

'Not me, but I've known what it is to be poor, the same as them. And besides, Liz could die. It's an accident, but you'll distort the evidence, make it out to be manslaughter.'

'Mr Winters, we do not distort evidence.'

'Sorry. I'm just angry that this has happened.'

'Do you like the two women?'

'I've nothing against them. It's alright if you win the lottery, but others have to survive, kowtow to those who've had the luck, even if they did not deserve it.'

'We're not here to discuss the injustices of life,' Clare said, realising that if life were just, then Harry Holchester, her fiancé, would still be alive, but he wasn't, and that was fate, nothing to do with luck.

Tremayne arrived to find Clare and Gerry Winters sitting in the waiting area. 'What's happened? he asked.

'There's been an altercation between Liz Maybury and Mavis Winters,' Clare said. 'If the woman dies, it's manslaughter.'

'It's an accident,' Winters said.

'We'll take the statements later. We'll decide then,' Tremayne said.

Clare could see that he was reluctant to consider laying charges against Mavis Winters; she realised it was understandable under the circumstances.

Polly Bennett came through the doors that separated the waiting room from Intensive Care. 'She's under sedation. They think she'll pull through,' she said.

'Her parents?' Clare said.

'I've phoned them. They're on their way. I want to press charges against Mavis Winters.'

'That's up to us,' Tremayne said. 'We'll take statements from everyone before we decide on a course of action.'

'She did it on purpose. Gerry was there, he'll tell you.'

'Miss Bennett, Polly, we've got to consider your friend first. Standing here debating what we're going to do does not help her. We'll need to talk to her first,' Clare said.

'You're right, I suppose, but I need somewhere to stay tonight. The bitch has kicked us out.'

'That's not true,' Gerry said. 'She's given you forty-eight hours. Under the circumstances, she'll reconsider, give you longer. She was angry; you know she had every right.'

'You'll not take our side?' Polly asked, miffed that the man was hedging his bets.

'I'll tell the truth. An accident, unfortunate maybe, but she only wanted you and Liz out of her life.'

'Was she angry enough to hurt the woman?' Tremayne asked.

'Angry, but she had been provoked. Liz was hurling insults. Apart from that wall, it would have ended there and then, and I would have evicted them that day. As it is, they can stay until Liz is better.'

'You bastard. After the way we treated you,' Polly said.

'What does that mean?' Clare said, looking at Gerry Winters.

'The Alan Winters treatment, what else?'

'What else indeed,' Clare replied, knowing full well what the treatment entailed. She realised that Mavis Winters' summation of the two women was spot on: they were a couple of whores.

Chapter 7

Bertie Winters: dissolute, reprobate, of little worth. As good a definition of the man as any, Clare thought. He had not been hard to find after checking out of the facility where his mother had placed him in a last-ditch attempt to save him.

'What do you want?' the young man said after he had opened the door at Cyril Winters' house.

'Sergeant Yarwood, I've a few questions.'

'You'd better come in,' the twenty-two year old replied, his straggly hair touching on his collar, his three-day stubble clearly seen. Clare had to admit that behind the unkempt appearance there was probably an attractive man. The smell of marijuana pervaded the air.

'No cocaine?' Clare said.

'That costs money.'

'You've got plenty.'

'Not anymore. That bitch of a mother has cut me off, told me to get a job.'

'Your sister wants to work.'

'Why should I? My father had plenty, and he did nothing for it. I'm entitled to do what I want.'

'Your father had been lucky. Are you expecting to win the lottery anytime soon?'

'I've got my legal rights. I'm entitled to some of the money.'

'Legally, you're probably entitled to nothing.'

Clare could see the man looking her up and down. It made her feel uncomfortable. She had sometimes seen it at Bemerton Road. There they were careful not to be too obvious and smart enough to keep their comments in check, but she knew that Bertie Winters would get around to it soon enough.

'What do you want anyway? I saw you round at my house the other day.'

'Your father's been murdered. Aren't you concerned?'

'Should I be? The man had a good time, plenty of good-looking women, and what did I get? Nothing, that's what. Just an old Toyota to drive and an allowance. I'm not a child doing chores to receive pocket money, I'm a man. I need my own place, my own money, a few women. Dad, he wasn't much, but he respected me, gave me money.'

'He wouldn't buy you a fancy car.'

'He would have in time. I knew about him and those women. He'd have paid for me to keep quiet.'

'If you're referring to Polly Bennett and Liz Maybury, your mother knows.'

'Not that.'

'What then?'

'There were others.'

'And why are they so important? Your father is dead, your mother needs your support. You should be with her.'

'Why? She doesn't care if my father's dead,' Bertie said as he puffed on his joint. 'Do you want some?'

'No thanks,' Clare said. She'd tried it at boarding school once, everyone had, but she had not enjoyed the experience, and besides drugs were not her thing, and sitting down with Bertie Winters did not appeal. It was clear that the lottery win had helped some people, Mavis and Rachel Winters, in particular, but it had destroyed or was about to destroy others. Alan Winters had died because of his money, and Bertie, the son, was a sure-fire candidate for premature death in the next few years, even if he went back to drug rehabilitation, moved back into the mansion in Quidhampton. The man was lazy, as had been the father, as was Cyril, and even with an old Toyota, he was bound to have an accident at some stage.

'Your uncle? Where is he?'

'Down the pub, I suppose. He likes to drink.'

'The same as your father.'

'Maybe, not that he'll be able to impress any of the women.'

'Mr Winters, did you kill your father? Would you kill your mother if she does not give you what you want?'

'Are you mad? Why would I do that?'

'For the money. Without your parents, the money would be yours and Rachel's.'

'Would it? It's a good idea.'

'I'm a police officer, yet you continue to smoke an illegal substance.'

'You're uptight, and besides, you want to find out who killed my father. Arresting me for a minor misdemeanour won't help your investigation.'

'Why?'

'I've seen things, know things.'

'It's a maximum of five years in jail if I arrest you.'

'What's the point. Mum, even if she won't give me what I want, she'll ensure that I have the best lawyers.'

'It's clear that you are not without some intelligence. Was your father intelligent?'

'He could be. He was lazy, the same as I am, and then he was rich. I'll be rich one day.'

'How?'

'You've just told me. If my mother dies, then I get half of what's left. It'll be enough for me.'

'Your mother could disinherit you, give it all to your sister.'

'She can't do that.'

'Yes, she can.'

'Then I'd take her to court.'

'With what? You'll have no money. You'll not win. Mr Winters. I'll put it to you again, did you kill your father because he would not buy you a better car? Are you planning to do the same with your mother? Are you aware of any will?' Clare knew that she was using a trick of Tremayne's in throwing rapid-fire accusations at the person, knowing full well that it would test

66

their resolve to deflect the answers, and would confuse and divert them.

Bertie Winters stood up, made for Clare, attempted to grab her. She took one swipe at him, causing the man to fall back onto his bean bag. 'You bitch, I did not kill my father. He was a lovely man, the only one that cared. That Rachel, with her stuck-up manner, her ambition. That bitch can go to hell. If my mother dies, then I'll take it all for myself, I'm telling you that.'

'Thank you, Mr Winters, you've told me all I need to know.'

'What's that?'

'That you are a weak excuse for a man and that you have not killed your father.'

'How dare you insult me.'

'I'll do what I want. What are you going to do? Complain to the police?'

'I'll remember, that's what I'll do.'

'And that's all. You should be grateful that I'm not arresting you today. Another day I might not be so generous. You did not kill your father, you'll not kill your mother.'

'What makes you so sure?'

'Because you're like your father, like your uncle. They are, were, both lazy, boring and fat men, full of bravado with a few pints in them, but up at Stonehenge on a cold night, a knife in their hand, they'd be running home to their mother, the same as you will eventually once the money runs out. Cocaine, marijuana, beer, they all cost money, and you don't have enough, or do you?'

'I've got some.'

'Enough to register the car? Enough for drugs? Enough to keep you here in this depressing little council house when there's a beautiful house not far from here? I don't think so.'

'If you weren't a woman…'

'Then what? You'd take me outside and kick my arse, is that it?'

'That's it. I'll not let any man talk to me like that.'

'But you'll let a woman, you'll let your mother. I suggest you get yourself back into rehab before your brain is totally addled.'

Clare left the house, phoned Tremayne. 'Bertie Winters did not kill his father,' she said. 'He's a drugged-out reprobate of no consequence, but not a murderer.'

'Can you be sure?'

'We can never be one hundred per cent certain, but I pushed him hard, rapid-fire questions. He'd have let slip something if he was guilty, and besides, he'd still need an accomplice. Alan Winters' death needed forethought and planning, and Bertie Winters is capable of neither.'

***

Liz Maybury, under mild sedation for ten days, was slowly brought back to full consciousness. The private ward, the specialist treatment, were paid for by Mavis Winters on legal advice. The woman's death or incapacity would reflect poorly on her if Mavis had not ensured the best medical care.

Liz Maybury's parents had taken turns to be at her bedside since the injury; Polly, her friend, visited every day. Liz's parents had not been pleased when interviewed by Tremayne and Clare, upset when told the reason for the altercation.

Polly was still living in the flat supplied by Alan, a possible payoff from Mavis if necessary. As for the furniture store, it was closed and up for sale, at a bargain price if anyone was willing to pay.

On the eleventh day, Clare was let into the ward, as long as she was willing to keep her questioning low key, no loud voices, no anger, and nothing that would disturb the fragile condition of the patient. Tremayne was not given permission; his presence was deemed not agreeable.

'Liz, Sergeant Yarwood. How are you feeling?'

'Fine, I think. They told me I've been here for nearly two weeks.'

On a chair in the far corner sat Liz Maybury's father.

'Do you remember what happened?'

'The woman went crazy, accusing Polly and me of seducing her husband, telling us to get out and on the street. We're not like that, really.'

Clare looked over at the father; he seemed uncomfortable about his daughter's revelations, although he had already been told, as had his wife, of Polly and Liz's relationship with Alan Winters. Clare could only feel compassion for them, as they seemed to be good people with a good daughter who had been swayed by the lure of an inordinate amount of money and luxury and a bad influence, namely Polly Bennett.

Clare had had to agree with them, it seemed to be the only right thing to do, but her investigations pointed to the woman in the hospital bed as the worst influence.

'Did she slam you into the wall intentionally?'

'It was an accident. She was angry, we all were, and Gerry, he stood there and did nothing, only held Polly's arm. Alan's wife, she was crazy, crazy angry. I suppose I can't blame her, but he didn't love her.'

'Did he love you?'

'Not us, but he was going to see us right.'

'Did you like him?'

'Not really. He was okay, but he was not an attractive man.'

'Only rich.'

'As you say. I've no regrets, neither has Polly.'

'And your relationship with Polly?'

'We're friends, that's all.'

'Lesbian?'

'Not me, not Polly. We like men.'

'Richer the better?'

'Maybe, and now Alan's dead.'

'We've spoken about this before. Are you sorry that he's dead?'

'Not really. When can I leave here?'

'That's not up to me. You need rest.'

'There's a place at home with us,' the father said.

'Not there. I want to be with Polly.'

'She's still at the place that Alan gave you.'

'That's what Polly said. Why? I thought his wife wanted us out.'

'You would be if you weren't here. Mavis Winters is paying for your treatment, did you know that?'

'Why?'

'Guilty conscience, legal advice. Whatever the reason, be thankful.'

'And after I'm out of here?'

'You'll need to talk to Mavis, not me.'

Outside the ward, the father spoke to Clare. 'Is it true? Liz and her friend were trading sexual favours for the place where they live, the cars they drive, the furniture store?'

'You've been told this before.'

'I know we have, but I need to check again.'

'I'm sorry, Mr Maybury, but yes, Polly Bennett and your daughter were doing just that.'

'It's not something you expect to hear about your children. A daughter who is no more than a prostitute.'

'I can't offer you any words of consolation, I'm afraid. We're conducting a murder investigation. I can't ignore certain facts which are relevant to the case in an attempt to hide the truth, protect the feelings of loved ones.'

'I understand,' Maybury said. Clare left a sad man talking to his wife.

***

Tremayne and Yarwood met in the office at Bemerton Road. The Homicide department was not busy, a sure sign that Superintendent Moulton would be on the warpath soon. There was another letter from Human Resources with an improved retirement package on the desk. Tremayne pushed it to one side.

'It's worth considering,' Clare said, although she didn't know the amount specified, only noted her senior's look when he had seen the figures.

'And leave you here on your own. Not a chance.'

'We need to talk about this case. What do we have so far?'

'A motive.'

'The money. Can there be anything else?' Clare said.

'It's this Stonehenge connection that I don't get. A death up there must be symbolic, but what is it?'

'Who are we discounting as the murderers?'

'Cyril Winters, too lazy, and nothing to gain. He's received some money; no doubt would have received more from Alan if he had asked. Mavis won't be so easy.'

'I'm discounting Bertie Winters, the son, for the same reason, although with the mother dead, he'd inherit. But he's still lazy, not enough energy to cross the road let alone drive up to Stonehenge,' Clare said.

'Mavis Winters has the strongest motive, but she's smart enough to know she'd be a primary suspect. And she'd still need an accomplice.'

'No one has an immediate motive; no one was going to gain in the short term.'

'Dean Winters. He says he's not interested in the money, but he's angry enough to want their lives destroyed.'

'He'd still need an accomplice.'

'If it's Dean, then who could be his accomplice? His wife maybe. We didn't interview her, saw no point at the time. If Stan and Fred, the two brothers, were not in prison, I'd consider them as potential murderers.'

'What about the man who raped Margie? The other live-ins of the mother? Did they kill them or frighten them off?'

'Raping their sister? I'd say they killed that man, not that you can blame them.'

'It's still murder.'

'I know it is, and I'd arrest them if there were a case, but it's not part of the current investigation. Could either of the two brothers have been capable of organising Alan Winters' death from behind bars?'

'What would they have to gain? Assuming Alan Winters is dead, then the money goes to his wife, then his children.'

'And what about Alan Winters' father? What happened to him?'

'The mother may know.'

'We'll interview the mother today. I'll arrange to meet up with Stan and Fred later in the week.'

Chapter 8

The house in Quidhampton was abuzz with decorators on Tremayne and Clare's arrival. They had phoned ahead, spoken to Mavis Winters, told her the reason for coming.

'You'll not get much out of Alan's mother,' Mavis Winters said.

'Why?'

'Inconsolable grief, although it's too little, too late. She should have thought about her children when they were young.'

'She'll talk to us?'

'She'll talk, not that she'll make much sense.'

Tremayne could see an angry woman, remembered a girl of sixteen. It was as if she was two separate people, but then he had changed too. Back then, when they had made love, or more accurately fumbled around in the dark, somehow consummating the relationship, he had been young and dark-haired, with a sideways profile that was as flat as a board. She, he remembered, had been firm and tender, and compliant in his arms. And now she was rich when she had been poor. He was not rich, never wanted to be, although the offer from Human Resources was indeed generous, certainly more than enough to redecorate his house to allow Jean to move in, even if it was only on an occasional basis. He kept thinking of her, knowing that she was a good woman, loyal to a fault, comparing her to the Winters. They may be as rich as Croesus, but they had nothing that he wanted. The lottery win, all sixty-eight million pounds, had transformed their lives, not enhanced them. Alan had died, Mavis was in despair over her son and worrying about who was after their money. The only one who was immune appeared to be the daughter, Rachel. Yarwood had admitted to liking the woman, believing her not to be involved, but she, it was assumed, was in for a half-share of a fortune when her mother died; enough to turn a saint into a sinner, and Rachel Winters was no saint, only a woman of flesh and bone.

Alan Winters' mother was upstairs in her room. Clare could see that it was large enough, although its condition was far from ideal. The woman did not look after herself. In the bathroom, clothes were hanging from the shower curtain rail. 'I'm not going down there,' the woman said.

'Your name is Betty Winters?' Tremayne said. The three were sitting on some chairs close to the window. Clare wanted to open the window to let in some fresh air, but did not. Betty Winters sat on the edge of her chair, her feet barely touching the ground. Tremayne remembered her vaguely from years ago, had seen her in the house since her son's death, but he had not realised how haggard she was. Before, downstairs in the kitchen when she had been preparing a meal, with Mavis Winters abusing her, the woman had seemed upright and hard-working. Now she was bent over, wearing just a pink-coloured dressing gown. On her feet, she wore a pair of slippers.

'She killed him, the bitch.'

'Who?'

'Who do you think?'

'Mavis?' Tremayne said.

'Yes, her. She never liked him, always screwing around she was.'

'We've found no evidence of that,' Clare said.

'I know her type. String a man along, milk him for all he's worth and then dump him.'

Clare thought it sounded like an apt description of the woman they were talking to.

'Tell us about Alan,' Clare said.

'He treated me well. He was my favourite.'

'Why? Because he let you live here? Because he had money?'

'She wants me to go and live with Cyril.'

'Will you go?'

'What option do I have? Cyril hates me, they all do, a poor old woman.'

74

Clare could not feel any sympathy for the woman if what they had been told was true. 'We've been told that your husband moved out of the house.'

'After he'd given me seven mongrel children.'

'We've spoken to all of them, except for Stan and Fred. Have you seen them?'

'Not them. They're ashamed of their own mother, and there they are, in prison. They've no right to stick their noses up at me.'

'We've been told that after your husband left, you had a number of men.'

'I was still young.'

'We're not criticising; we just need to ascertain the background to this investigation. To see if your children's upbringing has any bearing on the investigation.'

'I was on my own. I did the best I could.'

'What about the men who abused your children? What about the man who raped Margie?'

'Margie was a tart, even back then.'

'Margie was an adolescent. It was up to her mother to protect her,' Clare said. Tremayne could see that his sergeant was becoming upset, imagining the horror that the woman's daughter had gone through.

'Mrs Winters, Margie was a child in the eyes of the law. It was your responsibility to have her checked out by a doctor and for charges to be laid against the man. Why didn't you?' Tremayne said.

'I used to see her, short skirts, stuffing toilet paper down her bra. What man can resist?'

'Were you abused as a child?' Clare asked.

'Who wasn't, but we didn't end up on the street as a prostitute. Margie was always weak.'

'You knew, yet you did nothing. Was the man more important than your daughter?'

'I hated them all. I only cared for Alan. He was the only one who looked after me.'

'What happened to the man who attacked Margie?'

'He disappeared. I don't know. They never lasted anyway, too many children for them to care about.'

'You neglected the children, blaming them instead of your husband. What happened to him? Where can we find him?'

'I've no idea. Ask Dean, he may know.'

'Why Dean?'

'He's the smart one, not that he cares about me, never a birthday card, never a phone call.'

'Mrs Winters, I'm afraid you don't deserve anything from your children. You knew that your daughter had been raped, yet you did nothing. What were you planning to do? Sell her off to the local perverts? What sort of mother are you? Did you kill Alan, arrange for someone to take him up to Stonehenge and cut his throat?'

'Why would I do that? He was my son, I loved him.'

'Mrs Winters, you love no one. You are beneath contempt. If Mavis wants you out and with Cyril, then she is within her rights.'

Downstairs Tremayne and Clare found Mavis Winters involved in the redecorations. 'What do you reckon? Mavis asked.

'She's a hard woman,' Clare said. 'She knew about Margie.'

'Poor Margie, she's beyond hope.'

'Bertie?'

'He said you had given him an earful. Thanks for that.'

'Will it help?'

'He's back in rehab, but no. He'll try if pushed and I'll maintain a firm hand, but he's an adult. Apart from keeping him out of trouble, it's up to him, and I'm afraid he just doesn't have it in him.'

'Rachel?' Clare asked.

'She'll do well. Maybe she'll be able to look after Bertie when I'm gone.'

'You're only young,' Tremayne said.

'I suppose so. I'm just hoping that Bertie will outlive me.'

'Will he?'

'He's entitled to some of the money. There's not much I can do to stop it. Our solicitor set it up. When he reaches twenty-five, he's entitled to ten per cent, so is Rachel. It's a shame Alan died.'

'Why?'

'If he had lived, it would have been ten per cent of nothing. I've limited the losses; there'll be over thirty million, and with some investments, it should be more. I'm learning economics, money management on the internet.'

'Polly Bennett and Liz Maybury?'

'I was angry that day, but I didn't intend for one of them to end up in hospital. I've spoken to Polly, told her that the two of them can keep the flat and the cars. They'll still belong to me, though.'

'The furniture store?'

'Maybe they can manage it for me, as long as Gerry keeps away.'

'Will he?'

'They'll not give him the time of day if he doesn't have any money.'

'You'll ensure that?'

'He's got a job here. I'll pay him twice what he's worth, but it's nothing like the money that Alan had. They'll not waste their time on him.'

'And Alan's mother?'

'There's Cyril's place. She doesn't deserve any better.'

Clare could only agree. She knew she needed a drink. The time with the mother had left her feeling upset and down. The lot of a police officer is what Tremayne would say, but it still didn't alter the fact that she had spent time upstairs in that house with an evil woman.

***

Gerry Winters was not the most pleasant of men, in that he had a history of low-level violence in the city: drunken brawls, arguments with the neighbours, roughing up one of his girlfriends.

The first time they had visited the house in Quidhampton, he had been at the entrance keeping away the media and the general public after the death of Alan had become known. And whereas the media interest had waned, the beaming face of Alan Winters holding the cheque for sixty-eight million pounds still graced some magazine covers, the story inside plotting the fall of the luckiest man in England from infinite wealth to eternal death, the murder described in as much detail as possible. Stonehenge, the location of his death, was open to the general public again, although as always, the inner circle was restricted to just a few visitors, apart from during the summer solstice when the Druids and the other lovers of nature made a pilgrimage to the site.

'What do you want, Tremayne? Haven't you caused enough damage as it is?' Gerry Winters said. He was propping up the bar at the Old Mill in Harnham, the Bentley not visible outside.

'It's a murder investigation. A few eggs will be cracked on the way, and besides, what do you mean? Nothing's happened to you.'

'She's put me on wages, her own brother-in-law. What right does she have?'

'It's her money.'

'It's not. I drove him to that newsagent. I lent him the money to buy the damn ticket and then what happens? He goes and wins.'

'He repaid your loan?'

'We always joked that if either of us won, we'd share it with the other.'

'And he reneged on the deal?'

'It was her. She wouldn't let him.'

'Are you sure? Or is it just a few pints of anger and bitterness?'

'I've only had two.'

Tremayne looked over at the barman. He shook his head, raised one hand, palm forward, all five fingers.

'How about you and the two women?' Tremayne asked.

'Not a chance there. I liked Polly, but she only wants rich money.'

'You could borrow the money from Mavis, set up your own business,' Clare said. She was sipping from a glass of wine, Tremayne was on his second pint of beer. If Gerry Winters was feeling sorry for himself, drinking more than he should, then an otherwise hidden fact might be revealed.

'What skills do I have?'

'You must be good at something.'

'Hard work is for mugs. Alan didn't do anything with his life, and he ended up rich.'

'Rich and dead,' Tremayne said.

'What can you tell us about the night? Where were you? And what's the truth with you and Mavis?'

'I thought I could take her off Alan's hands after he died.'

'And before?'

'What do you mean?'

'According to Polly Bennett and Liz Maybury, on one of the occasions he took them back to his house, Mavis was occupied in another room. Any truth to that and was it you?'

'Not me. And I don't believe it. Mavis was a decent woman, still is, and whereas Alan was a waste of space, she was the one who kept the house together.'

'Apart from Bertie?'

'It runs in the family.'

'What? General apathy and disinterest in anything other than screwing and getting drunk. And what about Margie? She's in a terrible state. Don't you care about her?'

'What are you, Tremayne, a bleeding social worker or a police officer? How we run our lives is none of your concern, nor your sergeant's, granted that she's prettier than you. How about it, luv? Fancy a man down on his luck?'

'I've spent an unpleasant forty-five minutes with your mother. You don't want my answer and don't treat me as one of your tarts. We know about your arrangement with the two women. How you'd look after their interests, how they'd look after you.'

'I told you that.'

'They'll not be interested now. You've got nothing to offer, not even a ride in the Bentley.'

'Mavis has me trapped. She knows I'll keep working for her. I'm no better than a lap dog.'

'It's better than the alternative. There's always a spare bed at Cyril's house, or maybe you can lodge with Dean, although his wife would have you jumping through hoops.'

'Another bitch.'

'What do you mean?'

'She wears the trousers in that house. If it weren't for her, we'd be able to go down there, Dean would come up here. As it is, he keeps his distance.'

'He's never asked for money.'

'Dean, he knows the value of money, but she's extreme, believes that hard work, not charity, is the solution. She'd rather sleep on the street than come up here and ask for help.'

'She sounds a decent woman, a person who believes that it is the individual who determines their future, not a lottery ticket.'

'Lovely words, no doubt, but do you believe that rubbish? Dean's wife is a bitch; the one time we saw her, she launched into a tirade about how she was going to make one of the Winters into someone respectable, and as far as she was concerned, the rest could go to hell, especially the mother.'

'What did you do?'

'I hit her, right across the face.'

'And then what?'

'She hit me back, harder than I hit her. Dean stood there, his mouth wide open. She grabbed him by the arm and shot out of the house. None of us has seen her or Dean since, apart from Alan that one time.'

'How long ago since you've seen Dean?'

'It must be fifteen years.'

'Not even your mother?'

'She doesn't care anyway.'

'You dislike your mother the same as the others?'

'Dislike? That's probably right. She wasn't there for us when we were young.'

Chapter 9

Tremayne, back in the office, sat at his desk. He was leaning back, eyes closed, the front two legs of the chair off the ground. Clare could see that he was mentally going over the case so far; she decided to give him a few minutes until he'd concluded, or until the chair collapsed under his weight. The man was neither small nor light, and the chair was not heavy-duty.

Clare continued with her paperwork, an unfortunate result of the computer age, where the administrators enjoyed thinking up new ways to keep people confined to their desks. Superintendent Moulton relished reports. Tremayne was dismissive of their superintendent, but she was not. To her, he was trying to keep the police station efficient without being overly authoritative.

Clare typed away, pleased that she was capable with a keyboard, and a couple of hours every few days was enough for her to get through the bulk of the administrative tasks. Not that it helped Tremayne, who'd labour over every report he had to prepare, cursing under his breath as he pressed each key one after the other. It was painful to watch, and if he had wanted, she would have helped, but she knew him to be a proud man.

Her boss, she knew, was a stereotype of the archetypical policeman: dedicated, terse in manner, economical in compliments, determined to leave no stone unturned, no matter how small it was. She saw him as an excellent character for a television series; he fitted the mould perfectly, though he would not have appreciated her analysis of him.

Clare looked again. The man was now sitting on his chair, the four legs firmly on the ground again. It seemed the time for her to approach. 'What's the verdict, guv,' she said.

'What verdict? We've got nothing.'

'We've got a lot of people. There's a few in there who could have killed him.'

'Mavis is the most likely, but she would have needed help. The man, we know, had some medical issues, even if he did not know about them, or didn't care. Who would think that Stonehenge would be the ideal place? And the only people who would gain from his death are the immediate family. There's no question that it was Alan Winters who purchased the ticket, or is there?'

'I've checked. The man won the prize fair and square. The newsagent said he was a regular in the shop, always bought a ticket every week, before heading over to the pub. He placed a sign outside the shop after Winters had won. You know the sort of thing, buy your ticket here, you could have the same luck.'

'And they fell for it as if the shop was blessed by the god of good fortune.'

'Why not? People believe that if they see a four-leafed clover, it somehow foretells their future. Even you hold up your betting slip and say a few words as the horse lumbers around the track.'

'That's just fun, at least for me.'

'For you, but some people believe in the rituals. We've spoken about this before, but there are some who would see Winters' death as a rite of passage, the transference of his good fortune onto the murderer.'

'Dean Winters said there was mongrel DNA. Maybe he knew something.'

'He'll not appreciate another visit, or his wife won't.'

'And you care, Yarwood?'

'Not at all. If there's a screw loose somewhere, we need to know. Maybe all of them, although some are just too lazy to do anything about it.'

'Gerry Winters would, and he's angry enough, believes that he was cheated out of his fair share of the money.'

'Why was he? Legally he didn't have a leg to stand on, but Alan was his brother. According to him, it was Mavis who did not honour the agreement, and if she had so much sway over her husband, why did she allow him to play around with other women?'

'A visit to Mavis first, then on to Dean, is that it?'

'I reckon so. I'll make the phone calls.'

'Don't bother. We'll just knock on the doors, judge the reaction,' Tremayne said.

***

Compared to their previous visits to the Winters' house, it was quiet. The cleaners, the interior decorators, the general hubbub of family visiting to offer their sympathies no longer apparent.

'She's gone,' Mavis Winters said as she opened the door.

'Who?' Clare asked.

'His damn mother.'

'Gone where?'

'Back to that depressing council house. She came down from her room, a stinking mess by the way, cost me plenty to get it fumigated and cleaned out, and she was in the kitchen accusing me of killing her beloved son. She's one to speak, the old trollop. She didn't care when he was alive, not even as a child, and there she is, lecturing me for all her worth.'

'She went voluntarily?' Tremayne said.

'Not a chance. I grabbed her suitcase, stuffed a few of her belongings in it, and shuffled her out the door. Gerry dropped her off at Cyril's house. It must have been some homecoming.'

'And you don't feel a little sad at what you've done?' Clare said.

'She was a wicked old woman, not deserving of any kindness. We reap what we sow, that's something I remember from Sunday school, and she sowed plenty of weeds.'

'It's still sad,' Clare said, remembering her grandmother who had passed away not long before her initial move to Salisbury. The grandmother had been loved, even though as she aged she became progressively more cantankerous, and here was

84

a woman who professed no compassion for an old woman. Maybe it was right, in that the woman was demanding and embittered and had led a fruitless life, full of malignancy, but she was still an old woman, not more than a few years left in her. It just didn't seem right to Clare.

'Anyway, what are you here for? Not to talk about Polly Bennett and Liz Maybury?'

'What's happened to them?' Clare said.

'I've met up with Polly. I don't mind the woman, apart from what she did. She's smart enough, a bit of a tart, but then most of them are these days. No sooner are they out of their school uniform and they're down behind the bike shed with the local stud.'

Or in the other room with a young police officer, Clare thought but did not say it out aloud.

'What have you agreed with her? Tremayne said, noticing the smirk on his sergeant's face. He knew what she was thinking.

'The two women can run the furniture store, keep the flat and cars. It's a purely financial agreement. I need to consider the future, make some investments. They know that if they don't make a go of it, they're out on the street.'

'You've forgiven them?' Clare said.

'It takes two to tango, or in their case, three. Men, they're all the same, a tight arse, a wiggle, a heaving bosom pressed against them in the pub.'

Clare, who had warmed to the woman since their initial meeting, could see a hardness developing. She wasn't sure that she liked Mavis's attitude. For the first time, she felt that Mavis could indeed be capable of murder.

'We had come here to talk to you about two issues that give us concern, although I believe that you've answered the first one.'

'Why I let him play around?'

'That's the first.'

'What else could I do? The man's flush with money; he's driving a Ferrari until he prangs it, then it's a Bentley. The man was not a saint, and besides, I was busy enjoying myself as well.'

'Other men?'

'Not me, although there were opportunities. I was into expensive clothes, beauty treatments, eating at expensive restaurants, no longer looking in my purse wondering if I could afford to buy the brand-name food rather than the generic. We were both mad for a few months, and by then, Alan's well entrenched into his lifestyle and I'm into mine. And then this house came along, and I'm busy indulging myself. Having unlimited money is seductive. It's a mistress you can't refuse, you know you should, but it's impossible. It destroyed us in many ways, enriched us in others. Unless you've experienced it, you'll never know.'

'You could have given it away,' Clare said.

'That's never an option. As much as you believe it's the right thing, you will never do it.'

'Did Gerry ever stake a claim on the money?' Tremayne said.

'That old chestnut, the belief that he was entitled to a half-share because he had driven Alan to the newsagent.'

'Something like that.'

'How many times have you heard it? When I win the lottery, we'll share the proceeds.'

'Plenty, but no one ever does.'

'We all used to joke about being rich, everyone does. It's harmless make-believe, a fantasy.'

'Your fantasy came true,' Clare said.

'It did. And then the people came. All of the relatives, Gerry at the front of the queue, even his mother, who somehow believed that giving birth to the winner gave her some rights.'

'Did it?'

'Nothing, although she's been looked after, we even paid for a hip replacement, fixed up a few health problems. Apart from the relatives, there are the friends we never knew we had, even the newsagent where Alan bought the ticket. He thought he was entitled to at least fifty thousand.'

'What did he get?'

'Nothing. He had the ticket, could have purchased it for himself, instead of allowing the suckers to spend their wages on a frivolity.'

'Not a frivolity in your case.'

'Good luck, nothing else. Anyway, the newsagent got nothing. The brothers each received a cash payment of one hundred thousand and a solicitor's letter to sign.'

'Even Stan and Fred?'

'Even them.'

'And Dean?'

'It was offered.'

'What happened?'

'That stupid wife of his. Have you met her?'

'Not yet.'

'Don't bother. She's a venomous toad of a woman. I've no idea what Dean sees in her, although he's a weak man, the same as the others.'

'He's been successful.'

'I'll grant you that. Dean was the only one who did well at school, and he can be academic. Then he meets up with her, and she's pushing him forward. Heaven to him, hell to anyone else.'

'You never answered the question about Gerry. Was he entitled to a half-share?'

'Just because he drove Alan to the newsagents? Get real. The man was entitled to nothing, the same as the other bloodsuckers. He got his hundred thousand, even Alan's women, Polly Bennett and Liz Maybury. What else does he need?'

'He's fond of you,' Clare said.

'He's not a bad man, but I've no need of him. I've just got rid of his brother. What makes you think I'd go back for seconds?'

'Got rid of!' Tremayne said.

'A figure of speech, and you know it. It was luck on my part that he died, my lottery ticket if you like, and now the money will all be mine in another week.'

'Why's that?'

'You're releasing his body. We'll have a get-together here after the funeral. You'll come?'

'We will.'

'Come and enjoy yourself. Don't come here as a police officer.'

'But that's what we are. You realise that his murderers could be among the mourners?'

'I'm aware of it, but do you honestly believe this is related to the money?'

'It's the only motive that makes any sense, and now you're the person with the money.'

'I'll make sure I have security.'

'So did Alan and he ended up dead.'

Chapter 10

In one house, a woman, even if she could be hard with her relatives, had been friendly. In another, that of Dean Winters and his wife, there was no friendliness, and the hardness was like a brick wall.

'Why do you keep bothering us?' Dean Winters' wife said. Tremayne and Clare were in the house, just. Further entry into somewhere more conducive was being prevented by a woman with a scowl on her face. In the background, peering through a slightly open door, the husband's countenance.

'Mrs Winters, a man has been murdered. If we need to come here a dozen times, we will, or else we can meet at the police station,' Tremayne said.

'Are you threatening us?'

Clare could see that she was an unpleasant person, venomous as described. 'Mrs Winters, DI Tremayne is correct. We can summons you to the police station, even arrange a police car with flashing lights and a siren to pick the two of you up, or you can show us civility and invite us in. The decision is yours, but we will question your husband, even you, if it is necessary.'

'Very well, come in. And watch where you put your feet. I've just vacuumed the place; I don't want you dirtying it again, or I'll send the police a bill.'

'Mrs Winters, they'll not pay. I suggest you stop your bellyaching and let us in.'

'You can't talk to me like that. It's police brutality. Dean, take a note of what they've just said. In my own house.'

Tremayne turned to Clare. 'How long before you can get a marked police car here?'

'Ten minutes. I've got a friend at the local police station. Do we need handcuffs?'

'Tell them to bring them just in case. And remember, we want the siren as well.'

'The kitchen,' Mrs Winters said.

'I'll put on the kettle,' the husband said.

'Don't you bother. They're not staying long.'

'I'll have mine with two sugars, milk. No sugar for Sergeant Yarwood,' Tremayne said. He'd met enough awkward people over the years. He had no intention of letting this woman get the better of him.

In the kitchen, not one thing was out of place, there was not a dish in the sink nor an animal in the corner. A table stood in one corner, and four chairs, each lined up in perfect symmetry. Tremayne pulled his chair back so he could sit down, making sure to drag the chair's feet across the tiled floor. Clare looked at Mrs Winters, could see she was angry.

Clare took her seat, careful not to aggravate the situation. The husband came over with the tea: four cups and saucers, a sugar bowl, and the milk in a jug. All the cutlery matched. 'Make sure you use the table mats,' Mrs Winters said.

'I'm sorry,' Dean said. 'Barbara likes a tidy house.'

'And no interruptions.'

'Mrs Winters, do you want it recorded that you are a hostile witness?' Tremayne said.

'I'm not hostile. We have no dealings with those people. Why should we be subjected to questioning as if we are common criminals?'

'You are assisting the police,' Clare said. The woman opposite was clearly a tyrant who controlled her husband, even though she was significantly shorter than him, even slight in stature. One puff of wind and she'd blow over. She was no doubt keen on eating sensibly, dragging her husband along for the ride whether he liked it or not.

'Mr Winters, you say that you've not been to see Mavis Winters since Alan died,' Tremayne said.

'That is correct,' Dean Winters said. He was sitting next to his wife, ensuring that he did not put his elbows on the table.

'Yet your wife, who is clearly hostile to your family, is upset that you have not offered your condolences in person. Why is that?'

'I'll answer that,' Winters' wife said. 'It's the Christian thing to do, that's why. We're strong believers in the Lord.'

'Yet you do not want your husband to associate with them?'

'A family of criminals, that's what they are.'

'Mrs Winters, what is your background?'

'I'm from Southampton. I met Dean at the place where he works.'

'The boss's daughter,' Dean Winters said.

'My father was a hard-working, God-fearing man. He's worked hard all his life, never cheated on his taxes or my mother.'

'When did you first meet your husband's family?' Clare asked.

'He took me up there after we were engaged.'

'And you disapproved?'

'Of course. They were living in a slum. The place was dirty, there were bottles of alcohol everywhere. And do you know where they took us for a meal?'

'You tell us.'

'A pub lunch: mushy peas, soggy chips, and a limp piece of undercooked fish. It was an insult, and then they expected Dean to pay.'

'You did?' Tremayne asked, looking over at the husband visibly shrinking in his seat.

'Yes. They had no money. Alan had spent his salary the night before getting drunk, Cyril was penniless, as was Stan.'

'And Fred?'

'He was in jail.'

'Mrs Winters, did you know about your husband's family before you went there?'

'Dean had warned me, but I didn't believe him. No family could be that bad, I was certain of that.'

'And were they?'

'Worse, and then his mother sits there and tells me about their father and the men she had been with. I'm still cringing to this day.'

'You still married your husband.'

'I made a commitment to God to look after him. I wasn't going to let him down. I have made it my life's work to raise Dean from that cesspool to become someone worthy of my family's name.'

Tremayne pitied the man.

'You've not mentioned Margie, your husband's sister.'

'She wasn't there. I never knew about her until after we were married.'

'How did you find out?'

'She ended up here on our doorstep after we had been married for two years,' Barbara Winters said.

'She had your address?'

'Dean, he'd kept in contact with her. Even been helping her with money.'

'She's my sister. I can't ignore her, the same as the others,' Winters said. Clare thought that he was a compassionate man.

'She was dead, is dead. How many times have I told you? She's given herself over to the devil. Let him look after her.'

'We've seen her recently,' Clare said.

'How was she?' Dean Winters asked.

'She was living in a terraced house near to Wyndham Road. Her condition was not good, although she seemed safe. There were a lot of cats.'

'That's where I last saw her.'

'Is she?'

'Say it out loud, will you. Is she still selling herself?' Barbara Winters said. 'If you're willing to bring your family's shame into this house, you may as well tell the police, tell the neighbourhood. Why I put up with you and your family, I'll never know. If it weren't for the Lord, I'd turn you over for someone else.'

'I apologise for my wife. The strain of Alan's death has affected us badly.'

'Talk for yourself. One less mongrel on this planet.'

'That's a cruel thing to say,' Clare said.

'The world is full of the deserving, and then that mongrel goes and wins a fortune. Where's the justice in that?'

'All of the brothers were offered a substantial cash payment. Did you accept yours, Mr Winters?'

'Dean did not,' his wife said.

'Why not? Surely you could do with the money?' Clare said.

'It is the result of gambling. It would be a sin to accept it.'

'You'd rather hold to your beliefs than accept the money?'

'God will remember us on the day of judgement.'

'Mrs Winters, you hated the Winters, especially Alan for his wealth,' Tremayne said. 'Was it enough to want the man dead? Not that you would have benefited financially, but spiritually you may have believed that you were doing God's work, and Stonehenge may have been another blow to those who hold different beliefs.'

Barbara Winters was up on her feet; Dean Winters stayed seated. Clare could see that he was enjoying the spectacle. 'That's slanderous. I'll sue you for everything you've got. I've no doubt your superiors will take action once I contact them.'

'Mrs Winters, my superiors will do nothing. You've shown your hatred for the Winters, your abhorrence of the money they have, ill-gotten according to you. Someone murdered Alan Winters, and all those who may be suspect will be subjected to rigorous questioning. I repeat yet again – did you murder Alan Winters?'

'Leave my house this instant.'

'We are leaving, but we will intensify our checks into you. A person who refuses to accept a substantial cash payment with no obligations must have some issues. You must now be a prime suspect. Mr Winters, did you assist your wife?'

'Not with Alan.'

'Why not?'

'He was my family. I cared for him, the same as the others. We all suffered as children in that house. It's a bond that cannot be broken. My wife doesn't understand.'

'You bastard,' Barbara Winters said.

'For once in your goddamn life, woman, just shut up.' It was the first time that Dean Winters had spoken to his wife in such a manner. He had to admit it felt good.

***

'You were tough in there,' Clare said on the drive back to Salisbury. As usual, she was in the driver's seat.

'We need to break through these people, push them to the limit. Barbara Winters is a clever woman, careful in what she says, how she says it. The only way she'll speak the truth is when she's angered,' Tremayne said.

'Did you break through?'

'Not totally. The woman shows her hatred well enough, her prejudices as well, but this not accepting the money still seems bizarre. Who could resist that much money?'

'Some people believe strongly in the concept of right and wrong. Let's accept her at face value.'

'And then what? Are you saying that she's innocent of all crimes?'

'Not at all. You were on the right track there. A lingering hatred, the confusion between how the meek shall inherit the earth, better a sinner repented, that sort of thing, and then one of the fallen had hit the jackpot, while she, no doubt devout, has won nothing, apart from a subservient husband. Mind you, he cheered up at the end, told her to shut up.'

'It'll be fun in that house for a while. What do you think happened after we left?'

'Fireworks. I'm not sure who would have got the better of the situation.'

'My money is on the wife.'

'Where are we heading?' Clare asked as they crested the hill on the A36, the sight of Salisbury Cathedral spire in the distance.

'Liz Maybury.'

'Why?'

'We've not spoken to her since her time in the hospital, apart from a gentle questioning. We know Polly Bennett's account as to what happened, but not hers.'

'She said it was an accident, so did Liz Maybury. And now Mavis Winters is letting them stay where they are. They'll not be truthful.'

'I know that, but let's see.'

The furniture store was again open, some cars parked outside. Inside, Polly Bennett was near the cash register, making phone calls. On the floor, Liz Maybury was attempting to entice a couple into buying a coffee table.

'Inspector Tremayne, we never expected to see you in here,' Polly said as the two police officers entered.

'How's Miss Maybury?'

'Liz, she's fine. Her memory of that day is a little hazy, but apart from that, there she is, selling away. She's a good talker.'

'You and Mavis Winters?'

'There's a legal agreement in place. It's not as good as what Alan promised us, but we'll go along with it. And besides, we both like to work.'

'You could have done that all along, instead of sleeping with Winters,' Clare said.

'We're not perfect, none of us is.'

'Why run this place when you could find another man?'

'Sergeant Yarwood, I'm a pragmatist, so is Liz. If a man is there, we'll take advantage. In the interim, we'll survive.'

'You're still looking?'

'Always.'

'Anyone else in Salisbury that interests you?'

'Gerry Winters would if he had the money.'

'That's unlikely.'

'It depends on whether he latches onto Mavis or not.'

'Why are you telling us this?'

'I'm testing you. You still don't trust Liz and me. You see us as lesbians, witches practising satanic rituals, breaking the golden egg on a golden altar at Stonehenge.'

'It's plausible,' Tremayne said.

'That's why I said it. I'm not a dummy, neither is Liz. If I can come up with it, so can you.'

'Tell me,' Clare said. 'Now that you don't have Alan Winters, what are you doing for a man. Surely you need someone in your bed.'

'The same as you without Harry Holchester, lots of cold showers.'

Clare realised that she had not thought about him for several weeks, even after driving past his old pub. She knew that she would visit his grave in the next few days; this time she would not go with Tremayne.

Tremayne and Clare moved away from the cash register; the interested couple had been swayed by Liz Maybury's eloquent sales pitch. Clare did not like the coffee table, could not see it fitting in with her decor at her cottage, although there was a bookcase that she liked, the price was reasonable, and she knew they'd give her a discount. She couldn't see any conflict of interest; she'd check with Tremayne first, register that she had had financial dealings with the two women in case it came up in a subsequent trial.

'Inspector Tremayne, Sergeant Yarwood, pleased to see you. It's worked out fine as you can see,' Liz Maybury said as she approached them.

'Unexpected,' Clare said.

'It wasn't what we expected, but we're pleased.'

'How are you?' Tremayne asked.

'I'm fine, the occasional dizzy spell, but apart from that I just carry on as normal. You've been speaking to Polly.'

'She says that Mavis Winters has been pleasant.'

'She has. We like the woman. She knows the way of the world.'

'It was her husband you were sleeping with.'

'We've done nothing wrong except being foolish. It's not so easy when there is that much money around. Mavis said that she had known Inspector Tremayne for many years.'

'We've known each other since she was in her teens.'

'Boyfriend, girlfriend,' Liz said.

Clare could see Tremayne blushing. 'Not at all,' he said. 'We lived not far from each other. We used to talk occasionally. I understand that Polly's mum was friendly with Mavis Winters.'

'She was. I'm not sure if they still are.'

'How about you?'

'I came here from Bristol, following a boyfriend.'

'And what happened to him?'

'He fell by the wayside.'

'Not enough money?'

'He had some, enough for me, but he wasn't ambitious, I am. He's still around. I see him occasionally, but he's pushing a buggy with two children in it, a pregnant wife at his side, and no doubt a mortgage. I could have had that, didn't want it.'

'And now, what does the future hold for you and Polly?'

'We'll run the shop, find ourselves a couple of men. Nothing firm, just ideas.'

'Alan Winters is being buried this weekend. Will you be going?'

'Not us. I don't think we'll be welcome. We may watch from a distance. Will you be going?'

'We'll both be there.'

'Ex-boyfriends of the deceased's wife excepted.'

'As I said, Miss Maybury, we were friends. I also knew Alan from back then, as well.'

Outside the shop, Tremayne lit a cigarette. 'What did you reckon, Yarwood?'

'There's no question in my mind as to their relationship.'

'Lesbian?'

'Probably bisexual, but yes, the two of them are not lonely in their beds; they've got each other.'

'Capable of murder?'

'Without a doubt. They could have engineered all of this, but it seems unlikely.'

'What do you mean? Forcing Mavis Winters to hand over the shop to them?'

'Only if they have some dirt on her.'

'Would they?'

'Who knows? Alan Winters in bed with those two would talk. Who knows what he could have said.'

'It's an angle worth exploring, Check it out, Yarwood. Let's go back to the station,' Tremayne said. 'You're driving.'

Chapter 11

Clare had not been inside a prison before, a situation for which she was thankful. She felt that Pentonville, C Wing, was not conducive to the rehabilitation of a criminal, only a means of removing a man from society for the allotted period of time deemed necessary by judge and jury.

Clare had driven. They had had an early start, and she had picked up Tremayne from Bemerton Road Police Station at seven in the morning.

'We'll see Stan today, Fred tomorrow,' he said. Tremayne had a newspaper with him, as well as a form guide.

'Stan and Fred Winters, character witnesses?'

'We need some background on the suspects.'

'Do we have any? None of them has any record of violence.'

'Gerry Winters does. That's why we're seeing Stan and Fred, to see if any of the others are capable. They can't have been involved, the perfect alibi.'

'In prison courtesy of Her Majesty.'

'That's it, although I suppose she doesn't come to visit them too often.'

Stan Winters, forty-one years of age, and a man whom Tremayne had known for over thirty years. 'Tremayne, what are you doing here?' Winters said when they met.

'They told you we were coming?'

'They did. You can't pin Alan's death on me.'

Separated by a table, Clare and Tremayne sat on one side, Stan Winters on the other. The man was not deemed violent, the reason they were allowed to be in such close proximity. In one corner, a prison officer. Both Clare and Tremayne had shaken the man's hand on entering, Clare noticing that he held onto her hand for longer than Tremayne's, even pulling her in closer. She realised that it must be hard for a man in his forties to be denied female company. It had made her uncomfortable, but she said nothing.

'We realise you're not involved, but we still need to find a murderer. Whoever killed Alan could kill again.'

'He was harmless. Apart from the money, that is. Not that it did me much good, and he refused to fund my appeal.'

'I've read your case file. You and two others were caught red-handed, and you've only got just over a year to go.'

Clare could see that the man was not pleased to be in prison, but that was understandable. She knew she would not have lasted there for long, as the place was functional but austere. As they had walked through the prison gates, and through the intervening secured doors, she had not seen any warmth in the surroundings. The building was spotless, she'd accede to that. It reminded her of a public toilet, the old-fashioned type with its porcelain implements, the brass pipes, the white tiles on the floors and the walls.

Stan Winters, a similar height to Gerry Winters, was physically impressive. It was apparent that he worked out in the prison gym. The tattoos on his arms and neck looked crude, prison style. Even so, he retained some politeness, especially towards her. With Tremayne, he was blunt. Tremayne had told her that it had been necessary to be tough, or seen to be tough, in the area where Winters had grown up, or else you were likely to find yourself face down in the mud.

'One of your police officers lied at the trial, that's all I'm saying. The man they claimed that one of us had hit, it wasn't true. He slipped and fell.'

'Stan, let it go. You can plead your innocence with me all you like, but I'll not buy it. Yarwood may, but she's willing to listen to any hard luck story. You were a hooligan as a child; you've not changed.'

Winters sat still, looking at Tremayne, glancing at Clare. She was pleased that she had worn a heavy jacket, buttoned up to the neck.

'Tremayne, you're a bastard, always were,' Winters said. 'What do you want to know?'

'Alan's murdered at Stonehenge. If anyone's after his money, then why there? And what's the point? The money goes to Mavis and then her children.'

'You're the police officer, not me.'

'It's their backgrounds we need to understand. We know that Mavis can be tough, Bertie, the son, is incapable, and Rachel, the daughter, does not appear to be interested.'

'What about Cyril and Gerry?'

'They're your brothers.'

'I'll tell you what you want to know. Not because I need to, but I'm glad of someone to talk to, other than the prison officers and the other prisoners.'

Tremayne knew that what he meant was that he was glad that Yarwood was with him.

'Give us a rundown of your family.'

'Cyril, lazy, Gerry, could be violent, not ambitious though. Dean, you've met?'

'And his wife.'

'I was there that day we went down the pub with her.'

'She mentioned it.'

'And what was her recollection?'

'Mushy peas, soggy chips, and a limp piece of undercooked fish.'

'The woman had us saying prayers, holding hands, before we ate. And it wasn't what she described. It was good pub food.' Tremayne knew what the man meant, having enjoyed a meal in a pub on many occasions.

'So why did she lie to us?'

'She didn't lie. That's how she sees us, the trash of society. If it were up to her, she'd have us all sterilised, let us die out. Poor old Dean, all that education, and what happens to him: hen-pecked, doing what he's told.'

'Instead of being in Pentonville,' Clare said.

Stan Winters laughed. 'You've got a sense of humour,' he said. 'At least I'll be free at some stage, he won't be.'

'Completely under the thumb?' Tremayne said.

'Completely. If she tells him to jump, he jumps.'

'If she tells him to kill Alan for whatever reason?'

'Hold on, Tremayne, don't go putting words in my mouth. Murder, that's serious. Just because Dean does what he's told, doesn't mean he'd be capable of murder.'

'Anyone in your family capable?'

'Fred can be violent, but killing someone is different, and why Alan? The man had the money, and he was generous.'

'But he wouldn't fund your appeal.'

'He still made sure I had a hundred thousand pounds.'

'You've still got it?'

'Yes. It's invested with the bank, not that they pay much in the way of interest. They lock you up for robbing a building society of a few thousand pounds, and they're ripping us off for billions. There's no justice in the world.'

'Life isn't fair. If it were, I'd be a superintendent, and you wouldn't have been caught.'

'Mr Winters, does anyone visit you here?' Clare said.

'Dean comes occasionally.'

'His wife?'

'Not her; she probably sits in the car, but she'd not come in here.'

'Anyone else?'

'Alan used to come occasionally, as did Gerry. Even Mavis.'

'Why did Mavis come?' Tremayne said.

'She's a decent person, you know that. You were friendly with her once. She's single now, maybe you two could get together again?'

'Everyone seems to know about us,' Tremayne said.

'I was just a kid, peering through cracks in windows. Don't worry, your secret is safe with me. And you were a decent man back then. You could have rounded us up. Why didn't you?'

'I'd grown up in a similar neighbourhood, played up the same as you had.'

'What happened?'

'I grew up, became a police officer.'

'And I became a criminal.'

'The dice rolls in the direction you want,' Tremayne said. 'And besides, you've not answered my question: why Stonehenge?'

'No one in my family would have done it. Dean's wife, she's crazy enough, but she'd not get Dean to do that. Anything else, but not murdering his own brother.'

'He refused to accept the one hundred thousand pounds.'

'He told me on one of his visits. I told him that he was mad. It got quite heated.'

'What happened after that?'

'He must have told her. I didn't see him for a few months after that.'

'She told him not to come?'

'Dean's a good brother, straight as they come, no petty crime with him. And yes, it was her. If you want someone mad, she's the person.'

'These women that Alan was messing around with?'

'I told him not to upset Mavis, but what's a man to do? These women are throwing themselves at him. How could he refuse?'

'Would you have?' Clare asked.

'Sergeant, we're not perfect, the flesh is weak. If I had won that lottery, I'd have been into the women and the good life, the same as everyone else.'

'If Dean had won?'

'She'd have given it to charity or refused to accept it.'

'Would she?'

'Ask her. Everyone's got a price, what's hers? Focus on that stupid woman, not my family.'

'We've seen Margie,' Clare said.

'Still the same?'

'Yes.'

'Even Alan with his money couldn't help her.'

'I can remember her as a child,' Tremayne said.

'Pretty little thing back then, not so pretty now.'

'Has she been here to visit?'

'Never. Mind you, I'd prefer her not to come.'

'Why?' Clare asked.

'You've seen this place. It's hardly a resort. I stay afloat, we all do, by focussing on when we get out, our first beer, our first woman. Sorry, Sergeant.'

'No need to apologise.'

'I maintain positive thoughts in here. I deal with the daydream, not the reality.'

'And Margie is the reality?' Tremayne said.

'You'll go away from here, distracted by other things. For me, I'll be thinking about her for days.'

'Sorry about that,' Clare said.

'It's fine. It's good to see friendly faces, even you, Tremayne.'

'The funeral is this weekend.'

'I've made a special request to attend.'

'Will it be granted?'

'They'll only agree to the church service, not the wake afterwards, and then I'll be with a police officer, probably handcuffs.'

'I'll see what I can do,' Tremayne said.

'No handcuffs, the prison officer in civilian clothes.'

'We'll deal with it.'

'I trust you, Tremayne. And find out who killed Alan.'

***

Some things can't be predicted in every murder investigation, even Clare knew that. On the drive back from London and Pentonville, a phone call to Tremayne.

'Put your foot down, Yarwood,' Tremayne said on ending the call.

'Another death?'

'Not this time.'

'Who?'

'Rachel Winters.'

'Why her?'

'How the hell should I know? Supposedly, she's been in a car accident. She's in the hospital.'

'Serious?'

'According to Mavis, it's not.'

Clare accelerated up past the speed limit, even for the motorway they took to get back to Salisbury. Tremayne leant over and switched on the grille mounted flashing lights. The just over two-hour trip reduced to one hour and forty minutes. At the hospital, out on Odstock Road, Clare parked next to the A & E. Inside they found Mavis with Gerry.

Mavis gave Tremayne a warm hug. 'Thanks for coming,' she said.

'How's Rachel?'

'She'll be fine. She's suffering shock, a bad concussion, but apart from that, nothing.'

'Do you know any of the details?'

'You saw the car as you drove up here?' Mavis said.

'By the side of the road. It looks totalled.'

'She was hit on the side by another car.'

'The driver?'

'The vehicle took off. That's all we know. Rachel's resting now. We can talk to her in a couple of hours' time.'

'We'll wait,' Clare said.

The four of them walked to a cafeteria and sat down. Mavis excused herself and went and organised a coffee for everyone. After driving faster than usual for an extended period, Clare would have appreciated a few minutes to close her eyes, but that was not going to be possible.

'What has Rachel said?' Tremayne asked as he sipped his coffee.

'According to her, she was driving home, only slowly, when a car pulled out to overtake and slammed into her on the driver's side.'

'Have you experienced this sort of thing before?'

'When Alan first won the money. Everyone thought they were entitled to a handout, some became aggressive. We had to hire a security firm to protect us for a few months. After that, Gerry has dealt with security, hired a few casuals as we needed them.'

'Is there any question that this was anything other than an accident?' Clare said.

'It's suspicious, but we've had no trouble for some time. And why Rachel? I'm the one controlling the money.'

'We've been to see Stan,' Tremayne said.

'How is he?'

'He's fine. Upset to be in prison.'

'He did the crime,' Gerry Winters said.

'It's still tough.'

'He'll be out soon, good behaviour.'

'How about Fred?' Tremayne said. 'We've not seen him yet.'

'We're not looking forward to his release,' Mavis said.

'Why?'

'You knew Fred. He's more aggressive. He'll cause trouble unless I pay him off.'

'Will you?'

'If it's necessary. I don't want him around the house all the time, or around the city, bad-mouthing us.'

'Would he? I thought you were a close-knit family. Stan said you were.'

'Close-knit if we're threatened, but there's bickering behind the scenes, you know that.'

Tremayne could see Gerry causing trouble. He had just heard Mavis offering to pay off his brother, Fred, and all he had was a salary and a hundred thousand pounds.

Two cups of coffee later, all four were back at A&E. A doctor came over, spoke to Mavis. 'It's okay. We can go in.'

'I'll go in with Yarwood later. We'll need a statement,' Tremayne said.

'Then you can go first. I'll be staying the night here, as will Gerry.'

'Very well.'

The two police officers found Rachel propped up in bed, a bandage around her head, another around her right wrist. 'I'm fine, just a little dazed,' she said.

Clare compared it to where they had met Rachel's uncle. There it had been cold and austere, here it was warm and inviting. In one corner of the room stood a vase containing flowers. Upon the wall, a flat-screen television. There was even a view out of the window. Stan's view, even in the prison yard, was of a brick wall.

'Do you remember the accident?' Clare asked.

'I think it was intentional.'

'Why?'

'I've driven down that road many times. There's plenty of room to overtake, and it was a clear day.'

'Did you see the car?'

'It was blue.'

'Any idea as to the make?'

'It was so quick, and no. I'm not interested in cars, not like Dad who was out buying anything he could. I'd know a Bentley, we've got one of those, but apart from that, it was large and blue.'

'If we showed you some pictures?'

'Maybe, but don't hold out much hope.'

'If it was intentional, any reason why?'

'Not with me. There are some crazy people out there, I know that. Maybe it was someone who was jealous of our good fortune.'

'Do you sometimes experience that?'

'Sometimes, but they are mostly harmless.'

'Did you see the driver?'

'Nothing. The car was bigger than mine, maybe it was a four-wheel drive. Apart from that nothing, sorry. Is Mum here?'

107

'She's outside with your uncle.'

'Could you ask her to come in. She'll only worry.'

Chapter 12

Dean Winters sat at the table in the kitchen of his and his wife's perfect house in Southampton. His wife was standing up. 'You've let that malignant family of yours rule your life. What did they ever give you?' she said.

Dean Winters knew he was hen-pecked; he didn't know why he tolerated the situation. He knew that his situation was intolerable. If he could speak to Mavis, instruct her to give him the hundred thousand pounds, then he could plot his way out to freedom.

'And then you want to visit your brothers in prison. What have I been doing all these years? I've been making a better man of you, haven't I?' No reply from her husband. '*Haven't I?*' she said with emphasis.

'Yes, dear.'

'And what thanks do I get? I'll tell you, nothing. And then all you can talk about is that whore of a sister.'

'She's my family. We stuck together as children, we'll stick together now.'

'Don't give me that story about how you were neglected, how you starved, what a bitch your mother was. I've met her; she is a bitch, but you're a man now. Stand up and be counted.'

'You'll never understand. You with your perfect childhood, your perfect family. Didn't your father ever make a fool of himself, chase your mother's friends after a few drinks?'

'He never drank in his life. It would be a sin against the Lord.'

'It's Alan's funeral this weekend. I expect you to attend.'

'I'll be there. I will do my duty. And don't expect to get drunk afterwards.'

Winters sat silently; there was no more to be said, no more that would serve any purpose. He knew why he had married her. He was a weak man who needed a strong woman. For the first few years of their marriage, it had been gentle encouragement coupled with love; now it was with force, and her approach was of anger and hatred towards him. They had started sleeping in separate beds a year before, her idea, and whereas he had agreed, he was still a young man. If only it had been him who had purchased that lottery ticket instead of Alan. What fun he could have had. But then Alan had died, and he was still alive. He wasn't sure if he was the lucky one, or his brother.

'Are you going to sit there all day? There's work to do.' A jolt of reality from the other side of the room. Dean Winters raised himself from his chair, taking care to push the chair back in position, conscious of the need to maintain a parallel spacing to the chair on its left-hand side, alignment with the chair on the other side. He walked away and headed off for whatever it was she wanted him to do.

One of these days, I will strike back, he thought. He knew it would not be today.

***

An all-points had been issued for the car that had struck Rachel Winters' vehicle, not that anyone thought that anything would come of it, although if the damage were appreciable, then the other vehicle would be lodging an insurance claim. Clare, once she had left Salisbury Hospital, and after she had deposited Tremayne at Bemerton Road, struck out on her own for Avon Hill. 'I've got to go,' she said to Tremayne.

'Do you want me to go with you?' Tremayne offered.

'It's personal, I'll be alright.'

Tremayne wasn't so sure, but she was a grown woman, a seasoned police officer. He had no option but to comply. 'Give me a call if it becomes too much.'

'Two hours, and I'll be back.'

'I'll send out the troops to look for you if you don't return,' Tremayne said in an attempt at levity. He could see it was not well received.

110

Inside the station, the ominous presence of Superintendent Moulton. 'Have you wrapped up that case?' he said.

'I thought you were going to talk about the other matter.'

'Not every time. Sometimes I like to follow up on a case, check how my people are.'

'I'm fine. Yarwood went out to visit Harry Holchester's grave.'

'Will she be alright?'

'She'll be fine. No doubt she won't be too cheerful when she returns, but under the circumstances she's handled Salisbury better than I expected. I never thought she'd come back.'

'Any leads on who killed Alan Winters?'

'There are some with motives, but so far not an arrest. His funeral's this weekend. I'll be attending, along with Yarwood.'

'As representatives of the police?'

'Not me. I've known the family for a long time.'

'You'll be keeping an eye out?'

'Never off duty, you know that. There's some tension behind the scenes. Whether it's enough to murder the man with the money is to be seen.'

'Keep me posted.'

Tremayne phoned Jim Hughes, the crime scene examiner, a friend. 'The two who carried Winters' body from the road up to Stonehenge, male or female?'

'Either. Adidas trainers, nothing special. You can purchase them in a dozen shops in Salisbury alone.'

'Size?'

'It's in my report.'

'I'm sounding you out. Yarwood's not here.'

'You're feeling lonely, is that it?'

'Not you as well. I get enough from Yarwood. She's becoming good at the smart comment.'

'She's had a good teacher. Anyway, Adidas trainers. The grass was wet up there, muddy in places, so the sizing is not precise. But female is a definite possibility. It'd still require a certain amount of strength. Don't go looking for a couple of weaklings.'

'Thanks. Any more on the weapon?'

'In my report. Nothing special, just a very sharp kitchen knife. We've got one at home that could cut a throat. I nearly sliced the top of my finger off with it the other day.'

Tremayne opened his laptop, saw a few emails, a reminder of overdue reports. He checked the emails, one or two needed answering; the others included the usual reminders. Also, there was to be a change in administrative procedures. Not again, he thought. Another email to let all staff know that entry to the building would be by fingerprint recognition instead of a magnetic security card, with a transition period of fourteen days. If it was as good as the fingerprint recognition on his laptop, Tremayne thought, then it was going to be a disaster. He had been content when there was a key to the building, a person in reception, a book to sign in and out.

Two hours to the minute, Clare walked back into the office. Tremayne felt as if he wanted to put his arm around her, give her a reassuring hug, but did not. 'I'm fine,' she said. 'It was a nice day down there. I put some flowers, said some words and came back here.'

'I'm glad that you're back. We've got to put the lid on this case, or Moulton will be after me again.'

'He's been here?'

'Remarkably pleasant.'

'I've told you that he's a decent man.'

'I know that. It's just that he keeps going on about my retirement.'

'What does Jean want you to do?'

'If we get together again, she'll want to take trips here and there, but apart from that, she'll not be demanding. We're past the young and silly stage.'

'And I'm not?'

'You're not the cloistered nun type. You need to find yourself another man.'

'They're not so easy to find. Most of them want to buy you a meal and then back to their place.'

'That's not your style.'

'Harry was my style, and that didn't turn out too good.'

'It's like riding a bike; you've got to get back on it again.'

'I will. Anyway, my love life is not what we're here for, is it?'

Both of the police officers helped themselves to coffee.

'Jim Hughes reckons it could possibly have been two females up at Stonehenge,' Tremayne said.

'Polly Bennett and Liz Maybury?'

'What do we know about them?'

'I would have thought we knew plenty,' Clare said.

'List them.'

'Promiscuous, competent businesswomen, ambitious, not afraid of hard work, probably bisexual.'

'Is that it?'

'But why kill Alan Winters?'

'Maybe he was about to dispense with them, get some others.'

'The man was making up for lost time. All his life he had been poor, unable to get a woman, except for Mavis,' Clare said.

'She was a good catch when she was younger.'

'I didn't mean that. She's still a good catch. If it doesn't work out with Jean…'

'Don't go there, Yarwood. Stay focussed on the murder. Alan Winters dies on a slab of stone at Stonehenge. Who would benefit?'

'I just don't see how the two women would benefit unless they had an agreement with Mavis in place.'

'Or Gerry?'

'But why Gerry? The man's got no money, and there's no way that he'd convince Mavis to part with a share of hers.'

'Why? He reckoned he was entitled to a half-share, and that it was Alan who was refusing due to Mavis. What if Alan would have reconsidered without Mavis?'

'Then why didn't they kill Mavis? She'd be the easier solution, and then, if she weren't around, Alan would have been looking for a shoulder to cry on.'

'Or two shoulders?'

'It's a complicated plan. It could have backfired.'

'If Liz Maybury had not hit that wall, then the two women would have ended up with nothing, and Gerry's no closer to the money.'

'I don't like it. Too many uncertainties; too easy to fail.'

'I'll leave it to you, woman to woman, maybe find out where they're having a drink of an evening. See if you can slip under their guard.'

'What about Dean and Barbara Winters?' Clare said.

'Now there's a woman that's easy to read.'

'What do you mean?'

'How do you sum her up?'

'Aggressive, biased, a snob, a nagger, and someone who detests the Winters, even her husband probably.'

'Then why marry him?'

'She wanted her ideal husband. She knew she wouldn't find anyone the normal way, so she decided to create her own.'

'She's done a good job.'

'Not totally. There's still some bite in the man.'

'More a gnawing. He's just about worn down.'

***

Clare had to admit that her initial impression of Stan Winters had been wrong, and that, apart from his being a criminal, he was agreeable. The same could not be said for Fred, the oldest of Betty Winters' seven children.

'Tremayne, what do you want? Haven't you caused enough trouble?' Fred Winters said on entering the interview room at the prison. Clare could tell from his bearing that he was a man who intimidated, a man who had a history of violence.

Tremayne had warned her that the reception from Fred, closer in age to him than the other Winters' children, would not

114

be good. Fred Winters, taller than average, though not as tall as Clare, not as tall as Tremayne, bore the marks of prison life: the tattooed knuckles on both hands – love, hate – as well as tattoos on his arms. His sleeves were rolled up, indicative of the warmth in the room.

'Fred, you know the drill,' Tremayne said. 'Your brother's been murdered. It's up to us to conduct interviews, investigate, arrest the person or persons responsible.'

'Alan, he may have been my brother, but he was a fool.'

'Why?'

'Look here, Tremayne, you were a pain in the rear end when you lived near to us, and you still are.'

'Still smarting over that hiding I gave you, is that it?'

Clare looked over at Tremayne, not sure what he meant.

'I caught Fred vandalising a car once. I laid him flat on his back, gave him a black eye and a sore head.'

'You wouldn't do it again. From what I can see, you're past it.'

'I may be, but I didn't arrest you back then, did I?'

'Okay, Tremayne. We'll declare a truce. I don't forget people who've wronged me, but you treated us fair. We were troublemakers, still are, especially Alan. That man could upset people.'

'What do you mean?'

'He had a mouth as a youth, always shouting off, accusing someone of being gay, queer back then.'

'Kept his distance when he was hurling insults,' Tremayne said.

'His only defence. He wasn't the toughest kid, although he tried to pretend he was. He got a few smacks from me.'

'You were violent back then, still are.'

'I make no bones about it. I'm a hard case, always will be, and in here, no one gives me aggravation.'

'This is Sergeant Yarwood, by the way.'

'Pleased to meet you. Gerry said you were a looker. He wasn't wrong.'

'Yarwood is a serving police officer,' Tremayne reminded him.

'No disrespect, Sergeant. It's not often I get to see a woman these days. I just said it as it is.'

'No offence was taken,' Clare said.

'Gerry has been here?' Tremayne said.

'And Mavis.'

'Is that unusual?'

'Not really. Gerry sometimes comes, and Mavis occasionally. She's a good woman, better than Alan deserved.'

'What did they speak about?'

'Alan's death initially. It came as a shock to all of us, or his murder did. Alan was always an idiot. If he had died at the wheel of a car, then I would have taken it in my stride, but murder, and up at Stonehenge, I can't go for that.'

'What do you mean?'

'It makes no sense. I know that he was showing off, and supposedly he was messing around with a couple of tarts.'

'We know who they are.'

'If it had been you who had won the lottery?' Clare said.

'No tarts, just one woman. And as for showing off, it doesn't interest me.'

'You'd not follow in your brother's footsteps?'

'I'd have kept the win secret, and if I couldn't, I'd have bought myself a place in the country, settled down, even farmed the land.'

'I never knew that about you,' Tremayne said.

'Nor did I. In here they have a farm, or at least a few acres. There are chickens, a few pigs, a chance to grow vegetables.'

'And you're there?'

'Every day. There wasn't much chance where we grew up, although in Salisbury we were never far from the countryside. Now, all I want is the chance to farm.'

'If you had money?'

'That's why Mavis was here. She's worried that I'm going to cause trouble when I get out.'

116

'Are you?'

'A lousy one hundred thousand. Of course I am. The Winters' family, or the children, look out for each other, always have, always will. Mavis's idea of money is not mine. Alan would have given each of us a couple of million. He'd have still had plenty left.'

'Is that what you want?'

'I've thought it through. I want two million, plus another three as a loan. I've done the sums, I know it's viable. I'm not looking for charity, I only want what is mine.'

'Is it?'

'Alan would have eventually agreed. Mavis is reluctant.'

'Do you blame her?'

'No, but she came from a decent family, we didn't.'

'Your father, any idea where he is? He'd have to be in his eighties.'

'Dead I hope.'

'And your mother?'

'Dead are far as I'm concerned.'

'We've met Margie, interviewed your mother.'

'My mother can go to hell, Margie is important.'

'She's not in a good way,' Clare said.

'That's what I've been told. Mavis, I know, makes sure she is safe, and that she has food and medicine.'

'You have a lot of respect for Mavis?'

'A lot, apart from her wanting to hang on to the money. She'll look after the family better than Alan ever did. He was a brainless fool, Mavis isn't, you know that.'

'I do.'

'She was keen on you once,' Fred Winters said, 'before you became old and grey.'

'Still good enough to give you a hiding,' Tremayne said.

Clare could see a grudging respect between the two men: one a criminal, the other an officer of the law. There was a history between them that the years had not destroyed.

'Your brother's funeral, will you be attending?' Clare said.

'I would have liked to, but they'll not let me out.'

'Any reason, anything I can do? Tremayne said.

'I lost my temper with another prisoner, a lifer. He walked on my vegetable patch, thought he was smart, although he probably fancied a few days in the prison hospital.'

'What happened?'

'I gave him his few days.'

'Any increase in sentence, restrictions placed on you?'

'None. The warden, he's not a bad man, he knew what had happened, and besides, some of the vegetables were for him. Anyway, they'll not let me out, classified as violent.'

'Are you?' Clare said.

'I defend my own. But yes, I'm violent. Not drunken violent, but if anyone gets in my way, I'll push through or punch. Not many can stop me. Only Tremayne when he was younger. Now he looks as if he'll struggle to get out of his chair.'

'You're not looking so great,' Tremayne replied.

'Whatever you do, look out for Margie. There's not much hope for her, but we all try.'

'Mavis will do the right thing,' Clare said.

'You like the woman?' Fred said.

'Yes, I do. Very much, actually.'

'I know she's worried about when I get out, they all are, but it'll be fine. With Alan gone, we'll come to an agreement.'

'Your brother Dean?'

'You've met his wife?'

'Unfortunately.'

'If she had the money, nobody would get anything.'

'She portrays herself as charitable.'

'Her, she's a bitch. She hates us, we hate her. It's mutual. Watch out for her. If there's an opportunity, she'll take it.'

'And your brother?'

'Poor Dean, the smartest in the family, now under her control. I doubt if he can go to the toilet without her permission. I nearly said that in the vernacular.'

'What stopped you?' Tremayne said.

'Lady present.'

'I've heard it all, no doubt said it myself occasionally,' Clare said.

'Still, I must show some respect. Next time you can come on your own, don't bring Tremayne. I've seen his ugly face enough times,' Fred Winters said, a grin on his face.

Chapter 13

Clare had not been to many funerals: just her grandmother's and a school friend who had died in a car accident. Tremayne had been to too many.

Neither expected the horse-drawn hearse, the funeral director and his assistant dressed in top hat and tails. In the street the police had erected barriers. It wasn't often that the county's wealthiest inhabitant was buried, having been murdered.

Tremayne knew that it would be magazine fodder within a week. The life story of an unremarkable man who by chance had become wealthy beyond belief, dead before his time, the victim of murder by persons unknown. He knew of the speculation: some wild and crazy, some logical.

Inside the church, Mavis sat at the front with her two children: Rachel, a bandage still on her arm, and Bertie, neatly-dressed, clean-shaven, and in a suit. Further back, Gerry and Cyril Winters. Alan Winters' mother sat next to Mavis at the front, the two women pretending to be united in sorrow, but Clare noticed the space, small though it was, that separated them. In the same pew, Stan Winters and Margie, his arm around her. And in that church she seemed at ease, although her look was vacant and she did not appear to want to speak, only nodded her head if someone talked to her. In another pew, Dean Winters and his wife. Clare had noticed him speaking to his family on arrival, saw that his wife had ignored them.

'Thanks, Tremayne,' Stan Winters had said on his arrival at the church. The man had reason to be thankful. Tremayne had received special authority to take responsibility for the convicted felon during the funeral and afterwards at the wake. A prison officer, outside and in plain clothes, would wait in his car to ensure that procedures were followed. After the evening had concluded, he would drive Stan back to prison.

'If you stuff up, it's my head.'

'I won't. You've done right by me, I'll do right by you,' Winters said. He was wearing a suit as well, new by the look of it, supplied by Mavis.

At the appropriate time, the coffin was brought into the church. Six men supported it on their shoulders: Bertie as the deceased's son at the front, as well as Cyril, Gerry, Stan and Dean. The funeral director completed the six, maintaining equilibrium as the other five men swayed under the weight of the coffin.

Clare could see the tears in Mavis's eyes, even had them in hers and she had never met the man. Alan Winters' mother held a handkerchief too, as did Margie. Barbara Winters looked impassively forward in silent prayer. Clare knew that she wanted her to be the guilty person in the murder, not because she thought she was, but because she did not like her.

She imagined the funeral was similar to Harry's although she did not know. His relatives had offered to send her some photos, but she had declined.

The coffin arrived at the front of the church and was placed on a trestle, sombre music echoing throughout the church. The men resumed their seats. A few words from Barbara Winters to her husband; derisory, Clare assumed.

Clare turned around, could see that Polly Bennett and Liz Maybury had slipped in by a side door, their presence unobtrusive. She had known they would be present, a special dispensation from Mavis Winters. 'They wanted to come. It shows some decency on their part,' Mavis had said when Clare had asked her why.

Rachel gave a reading from the Bible, Stan said a few words, as did the other men in turn. Mavis did not move from her seat. She kept looking at Margie, checking she was alright. Alan Winters' mother did not acknowledge anyone other than Mavis. She continued to look forward or at the coffin. At the conclusion of the ceremony, the coffin left, the entourage following, the Bentley at the front, the other cars, three Rolls

Royces, following behind. Tremayne drove with Stan, Clare stayed back at the church.

Tremayne, not immediate family, would not enter the crematorium, where a few more words would be said before the coffin passed through some curtains on its way to the cremation of the body. Tremayne had only joined the entourage as part of the requirement to keep Stan Winters in his sight at all times.

Once free of the crematorium, Tremayne drove back to the Winters' house.

'Thanks, Tremayne. I'll not let you down,' Stan Winters said yet again.

'That's why you're here.'

At the house, there was security at the front gate. Tremayne drove straight through. A catering company's van was parked to one side of the driveway; the other cars parked one behind the other. Clare, Tremayne could see, had arrived and was talking to the prison officer assigned to look after Stan Winters.

'Prison Officer Dennis Marshall,' he said. Not that the introduction was necessary as Tremayne and the officer had signed the papers earlier in the day at Bemerton Road agreeing to Tremayne accepting responsibility.

'We'll make sure to get you some food and drink,' Tremayne said.

'Thanks. I'll be back within an hour.'

'Don't worry about me,' Stan said. 'I'll do nothing wrong.'

'Just following orders, you know that.'

'So is Tremayne. I've known the man since my teens, a family friend. If you don't mind driving someone who's drunk some alcohol back to Pentonville.'

'That's fine, not that I'll be drinking.'

Dennis Marshall got into his car and drove off down the road. 'He's got an aunt who lives not far from here. He's gone to see her,' Clare said.

'He seemed a decent man.'

'He is. It appears that he and Stan Winters get on well enough in Pentonville. That was why he volunteered to bring him down here today.'

122

Stan Winters left the two police officers and went inside.
'Any observations?' Tremayne said.

'Nothing especially. The two women were at the church.'

'Are they here?'

'No. Mavis wouldn't allow them, and besides, I doubt if they'd want to come.'

'They know the house well enough.'

'Barbara Winters?'

'She briefly hugged Mavis, more out of obligation than anything else.'

'And Margie?'

'Vague, staring into space. Apart from that, nothing to say. She's been cleaned up for the occasion.'

'She'll be the next funeral,' Tremayne said.

'That'll be a lot sadder than this one. I doubt there'll be a wake for her.'

'There will be, only it won't be a time for getting drunk and remembering the deceased with humour.'

'Not much humour from Barbara Winters, nor Alan's mother.'

'They're both a pair of miseries.'

Tremayne and Clare left the front porch of the house and went inside. Clare felt a little out of it, knowing full well that she was not a family friend, although she had become friendly with Mavis since her husband's death. Dean Winters sat in one corner, a glass of wine in his hand, his wife keeping a close watch on him. Clare could see that he wanted to join in.

Tremayne, a man who would have drunk more than his fair share but cognisant of his responsibilities, kept to the one beer. 'Damn nuisance,' he said to Gerry Winters. 'I can't drink.'

'Stan will do nothing. We'll not let him. Have a drink, more than what you're drinking now.'

'You're right, but he's my responsibility. Once he's on his way to prison, I'll be into it.'

'I'll join you if I'm still sober.'

'The way you're hitting it, I don't think so.'

'It's a good send-off for Alan. Did you see Polly and Liz at the church?'

'Are you still getting around to their place?'

'Occasionally. They know that I've been putting in a good word for them with Mavis.'

'They're using you, you know that. If it's not you, it'll be another man.'

'I'm using them. Polly and Liz are a lot of fun.'

'Mavis has clipped your wings; any animosity?'

'At the time, but she's easier to deal with now. I'll soon have the Bentley.'

'You were there when Mavis indicated that she'd pay off Fred. What did you think?'

'We've had a family meeting. At least, Mavis, Cyril, and me.'

'What was decided?'

'Fred wants two million, so do we.'

'Mavis?'

'Now she's got control of the money, she'll be agreeable. You've met Fred?'

'We have.'

'What did you think, be honest?'

'He'll cause trouble.'

'With two million?'

'He's a bully, even if he was polite to Yarwood. He'll aim to take control of Mavis, of your family.'

'We'll stop him.'

'How? Murder?'

'Mavis has a smart lawyer.'

'Fred won't listen to lawyers, nor police officers, you know that,' Tremayne said.

'Stan's fine. We're grateful for what you did.'

'He was eligible to come. I just added my weight to his application.'

'You did more than that. You acted like a friend. The Winters family will not forget.'

124

'They may. One of you is a murderer. It can only be people close to him.'

'I don't see it. What about Polly and Liz?'

'Where's the motive?'

'I don't know, but it can't be his own flesh and blood.'

***

A banging of a metal tray, a hushing of the hubbub in the house. 'Ladies and gentlemen, thank you for coming,' Bertie Winters said. He was standing on a chair, a glass of champagne in his hand. 'As sad as this occasion is, my father would want us to be here and to have a few drinks on his behalf. My mother, Mavis and my sister, Rachel, thank you for coming. Please enjoy yourselves. There is plenty of food and drink for everyone.'

Tremayne could see the caterers in the large kitchen. He joined the queue, as did Gerry, two people behind him. He was talking to Clare. In front of Tremayne stood Dean Winters. 'Your wife, she's not eating?'

'My wife is here under duress, you know that.'

'Where is she?'

'Outside in the car.'

'A tough woman.'

'She came here out of an obligation, to pay her respects to the dead. Apart from that, she wants nothing to do with this family.'

Tremayne could see that the man had a stiff drink in his hand, and he was on his way to being drunk, the reason for his loose tongue. 'Why do you let her control your life?' Tremayne said.

'You've only seen her bad side,' Dean Winters said.

Tremayne knew after years of policing that people such as Barbara Winters only have the one side. Dean Winters' life was a living hell. He knew that later on, when they drove back to Southampton, Dean would be on the receiving end of a severe ear-bashing and that he'd be in the dog house for weeks. And every time there was an argument, his behaviour at the Winters' home that day, his family of criminals, his mother, would be brought up.

Tremayne took his plate, full to overflowing. He knew he couldn't drink, but he could eat. 'Ten o'clock,' he said as he passed Stan.

'Don't worry about me, Tremayne. I'll be there.'

'Sober?'

'What do you reckon?'

'Not a chance. We need to make sure Prison Officer Marshall gets fed.'

'Don't worry. I'll take it out for him. He's decent, that is for a screw.'

'Margie?'

'We're trying to look after her. She seems better for being here. We're hopeful of getting her to move in.'

'Would that be okay with Mavis?'

'There's a small cottage at the end of the garden. Mavis will fix it up for her.'

'Will she come?'

'We remain optimistic.'

Tremayne walked through the group of people, stopping to converse as he went. He saw Yarwood sitting down, eating her meal. 'Barbara Winters is outside in her car. Once you've finished, go out and see if you can get her to talk.'

'She's missing out on this food?'

'As far as she's concerned, it was prepared by the devil.'

'Instead of a catering company.'

'You know that someone here is probably a murderer?'

'It's a shame. The Winters may be rough around the edges, but I like them, even Fred.'

'He's trouble. Stan's been a fool, getting involved in crime, but he'll probably go straight after his release. Fred won't.'

***

A tap on the car window, a reluctant opening. 'Mrs Winters, do you have a minute?' Clare said. She could see Barbara Winters in the driver's seat, dressed in black. Her hair, as always, immaculate, her makeup perfect, her mouth pinched and unsmiling.

'If you must.' The door lock was released. Clare got in and sat in the front passenger seat.

'The food is excellent,' she said as a way of opening the conversation. It was not a formal interview, more a way of getting to know the woman better, to see if there was anything remotely agreeable about her.

'I'll eat at home.'

'You're unable to be in their presence for more than a few minutes?'

'I honoured the Lord at his place. I care about him, not these people.'

'It's not mushy peas and soggy chips.'

'I've no doubt. They don't have to worry about the cost.'

'Your husband was offered a substantial amount of money.'

'He refused. Money derived from gambling is a sin. If you've read your Bible, you'd know that.'

'And now your husband is drinking alcohol.'

'He has defied me, defied God.'

'The priest who conducted the ceremony, he's here having a drink of beer.'

'He is not a true disciple of the God that I serve.'

'Then what is he?'

'He is a blasphemer, the same as those others. He will pay for his sins in the fires of hell.'

Clare shivered in the woman's presence. To her, God was meant to be a benevolent, forgiving entity; to Barbara Winters, he was vengeful, looking for retribution, punishing those who did not maintain his ideals.

'What will you do with your husband after tonight?'

'He will pay for his sins, offer up prayers for forgiveness.'

'Maybe he'll stand up to you and refuse.'

'He will not. The Lord will give me the strength to deal with him.'

'Tell me, when you had heard that Alan Winters had died, what did you think?'

'I praised the Lord that there was one less sinner in this world.'

'No sadness for your husband that his brother had died.'

'Why should there be? Dean is better off without him.'

'And when you were told that he had been murdered?'

'It does not concern me how he died.'

'But you must have had some feelings.'

'All those who have benefited from the money will die. That is the Lord's will.'

'He's told you this?'

'Yes, in the Bible: "for what will it profit a man if he gains the whole world, and loses his own soul?"'

'Their souls are lost?'

'The Lord will reclaim them in their repentance. Otherwise, they will burn in the fires of hell.'

'And your husband.'

'There is still time to save him.'

'After a few drinks?'

'Constant vigilance, constant praise of the Lord, constant piety.'

'Mrs Winters, could you kill a sinner?'

'If the Lord commanded it.'

'In the Bible?'

'Yes. It is the word of God written down for us to obey.'

Clare wondered what planet the woman came from. She made her excuses and retreated back to the sanctity of regular people.

Chapter 14

Back in the house, Clare found Tremayne in conversation with Mavis Winters. She saw Bertie, the son of the household, sitting on his own, orange juice in his hand. 'Can I sit here?' she said.

'Sure. Why not? Have you found out who killed him yet?'

'We're continuing our investigations. How about you?'

'After time in prison?'

'A centre to deal with your addiction.'

Clare could see that the man's initial respectable appearance at the church was waning. His suit jacket was flung to one side, his tie loosened, the top shirt button undone, and the shirt hanging out of his trousers. It was clear that the young man preferred to be a slob.

'I'm only sticking it out at Mum's insistence.'

'You'd prefer to be on drugs?'

'Life's for living. What's the point of worrying if you've got plenty of money?'

'Your mother has.'

'It's mine as well. He was my father.'

'Your father never worried about life, did he?'

'Not at all. Rich or poor, he was always the same. He'd still have time for a drink, and with me he was generous.'

'But he wouldn't let you have the car you wanted.'

'That was my mother. She was always in his ear.'

'If you had it, what would have happened?'

'I'd have pranged it, but so what? There's plenty more where it came from.'

'And if you were dead?'

'At least I would have had some fun, pulled some women.'

'You're aware of your father's mistresses?'

'Polly and Liz?'

'Yes.'

129

'I'd have to listen to them sometimes in the room down the hall.'

'With your father?'

'Yes.'

'How did you feel about that? Your father with other women, your mother in the same house.'

'Horny.'

'Nothing more?'

'Why? Should I? Should I care about my mother when she's controlling the money? She knew he was playing around, did nothing to stop him. Not that I blame him. That Polly's a bit of hot stuff, so are you, come to think of it.'

'Don't try it, Bertie. I'm a police officer. I'll break your arm if you come near.'

'I'm even sober, and I can turn you off.'

'You're the indulged son of a wealthy family, one of the idle rich.'

'It's better than being one of the idle poor. That's what my father was and what did it get him?'

'A lottery ticket,' Clare said.

'That's justice for you, and the man knew how to enjoy it. Those two women were classy.'

'If you had the money?'

'What he was doing, a better class of women.'

'And dead up at Stonehenge?'

'Not me. I'm smarter than that.'

'How?'

'I just am.'

'Do you know something. Something that you should tell me.'

'Not really. I'm just making conversation.'

Clare left the man with his orange juice, sure that he'd be back into drugs once he returned to the house on a permanent basis. She felt unclean when she left him. She found Rachel, the sister, talking to her mother.

'How are you?' Clare asked. The mother moved away.

'It's a good send-off for my father,' Rachel said. There was still some slight bruising on her forehead, but apart from that she looked fine.

'Yes, it's good. Are you pleased to see your family here?'

'I'm pleased to see Uncle Stan.'

'He's a favourite?'

'He always was. He always remembered my birthday, always bought me something silly. Inspector Tremayne helped to get him here?'

'Your uncle was eligible to attend the church with a prison officer, but not the wake, and certainly not to be here drinking. DI Tremayne organised that.'

'I'll thank him later. He was a friend of my mum's once.'

'What do you know?'

'My mum told me last night. It was just the two of us; one of those reminiscing about life, over Dad, mum and daughter things.'

'How much did she tell you?'

'She told me she was young, the same as him. There was a party, they'd both had a few drinks.'

'And?'

'The two of them in another room.'

'What did you think?'

'I laughed, we both did. My mum and the police officer. They'd make a good pair, even now.'

'It was a long time ago,' Clare said.

'Mum needs someone to help her. I know Uncle Gerry would like to be with her, but I can't see it. With Inspector Tremayne, he'd deal with them all, including Uncle Fred.'

'We've met him.'

'None of us wants to see him.'

'He's coming back.'

'We know. If Inspector Tremayne were with Mum, there'd be no trouble. He's probably the only man who could handle him.'

'That's up to Tremayne and your mother.'

'She'd be interested. I can't think of anyone she respects more.'

'He's a curmudgeon, can be cantankerous.'

'Mum can be awkward. See what you can do. We'd all welcome him into the family.'

'Not after we arrest one of you,' Clare said.

'We'd understand. If someone is capable of murdering my father, then they'd be capable of murdering Mum, and then Bertie and me.'

'That's true. We've always thought that the money was the motive. What if it isn't?'

'It must be. What else? My father was inoffensive. He could get drunk, cause a ruckus at the pub, but apart from that he wouldn't harm a fly.'

***

Tremayne and Clare continued to move around the house; the atmosphere was very congenial. Everyone was singing the praises of Alan Winters, the good fortune that he had had, the fact that he had struggled for years, barely making enough to live on. It didn't move Tremayne.

Relegated to one beer and then orange juice, at least until Stan Winters was off his hands and back in the care of the prison officer, he and Clare, apart from Barbara Winters who was outside in her car, were the only totally sober individuals in the house.

Tremayne knew that in spite of the accolades accorded the recently deceased, he was a lazy individual of little worth, which was surprising considering that Mavis, his widow, Tremayne's one-time lover, was full of energy. It was strange how two people so dissimilar in many ways could have forged a successful marriage, brought up two children, one smart, the other impacted by drug abuse.

Margie Winters had withered under drug abuse, apparently the result of her childhood experiences, but Tremayne wasn't sure. He was convinced of the maltreatment, but maybe the woman had an addictive personality, was susceptible to drugs, the same as Bertie Winters, an inherited trait that passed some, affected others. Tremayne knew that he had tried to give up cigarettes many times, never succeeded, whereas his brother, younger than him, had never smoked. Not that it had helped him as he had keeled over in his early forties with heart disease.

Tremayne found Mavis Winters sitting on her own in another room. 'I'll miss him,' she said as he sat down beside her. 'He wasn't much use, good at nothing, yet he was like an unruly dog. Good to have around but a damn nuisance.'

'He was good at purchasing lottery tickets.'

'We're not happier for all the money. It's just another responsibility. I remember the carefree nights at the pub, a singalong, everyone getting drunk. It was alright for Alan, he didn't care, but now, if I go anywhere, they always look for me to pay, and then the shops want to show me the most expensive items. And as for the begging letters…'

'Tough?'

'Some of the letters break your heart, not that you'd know if they were genuine or not.'

'You helped some?'

'At first, but then the word got out that I was an easy touch. Once it was revealed, even though those we helped had signed a non-disclosure agreement, on the advice of our solicitor, there was a flood of letters.'

'What did you do?'

'Alan wanted to continue to give; I said no. They'd approach him down the pub, he'd give them five hundred pounds to go away, but with me, I'm not willing to give our money away that easy. You know the saying: a fool and his money are easily parted. Alan was the fool, I was the bastard who wouldn't help. There were times when I wouldn't go out of the door for fear of being hassled.'

'But you do now.'

'I couldn't solve everyone's problems, nor could Alan. He was burning more than a million pounds every three months. Can you imagine it, a million pounds? When we were young, we were lucky to have a pound to buy an ice cream, and there was Alan throwing it away.'

'You've solved the problem now?'

'Only because he died.'

'What do you mean?'

'We can't help everyone. I've funded a cancer unit at Salisbury Hospital, a piece of equipment somewhere else. Not that it stopped Alan wasting the money, but he was under some sort of control.'

'What sort?'

'I was checking the finances.'

'It didn't stop him buying the furniture store for Polly and Liz.'

'I know, and that still annoys me.'

'But you'll let them continue?'

'For the time being. I've not forgiven them, nor Alan, and if I pull the plug, then that's more money lost.'

'You seem to understand finance.'

'Understand, maybe, but I never expected to be dealing with this, and now I've got to pay out to the brothers.'

'Two million each?'

'And how long before they exhaust that? Cyril's stupid enough to manage, but he'll probably be evicted from the council house, and then he'll want another place, and you've seen the price of property.'

'I've seen it,' Tremayne said. 'My place is worth three hundred thousand, and it's not much.'

'And if Cyril is evicted, do you think he'll want to buy a place the same as yours? Look at this house, beautiful, isn't it?'

'Yes.'

'That's the problem. Even I look at this and think I'd like somewhere bigger, better, maybe with some history. Once we were happy with a ten-year-old Ford, now it's a Bentley. There's no end to desire, and Fred will cause trouble. He thinks he's into farming, and two million pounds represents a compromise.

That's not Fred. If he sees something, he wants it, and if he can't afford it, then he would steal it, but now, I'm the bank.'

'You don't want the responsibility?'

'Quite frankly, others may call me stupid, but I'd go back to the life we had, difficult as it was. This wake, how much?'

'Ten thousand pounds,' Tremayne said.

'And some. What with the funeral and the catering, there'll not be much change from forty thousand pounds, and what do we have to show for it?'

'It was a good send-off.'

'For Alan? He wasn't worth it. The family at the crematorium, a few drinks at the pub afterwards would have sufficed. It just never ends. Even with all this money, I'll need to make compromises.'

'It's not a problem that has ever worried me,' Tremayne said.

'We're very similar in many ways, you know.'

'Maybe we are,' Tremayne said, not certain where the conversation was heading. It was the woman's husband's funeral, and Mavis Winters was intimating something more. He was feeling uncomfortable, not sure what to say or do.

Tremayne looked at his watch. 'It's close to 10 p.m.' he said thankfully.

'Stan?'

'It's time for me to hand him over.'

Tremayne walked out to the other room, Mavis holding his arm. 'Stan, are you ready?'

It was clear that the prisoner was not sober. 'Ready when you are,' he said.

'Clare, give me a hand,' Tremayne said.

With that, the two police officers escorted Stan Winters back to Prison Officer Marshall's car and strapped him in, Stan attempting to give Clare a slobbery kiss, her avoiding it.

The others made their farewells, Tremayne signed off his responsibility, and wished Marshall well. 'Don't worry, he'll soon be back safe and sound. He wasn't meant to drink. I'm not sure how I'll square it with the warden,' Marshall said.

'Don't worry about it. I'll deal with it if it's an issue.'

Stan Winters left, Tremayne headed back inside for a beer. If Gerry were still sober, he'd find him; if he weren't, it would not make any difference. The detective inspector intended to enjoy the remainder of the evening. 'What have you found out, Yarwood?' Tremayne said to Clare who was sitting in one corner. The wake was coming to a conclusion, the caterers were packing up.

'Bertie fancies his chances, Rachel's a good person, the most likeable of them all, and Barbara Winters belongs on another planet,' Clare said.

'Stan?'

'He's okay, but he's not the murderer.'

'What about Dean?'

'Judging by the condition he was in when he left, he'll be doing penance for some time.'

'Self-flagellation?'

'Either he'll be whipping himself, or she'll be doing it for him.'

'The man's life must be miserable.'

'He chose which bed to lie in. Not really our concern, unless it's relevant to the investigation.'

'Yarwood, I'll make a detective out of you yet,' Tremayne said. He looked around the room, saw those who remained, Cyril and Gerry were close to comatose, their eyes closed. Rachel was helping her mother, and Bertie had taken off with his friends into town. Tremayne knew that would represent trouble, and he was only on temporary leave from the place that was treating him for his drug addiction. Margie sat outside in the garden, even though it was cold. Tremayne could see that she was shivering. He and Clare walked out through the French doors and put a coat around her shoulders. The woman gave no sign of recognition.

'Are you okay, Margie?' Clare asked. A feeble nod of the head.

'She needs medical treatment,' Tremayne said.

'She needs heroin,' Clare said.

'That's what I meant. I can agree with a doctor, the same as you. Neither of us can prescribe an illegal drug.'

'I want to go home,' Margie said. Apart from a few words at the church, they were the only other words she said that night.

'Mavis will have a room,' Clare said.

'I want my home, my cats.'

Tremayne knew that what she really wanted was her stash of drugs. Clare walked back inside, found no one able to drive her. She returned. 'I'll take her,' Clare said.

'I'll leave the same time as you.'

'Not drinking?'

'Not on my own, I'm not.'

Tremayne made his farewells, as did Clare. Mavis and Rachel gave Tremayne a big hug. Clare received a hug and a kiss as well. Margie was already in Clare's car, her seat belt buckled. Mavis held her for a long time as she sat there. Fifteen minutes later, Margie was back with her cats, twenty minutes later her shivering had stopped.

Clare phoned Tremayne. 'I've dropped her off.'

'She'll not last long, neither will Bertie.'

Chapter 15

Tremayne had barely had time to climb into his bed at his house in Wilton when the phone rang. It was Mavis. 'It's Alan's mother.'

'What about her?'

'She's dead, upstairs.'

'I'll be right over,' Tremayne said. He pulled himself up, rubbed his eyes to wake up and walked to the bathroom. For someone who had only drunk two beers, he was not feeling good. He looked for a toothbrush and toothpaste, took a quick shower, and left the house. The night had turned colder. He called Clare.

Upon arrival at the Winters' house, Tremayne found an ambulance and Yarwood's car.

'You were quick,' Tremayne said.

'I had just arrived home, not even opened the front door when you phoned.'

'Not like me.'

'I can see that. I suggest you button your shirt.'

'Thanks, Yarwood.'

Rachel Winters came outside. 'It's grandmother, she's dead.'

'Where?'

'Upstairs, her old room,' Rachel said. Tremayne and Clare hurried up the stairs; they knew the way, having interviewed the woman there once before. In the room was a medic, and Mavis, sitting to one side, looking at the body.

'If only I hadn't sent her to live with Cyril,' Mavis said.

'Who found her?' Tremayne said.

'I did. I was going to get Gerry to take her home, not that's he in a fit condition to drive. I may have let her stay here for the one night.'

'Any idea how she died?'

'Old age, grief. I don't know. I found her on the bed, the same as you can see her now.'

The medic stood nearby. 'Heart failure probably, but it's not for me to say,' the medic said.

'Pathology will tell us,' Tremayne said. He could see the woman, thought she looked peaceful, even saintly. Her arms were folded across her chest as if she knew her end was near. Clare found a clean sheet in a cupboard and placed it over her, only leaving her face showing. Rachel came into the room, kissed the dead woman's forehead.

Clare could see that the young woman had been crying. Even she could feel a lump in her throat.

'Don't say too much,' Mavis said. 'None of us liked her.'

'Please, mother, not now.'

Tremayne understood where Mavis was coming from; Rachel and Clare, younger and less cynical, less world-weary, did not. Tremayne had known about the Winters' mother back from his days when he lived nearby, the gossip about what went on in their house all too prevalent. He'd not heard about Margie. If he had, he was sure he would have taken some action, and now Margie had to be told that her mother had died. He'd leave that to Yarwood.

Jim Hughes arrived. The death of the old woman did not seem suspicious, but she had been the mother of a murdered man. Hughes was not pleased to be disturbed close to midnight. He set himself up near the bed, pulled back the sheet, took some photos. Another crime scene investigator checked the room, looking for anything suspicious. Mavis waited downstairs with Clare and Rachel. Cyril slept on a sofa in the living room; Gerry staggered around drinking black coffee, trying to sober up.

In the dead woman's room were Hughes, another CSI and Tremayne. 'You're not going to start asking me questions before I've finished, are you, Tremayne?'

'What do you think?'

'You're going to be a nuisance until I've given you something.'

139

'That's it.'

'Okay, a woman in her late seventies.'

'She was seventy-nine,' Tremayne said.

'Average height, marginally underweight, in apparently reasonable health for her age.'

'What makes you say that?'

'No immediate signs of injury to the body, a broken arm when she was younger. The body still retains some elasticity. Dead for two hours.'

'Conclusive?'

'Nothing's conclusive until I've finished and the pathologist's conducted his examination, you know that.'

'Is the death suspicious?'

'At seventy-nine, the funeral of her son? I'm not sure, but there's no sign of drugs in the room, no sign of injury to the body. Unless my examination and the pathologist reveal anything unusual, I'd say the woman died of natural causes. Nice house, by the way.'

'With their money, you'd expect it to be.'

'They can keep it. Too many hassles for me.'

'And for me,' Tremayne said.

'You know my next sentence?'

'Clear off and leave you to it.'

'Something like that.'

'Okay, I'll be downstairs.'

'Give me two to three hours, and we'll transport the body to Pathology. You can talk to the pathologist after that.'

'Thanks for coming.'

'It's better than having you on my back. Anyway, this soon after the death is always preferred.'

***

Downstairs, the mood was sombre. 'Poor granny,' Rachel said. Her mother sat to one side of her, her arm draped around her daughter.

'It was her time.'

140

Tremayne moved over close to Yarwood. 'How are they taking it?'

'Rachel's upset. The others are making all the right sounds.'

'A good woman, it's a shame, so young…?'

'Sort of. Cyril's still asleep; he's not been told yet.'

'Dean?'

'Mavis phoned him.' Clare said.

'And Stan?'

'He's been told, but he's still heading back to Pentonville. He'll need to apply for compassionate leave again.'

'I'll organise it,' Tremayne said.

'Someone will need to tell Fred, as well as Margie.'

'You'll not get much sense out of her tonight. You can visit her in the morning,' Tremayne said.

Tremayne walked over to Gerry, offered his condolences

'It's strange,' Gerry said. 'None of us liked her, but now she's dead, we feel sad. Why is that?'

'Don't ask me. Part of the grieving process, I assume.'

'I should get over and see Margie. She needs to know.'

'Will she be upset?'

'With Margie, who knows? We always thought she'd be the first to go, never considered that our mother would die, too mean-spirited to consider leaving us in peace. Cyril will not be upset. He had her back in his house, and she was giving him hell.'

'Dean?'

'He's got enough to deal with as it is. You saw his wife, the holier than thou bitch,' Gerry said.

'Yarwood had a talk with her.'

'Not in here.'

'Out in her car. She was not complimentary of your family.'

'A truly awful woman, even worse than our mother. Our mother only cared about herself, didn't aim to change us; we could have all gone to hell as far as she was concerned.'

'Why was she like that?' Tremayne said.

'Maybe it was something to do with our father; maybe that was her nature. We never knew, but then we were children. We survived, looked out for each other.'

'Except for Margie.'

'When she goes, there'll be a lot of sorrow.'

'For your mother?'

'Not much.'

Tremayne walked back upstairs, standing to one side as a stretcher was brought into the house. Jim Hughes came down the stairs. 'Pathology,' he said.

'Anything more?'

'Nothing else to report, if that's what you want. I could do with a cup of tea.'

'In the kitchen. You'll find the family, but they're fine.'

At 2 a.m. Clare and Tremayne left the house, along with Jim Hughes. Cyril was staying the night, Dean was coming up in the morning. Clare wondered if his bruises would be showing. Tremayne didn't care either way; he had a bottle of whisky at home, he'd have a couple of drinks before he went to bed. It had been a long day, a long night. He missed Jean.

***

To the south of Salisbury, a house, the same as all the others in the street. Inside a warring couple.

'She's my mother,' Dean Winters protested. His head still throbbed, it was three in the morning, and the woman was still going on about his condition when he had left his sister-in-law's house.

'I don't care. You're not going back there. You've got a job here, responsibilities, a wife.'

'What kind of a wife are you, sleeping in a single bed, denying me?'

'We're too old for that,' Barbara Winters said.

'Alan was older than me, and he never had any problem.'

'With that Mavis Winters, his tarts? What do you expect? The man was debased, not cognisant of his responsibilities to his

142

religion, to his family. There's that whore of a sister, I saw her there, the needle marks in her arms. Your nephew, that Bertie, what a disreputable individual he was, and as for your niece…'

'Don't say a word about Rachel. She's holding down a steady job, and she was polite to you.'

'I could see through her. It was only an act. No doubt she's screwing whoever she fancies.'

'Just because you were too pure to have children, not wanting to soil your hands changing their nappies, feeding them, don't insult my family, don't insult Mavis or Rachel.'

'If you like them so much, why don't you go and live in that big house with all their money?'

'It'd be better than here. I'm afraid to sit down in case I crease the fabric, and as for you…'

Barbara Winters came forward; she hit her husband across the face. Dean, inflamed, for once in his life hit her back, and hard. 'You bastard, how dare you?'

'Shut up and sit down, will you.'

'I will not. I'm off to bed.'

Dean Winters sat down after she had left, not caring if the chair was out of symmetry with the others. He felt good. He picked up the keys of the car, even though he was still sobering up, and left for Salisbury.

***

Polly Bennett and Liz Maybury, both fast asleep, both in the same bed, did not expect a knock on their door. It was past two in the morning, and they had to be at the shop by eight.

'It's Gerry,' a voice through the door.

Polly opened the door. 'What is it?'

'My mother died.'

'The same day as Alan's funeral?'

'Yes. I saw you and Liz there.'

'He did right by us, the same as you. You'd better come in.'

Gerry entered the flat, saw Liz sitting up in bed. 'Sorry, I just wanted to see a friendly face.'

'Stay here tonight,' Liz said. 'There's room for three.'

Polly brought a coffee: black and strong. She also turned on the shower. 'You stink of alcohol. You'll need a shower if you want to be with us.' Gerry took off his clothes and opened the shower door. He was pleased to be welcome.

In the morning, he would remember their kindness, attempt to put in a word with Mavis about how well the shop was going. That night, he would enjoy the distraction of Polly and Liz.

***

Clare slept for a few hours, waking up at six in the morning. She fed the cats and left her cottage. By six forty-five she was outside Margie's place. She thought it was too early, but decided to knock on the door anyway. After ten minutes Margie opened the door.

'My mother's dead,' Margie said.

'You've been told?'

'Cyril phoned me.'

'Has he been here?'

'No one comes here.'

'How are you?' Clare asked.

'I'm not sure what I feel,' Margie said. Clare realised that it was the first time that the woman had spoken other than in monosyllables.

'Are you high on drugs?'

'I was last night, not now.'

'Can I come in?' Clare said. Standing outside on the doorstep discussing a dead mother did not seem right to her.

Clare thought the woman to be much improved from the previous times she had met with her.

'She's was my mother, but I hated her. Is that wrong?'

'It's unfortunate.'

'Do you love your mother?' Margie said.

'She drives me mad sometimes, but yes, I do.'

'I never loved mine. Did they tell you?'

'Your brothers are all concerned, so is Mavis.'

'I like Mavis and Rachel.'

'So do I,' Clare said, 'Very much. Do you want to be with them?'

'Today, I would. Will you take me to their house?'

It was a remarkably verbose conversation with a woman who had barely uttered a word before. Clare was pleased that she had come so early.

At the Winters' house in Quidhampton, a warm welcome. Mavis thanked Clare, pleased that Margie was in the house, hopeful that she would stay. Clare knew that was unlikely. Bertie was still not home, and Mavis was worried.

'He was meant to report back for his treatment,' Mavis said.

'If I see him, I'll send him back,' Clare said, although the man was in his twenties, and there wasn't much she could do. Rachel, diligent as always, was back at work.

Margie thanked Clare as she left, even gave her a kiss on the cheek, demonstrative for a woman who had been lacking any emotion before the death of her mother, even before her brother's death, although Clare thought that the mother's death had brought memories flooding back, memories long suppressed.

***

Clare had never imagined that she would ever re-enter the Deer's Head, Harry's former pub, but Tremayne had been adamant. He'd had a tip-off that Bertie Winters was to be found there.

'Sorry about this, Yarwood. It was bound to happen at some time,' Tremayne had said.

Clare knew that he was right. She couldn't be a police officer in a city as compact as Salisbury and avoid places because they upset her. Inside, she found the pub had changed little, apart from a touch up of some flaking paint. The pub had been there for centuries, and it was the old-world charm that people wanted, not a modernised square with a poker machine in one corner, a bar in the other, a charmless landlord. The new publican, Clare had to admit, was not charmless; quite the opposite. 'Evan Bassett,' he said on introducing himself. 'First time in here for you,' he said to the two police officers.

'We've been before, often in fact,' Tremayne said.

'Apologies, I was insensitive.'

'You know?' Clare said.

'Not in detail, although I've heard the stories, and some of the regulars used to come in here before.'

'You've got Bertie Winters here,' Clare said, changing the subject. She looked around the bar, noticed the steps down to the cellar where she and Harry had almost made love, the stairs leading up to the small bedroom where they had. The table in the corner where Tremayne had usually sat was occupied. At least she was pleased that her senior, a man of habit, wouldn't have the chance to resume his usual place in the bar.

'Over there, sleeping it off.'

'Thanks. You know who he is?'

'I came from up north, never heard of the Winters family before I came here. One of the locals told me who he was. For someone with so much money, he doesn't look anything special.'

'He's not,' Clare said. 'One ticket and you could have what his family's got.'

'Not me. I'll keep to the occasional bet on the horses.'

'What do you reckon for the 2.30 at Newmarket?' Tremayne said.

'Sonny Boy.'

'I fancy Flash Comet.' Clare sighed; another horse racing aficionado. She could see the Deer's Head becoming Tremayne's favourite pub again. She was there as part of her job, she did not want to linger.

'Let's get Bertie Winters and get out of here,' Clare said.

'Excuse us, Evan. We need to take the young man back to his family.'

'I read that his father had been murdered.'

'We've not apprehended his murderer yet.'

'It must be hard coming in here, unpleasant memories,' Evan Bassett said to Clare.

'It is. Excuse me if we grab Bertie Winters and leave.'

'I understand.'

Tremayne and Clare grabbed Bertie by the collar and walked him out of the pub. The man was semi-conscious. Tremayne, Clare knew, wanted to stay and discuss horse racing. She knew that he would have to come back on his own. She had entered the pub once, she did not intend to enter it again.

Once they were back in Quidhampton, Mavis called for a doctor. Tremayne thought it a waste of money, as all the man needed was a good sleep and solid food.

Tremayne and Clare were surprised to see Dean Winters eating a steak with gusto, a newly-hired cook preparing food for the family. 'Too long on salads,' Winters said.

'Your wife?'

'Not here. She's back in Southampton.'

'You've got a black eye,' Clare said.

'She hit me fair and square.'

'It took you long enough to stand up to her,' Mavis said.

'Either she'll come around, or it's over.'

'What do you reckon?' Clare said.

'You've spent time with her. What do you think?'

'She has some very firm views on certain subjects.'

'The Winters family,' Mavis said.

'It was biased.'

'Her father was an unpleasant man, constantly haranguing his staff, paying them a pittance,' Dean said.

'Then why did you marry her?' Mavis asked.

'The same reason any man gets tied up with a woman when they're young and in love: rose-coloured glasses.'

Tremayne did not need to be told why. He had married Jean for the same reason, although she had been an agreeable woman, still was. They had broken up because of his policing, but he was about to reunite with her, not out of a youthful reason, more out of a need for companionship.

Gerry Winters walked in the door. 'You've been with them,' Mavis said. 'I hope they're making a good job of my business.'

'They are.'

Tremayne and Clare left for Bemerton Road. The Winters family was united in the one house, except for Stan and Fred. Tremayne phoned up both of their respective prisons, spoke to both men. Fred was derogatory about the woman who had died; Stan was more conciliatory. 'No chance before the funeral,' Tremayne said to Stan's immediate request for compassionate leave.

'Do your best,' Stan said. 'I'll miss Alan, not her, or not as much as I should.'

Chapter 16

Neither Tremayne nor Clare was in the best of moods. There was still a murder to solve, and emotional involvement with the primary suspects did not help.

Clare left the office early, an appointment to meet up with Polly and Liz at a pub. It had been Tremayne's suggestion to meet them where their guard would be down, to see if there were hidden depths to the women, a reason for them to want Alan Winters dead and Gerry Winters in their bed. It was clear that they did not need to be with Gerry, and there was no great love affair there, so why were they bedding him? His smile as he had entered the Winters' house earlier indicated that it had been full on with them. Even Mavis had smiled at the cheek of the man.

Tremayne remained in the office; there wasn't much for him at home. Superintendent Moulton paid another visit, the usual, but he was not pushing hard for a retirement. Tremayne thought the man may be suffering from his problem, so much time policing that it had taken over his life at the expense of family.

'Your reports are late again,' Moulton said. For once he had taken a seat in Tremayne's office, seemed content to stay.

'We're struggling with a breakthrough in the Winters' murder,' Tremayne admitted. 'We've suspects, but so far we've not been able to tie them together.'

'Do you need additional manpower?'

'Not really. It's a case of finding the significance of Stonehenge, and why the wealthiest man in the area had to die. It's not as if he wasn't generous, he certainly was to those he liked. His widow is not going to be such an easy touch; she'll want legal guarantees for any money given, payment schedules for money lent, and she's not about to throw it away on young lovers.'

'Alan Winters, he was into women?'

'It was in one of my reports.'

'I know that. I'm making conversation, just going through the case with you,' Moulton said. 'I know you see me as a pen pusher, but I was a regular policeman once.'

'On the beat, sir?'

'The same as you, the same as all of us. Sometimes I miss dealing with the criminals, being out on the street.'

'I thought you were a procedures man, enjoyed being in the office.'

'That's true, but it's no different from running a large business. The concern over budgets and KPIs. And then there's the constant battle about staffing levels.'

'And retirements?' Tremayne said.

'It's not you in particular. The modern police force is run along business lines. We're expected to be financially viable, and obtaining the necessary money to run this place, a yearly headache, is not easy.'

Tremayne realised that it was the first time that he and Moulton had sat down for a conversation. In the past, it had always been a letter on his desk, a discussion about retirement, a quick chat about the latest case.

'We think there's another element to this case,' Tremayne said.

'There are some crazy people out there with crazy ideas.'

'We've got one of those.'

'Any possibility there? You dealt with the paganists in Avon Hill, and they were rational people under normal circumstances.'

'This one's not,' Tremayne said. 'The woman breathes flames; her husband's life must be hell, although he walked out yesterday.'

'For how long?'

'Not for long. Some men want to be told what to do.'

'Not you, Tremayne.'

'Nobody's going to push me around.'

'Not even me.'

'Not even you, sir. I'll retire when I'm ready.'

'That's how I see it. Outside of this place, you're not sure what you'd do.'

'That's true enough. I only go home to sleep, watch the sports channel. I rarely eat there, maybe the occasional frozen pizza in the microwave, but nothing else.'

'Yarwood, how is she?'

'A good police officer; she should be an inspector.'

'She will be, but that wasn't the question.'

'I know that. She's bought a cottage in Stratford sub Castle; she's even been into Harry Holchester's pub. She'll pull through.'

'No man in her life?'

'Not yet.'

'Let me know what you need,' Moulton said. 'I'll not talk about your retirement for a couple of months.'

'Why's that?'

'The quotas have been met. Until there's another push, I'll leave you alone.'

Moulton left. Tremayne sat in his chair, somewhat stunned after his visit. He looked out of his office door and into the department beyond. Apart from a cleaner, the place looked depressing. He knew he needed company. He needed to discuss horse racing over a couple of beers.

The Deer's Head, the one place that Yarwood had not wanted to enter, although she had in the line of duty, and the one place he had never thought he would either, was welcoming.

'What'll it be?' the publican, Evan Bassett, said on his arrival. Tremayne remembered to duck his head as he entered. The pub had been built when people were a lot shorter, and the lintel above the door would have hit him in the centre of his forehead.

'The usual,' Tremayne said, forgetting that it wasn't Harry behind the bar but another man.

'And what's that?'

'A pint of your best. Any food?'

'Chicken pie.'

'I'll have one of those.' Tremayne instinctively made for his favourite seat. It was unoccupied. He took a drink of beer, opened up his newspaper, took out a pen. He felt at home.

'How did Sonny Boy go in the 2.30 at Newmarket?' the publican asked, remembering their earlier conversation when Tremayne and Clare had rescued Bertie Winters.

'Which horse did you choose?'

'Flash Comet, it romped home, 10 to 1.'

'Your skills are better than mine. Yarwood, that's the police officer that I came in with before, she reckons I'm wasting my time.'

'Do you ever get out to the Salisbury Races?'

'Whenever I can.'

'Next time you go, give me a call. We could make a day of it, have a few beers, a few bets.'

'What about the pub?'

'I'm not wedded to the place. I can always call in help, and my wife will serve behind the bar.'

'She's not here?'

'She is when it's necessary. Tell me about the former publican,' Evan said.

'Yarwood was engaged to the man. Harry Holchester was his name. I liked him.'

'He turned out bad?'

'Not according to Yarwood, but yes. He was one of those up at Avon Hill. Have you ever been out there?'

'Not yet. We're new to the area.'

'A pretty place. Most of the stone to build the cathedral came from a quarry nearby.'

'I didn't know that.'

'Most people don't. It's not the same as when we were there. Back then Avon Hill was a foreboding place where you hardly saw anyone. The last time I was there with Yarwood to put flowers on Harry's grave, it was more agreeable, children in the street.'

'Yarwood, will she come in here again?'

'It's unlikely. She'd not be pleased with my being here.'

A call from the bar for service and Evan left.

Tremayne ate his pie and drank his beer. After ninety minutes he left the pub; it just didn't feel right, almost disloyal to Yarwood.

***

Clare drank her wine. Polly Bennett and Liz Maybury were downing vodkas. Clare enjoyed their company, even though she knew their story, their willingness to use their bodies to gain what they wanted. She realised that ambition is achieved in many ways; she wanted to do it through competent policing, the two women, Polly clearly the more intelligent of the two, would use whatever was at their disposal.

'Why are we here?' Polly said. 'We're an open book, you know all about us, we know nothing about you.'

'What's to tell,' Clare said.

'Everyone's got a story.'

The three women were sitting in the Ox Row Inn. All of them had ordered. Clare knew she would be paying.

'You know about us,' Liz said. 'I don't think you approve either. Am I right?'

'I couldn't do what you have.'

'Alan?'

'And Gerry.'

'It was good to be chauffeured around in a Bentley. And Alan set us up in business.'

'That's what I don't get. Why, if you can seduce the man, do you bother with running a business?'

'Clare, we want our independence. Alan was fun, so is Gerry, no doubt another man will be, but we want each other, not them.'

'We've assumed you were.'

'Involved?'

'Does it worry you?'

153

'No. But why the men?'

'We swing both ways. It's not a big deal for us. We're not ashamed of using men if it achieves what we want. Alan was generous, and Gerry, well, he's a lot of fun.'

'Humorous?' Clare said.

'In bed,' Polly said. Both she and Liz laughed at Clare's apparent naivety.

'Clare, what's your story? You at least owe us that.'

'There's not much to say. I met a man, we were engaged, preparing to get married. And then he was killed.'

'We know more than that,' Liz said.

'If you don't want to talk about it,' Polly said, 'we'd understand.'

'No, you're right. I owe you the truth. I came here from Norfolk. We were involved in a series of murders, Tremayne and me, not all of them pleasant. We became aware of a group of pagans conducting ceremonies.'

'What sort of ceremonies?' Liz asked.

'Human sacrifice.'

'In Salisbury?'

'I've told you the story,' Polly said. 'I know all about it, Clare. You don't need to say anymore.'

'It's fine. It's good to talk. You're local, Liz isn't. Harry, he was the publican of the Deer's Head. We were in love, moving in together. And then DI Tremayne and myself are trapped out at Avon Hill, along with some others, and they're coming for us.'

'Who?' Liz said.

'Let Clare talk,' Polly said.

'Some of the others go for help, some try to make a run for it across the fields. Not all of them made it.'

'And then what?' Liz said. Clare could see that she enjoyed the macabre.

'We make a run for it. We take one of the police cars, there are four of us. We make it up the hill, no more than a mile, they catch us, tie us up.'

'And?'

'The chief elder invokes his gods, the others become desperate for a sacrifice. They decide I'm the first. They prepare to come for me, then some of them decide that it's gone too far. They start fighting amongst themselves. Some are killed, those left come for me. Harry, I didn't know he was one of the elders, releases me, tells me to get out of there with DI Tremayne and two uniforms. Harry then kills the elder, and they dissipate. Most are in jail now for murder.'

Liz had wanted to hear the ghoulish details, did not expect to be moved by the story. 'How sad,' she said.

'You must have read about it,' Clare said. 'It was the headline story on the television for a few days.'

'I remember it, but you were there. You were a witness.'

'I was meant to be dead.'

'And Harry?' Liz said.

'I don't know why I'm telling you this. It brings back painful memories.'

'You can't bottle them up forever,' Polly said. 'Maybe you see us as uninvolved. It's not something you can tell your parents, probably not even talk to the others who were there.'

'We have the same problem,' Liz said.

'What do you mean?'

'We want to tell our parents about us.'

'It may be best to sit them down and tell them the truth. It's never as bad as you imagine. I wanted to ask you about Alan's death,' Clare said.

'A few drinks and we'll talk, confess to the crime,' Polly said.

'I don't think you two did it, but you've been close to certain members of the family. You've been around to Alan and Mavis's house. The smallest piece of information helps in the final analysis. Something obscure may bring his murder to a conclusion.'

'We didn't kill him, although we slept with him. I suppose you see us as promiscuous.'

'Promiscuous is a term I would use.'

'You've been honest. We'll not hold it against you.'

The three women ordered more drinks.

'You never finished your story,' Liz said.

'We're safe, the four of us. Harry's still in the wood; he's killed the chief elder. Tremayne doesn't want me to go back, but I have to. I find him sitting down. He's guilty of murder, I can't ignore the fact, and he would be arrested. Before that can happen, a branch falls from a tree, hits him, and hurls him away from me. I saw him die.'

'It must have been awful,' Liz said.

Polly said nothing initially, overcome with emotion. 'I read about it. It seemed unreal then, but with you being there, your fiancé,' she said.

'It feels better for telling you. You two are the first people I've told the story to, probably the last. Now tell me about Alan and Mavis Winters.'

'There's not much to tell,' Polly said. 'We had a good time with the man. He looked after us, we looked after him.'

'Did he have other women?'

'He may have, but not that we're aware of in Salisbury. It's unlikely, though.'

'Why's that?' Clare said.

'Clare, don't be naive. One man in his late forties, two women. We were always available. He's unlikely to have had the energy for any others.'

'His relationship with his wife?'

'He was fond of her, even loved her. You can't blame the man, he was only human.'

'Why do you say that?'

'We're there and willing. What man could resist, especially if he had that much money?'

'Not all men are like that,' Clare said.

'They're all like that,' Polly said. 'It's part of the human condition; man, the hunter, woman, the mother of his children. Alan was just fortunate that he could indulge his fantasy.'

'Mavis Winters?'

'She saw us at the house once. Alan thought she wasn't there.'

'What happened?'

'She was upset. We were as well.'

'What about Alan?'

'He seemed to enjoy the spectacle, made up some story about she had another man.'

'Did you believe him?'

'Not really. We assumed it was Gerry, but we don't think it was.'

'Why's that?'

'He's been around to our place a few times. After a few drinks and us, he likes to talk. We know all about his family, the mother, the brothers, even Dean.'

'And Alan's children?'

'We asked Gerry why he'd never married.'

'What did he say?'

'After his childhood, his parents, he had never wanted to form a lasting relationship.'

'But he slept with you two.'

'He likes women. He was more active than Alan, but then he was a few years younger. Maybe that was the reason. He liked Alan's daughter, not so much his son.'

'You know his son?'

'We've seen him around. Spaced out, the same as his aunt.'

'You know her?'

'Not really. We know of her; Alan told us.'

'What did he tell you?'

'That she was in a terrible state, and not even he with all his money could save her.'

'Any more?'

'Not about his sister. We knew Cyril; he'd sometimes be with us.'

'Drinking?'

'We didn't sleep with Cyril. He didn't seem interested in us anyway.'

'What did Alan say about Dean?'

'He couldn't understand why he had married his wife; said she was a dragon.'

'Did you know her?'

'We saw her at the funeral, but apart from that, we'd never seen her, nor Dean and his other brother, the one in jail.'

'Stan.'

'If you say. We only went to the funeral. After that we came home.'

Chapter 17

Tremayne met up with Clare at Bemerton Road Police Station the next morning, 6 a.m. sharp. Clare realised that she had drunk more than she should have the previous night, even willing to admit that she had enjoyed herself. Tremayne had drunk a couple of beers at the Deer's Head and gone home. For once, he was looking the better of the two.

'Any further insights?' Tremayne said.

'No secrets revealed. The women are honest about why they were with Alan Winters, honest about their relationship and their plans for the future. Polly's the smarter of the two, but they're both well educated. I liked them.'

'That's the trouble with you, Yarwood, you like people. They could have been playing you for a fool.'

'I've not said they were not involved in the murder, have I?'

'No. Were they?'

'There's no reason. We'll need to look further afield for an answer.'

A phone call; Tremayne answered. 'Mavis Winters' house,' he said to Clare. A short drive and they were in Quidhampton, Tremayne having driven for once.

'It's Dean,' Mavis said.

'What's up? Tremayne asked.

'She came up, angry, out of her mind.'

'His wife?'

'Who else?'

'Where is she? Where is Dean?'

Clare had already moved into the house. Inside, lying on the floor of the kitchen, was Dean Winters. 'She went mad, she had a knife,' Rachel Winters said.

'From where?'

'From here. We've a drawerful.'

'Your uncle?'

'She stabbed him in the arm. She was aiming to kill him, but I pulled her away. She nicked me with the blade, but it's only a minor wound. Uncle Dean needs to be in the hospital.' Outside, the sound of an ambulance.

'Where's the patient?' the medic said.

'Over here,' the faint voice of Dean Winters said.

'Put out an all-points for Barbara Winters,' Tremayne said to Clare.

'Right away.' Clare made a phone call to instigate the process, opened her laptop and sent a photo and a description.

She returned to the kitchen to find Dean Winters sitting on a chair. 'It hurts like hell, but I'll survive.'

'Are you up to making a statement?' Tremayne asked.

'It was Barbara, not used to me standing up to her. It's the same with her family. They're all aggressive.'

'Why did you marry her?' Mavis said.

'I didn't know what her family was like.'

'Until they'd trapped you in their web.'

'Maybe I was, but it was good for a few years.'

'Not that we ever saw you.'

Clare looked around the kitchen. Apart from the blood on the tiled floor and the upturned chair, there was not much to see. 'Where is your wife?' she asked.

'Back in Southampton, I assume.'

'Mr Winters will need a few stitches.'

'We'll take him,' Mavis said. 'Unless he wants to go in the ambulance.'

'That's fine. I'll go with you,' Dean said.

'We'll need to take statements from everyone here,' Tremayne said.

The violence from Barbara Winters had not been expected by Tremayne and Clare. The woman's invective, her views on the Winters family, were well known, but a knife attack represented a new development. It was the second knife attack in the current investigation; the first one, fatal, the second, almost. Tremayne thought it was circumstantial, Clare was not so sure.

'We need to find Barbara Winters,' Tremayne said. 'I've phoned her local police station. They've been round to her house; she's not arrived yet.'

'We need her today,' Clare said. 'We need to know if her husband's stabbing is pre-meditated or an act of violence in the heat of the moment.'

'The latter, almost certainly, as the woman did not arrive with a knife, only found one in a kitchen drawer.'

'What do we know about this woman?'

'Enough to know that she's not pleasant.'

'Capable of murder?'

'Dean Winters would have been dead if Rachel hadn't interceded.'

The injured man left with Mavis and Rachel in the Bentley; Tremayne and Clare returned to Bemerton Road. At the station, the two police officers discussed the case. Clare was all for driving to Southampton; Tremayne was more circumspect.

'If she's not at the house, what then?' Tremayne said.

'We can check out her family.'

'What do we have? Have we interviewed them before?'

'She has a brother, two years older than her. Her father is retired, living in a home, dementia. We've just compiled the standard report on her, the same as the others in the investigation.'

'The father, any chance that he'll know where she is?'

'According to the report, he'll not be able to help. The brother is not far from Southampton.'

'Have you phoned him?'

'Not yet.'

'Then I suggest you do it right now.'

Clare dialled the number, no answer. She tried two more times, no success.

'Suspicious?' Tremayne said.

'Not really. He's a pilot. He may be out of the country.'

'Can we get the local police around to check him out?'

'It's only twenty minutes from here,' Clare said.

'Why didn't you say so?'

'You weren't listening.'

'You're driving. If she's not there, then we come back. When's the mother's funeral?'

'One week, maybe.'

'They've not set a date yet?'

'They need a death certificate. Her body is in Pathology.'

'Okay, first the brother's house and then Pathology.'

'Yes, guv.'

***

Clare took the A36 out of Salisbury, heading in the direction of Southampton. Ten miles from the centre of the city, she turned off to the right, and took the B3079 to the village of Landford, twenty-two minutes' driving time. The brother's house was not difficult to find. It was neat and tidy, the same as all the other houses in the village. In the driveway and on the road there was no sign of the car that Barbara Winters had used when she had driven to Salisbury. 'Wasted trip,' Tremayne said.

'We'll wait for twenty minutes. I'll park the car out of sight, and then have a look in the windows.'

'I'll stay in the car, in case she arrives. If she parks in the driveway, I can block her exit.'

Clare parked the car, made sure that the brother's house was visible. The owners of the house on the other side of the road, fifty feet away, expressed concern about a strange vehicle in their driveway. Tremayne flashed his ID, gave the lady a brief synopsis of the situation. 'They're a strange family. Arrest the lot of them for all we care,' she said. 'He's not sociable. If one of the children kicks a football over the fence, it comes back slashed with a knife, and if someone's dog defecates on the footpath outside, you'd think it was a criminal offence.'

'Have you seen his sister?'

'She comes here sometimes, doesn't speak to any of us. What's she done?'

'Have you seen her today?'

'Not today. She was here the other day, but not for long.'

'Do you know why?'

'Not me. I don't become involved. I'm only interested so I can keep my children away.'

'That bad?'

'They'll scream at the children if they go too near.'

'Is the brother married?' Tremayne knew the answer to the question, just wanted to check what else he could find out.

'There was a woman there once. She used to chat, but then she disappeared. One day she's there, the next she's gone. It was very suspicious; he was seen digging in the garden that night, as well.'

Tremayne noted what the woman said, but did not place too much credence on Barbara Winters' brother slaying a woman and burying her in the garden. It was too melodramatic for him, and a small village was a good place for gossip. However, he'd have it checked out.

Clare walked around the house. The back garden was the same as the front, neat and tidy with no flowers. The edges of the lawn were precise, the gravel paths freshly raked. She could see the family trait: the symmetry, everything in its place. Inside the house, there was no sign of movement. Clare heard a sound on the driveway. She peered around from where she was standing.

Tremayne moved over into the driver's seat of Clare's car. The neighbour was excited that she was there as the action unfolded. The local pub would be buzzing that night with the story of how the police had come to the village and arrested the woman.

Clare moved away from her hiding place; Barbara Winters got out of her car. 'Mrs Winters, we've a few questions for you.'

The woman, panicking, got back in her car, started the engine and reversed, stopping abruptly on seeing Tremayne blocking the driveway with Clare's car.

'I didn't mean to do it,' Barbara Winters said on getting out of her car for the second time.

Tremayne handcuffed her and put her in the back of the police car. Clare sat to one side of her, as Tremayne was driving. The woman could not be left free. On the other side of the road, the neighbour busily talking to another woman, taking in the scene, talking on her phone at the same time.

At Bemerton Road Police Station, Barbara Winters was taken into the interview room. Her legal representative was on his way, expected within five minutes. Outside, Dean Winters waited with Mavis. 'I want to see her,' he said to Tremayne.

'We'll need to interview your wife first.'

'For what?'

'It's a crime to stab someone with a knife; manslaughter if you had died.'

'But I haven't. Can't we forget about what happened?'

'Dean, shape up. She may be your wife, but if you keep whimpering around, she'll continue to make your life a living hell,' Mavis Winters said.

'But I love her; I need her. Without her I'm nobody.'

'You should have thought of that earlier before you stood up to her,' Tremayne said.

Barbara Winters' legal representative, Graham Davies, arrived.

In the interview room, Tremayne went through the procedure, informed Barbara Winters of her rights, asked everyone to state who they were and the time of commencement.

'Mrs Winters, you went to the house of Alan and Mavis Winters. Once there, you stabbed your husband, Dean, with a knife that you had found in the kitchen.'

'It was unintentional. I love my husband.'

'Are the facts correct?'

'Yes,' Barbara Winters said after conferring with Davies.

'This is a criminal offence. If your husband had died, you would have been charged with manslaughter, probably involuntary, and the punishment for such a crime would be custodial. Were you aware of this when you visited the house?'

'Not at all. I was angry. He had shamed me in front of his family.'

'A family you hate.'

'I do not like them, that is true.'

'Why?'

'They are common people, unbelievers. They are not my kind of people.'

'Your husband is one of them.'

'With me, he was not. At home, before his brother died, we were close.'

'And your husband defied you by drinking alcohol, by talking to one of his brothers, a criminal serving time in prison.'

'I do not want him associating with unworthy people.'

'But he is one of them. You were aware of the bond that exists between the children of Betty Winters.'

'Children of the devil, that's what they are. It is my duty to save Dean from them, to make him a better person.'

'Why do you feel that you can separate a person from his blood relatives? You are aware of the abuse that they suffered as children?'

'You knew them, and you were a police officer. Why didn't you do something?' Barbara Winters said.

'I'm asking the questions here, Mrs Winters. You have stabbed your husband, that is a crime that needs to be addressed. I put it to you that you came up to Salisbury fired up with anger after a night without your husband. You were angry; you wanted him dead. You approached him in that kitchen hoping that he would acquiesce and come back to you, the lost sheep that he was. And when he would not, you took the only action open to you. You stabbed him, you wanted him dead.'

'I was hurt, angry, but I did not want him dead.'

'This is intimidation,' Davies said. 'It is not within your right to conduct the interview in this manner.'

'I apologise,' Tremayne said. 'Alan Winters has been murdered, a knife in his heart; his brother Dean has also been stabbed. The crimes are similar.'

'I did not kill his brother,' Barbara Winters said. Clare could tell the woman wanted to get across the table and scratch out Tremayne's eyes. Davies had his hand firmly on his client's arm.

'Mrs Winters, Alan Winters was killed at Stonehenge. It has all the signs of a spiritual death, an offering to a god of a worthless man, an act of atonement.'

'He was worthless. All that money, not through toil and hard work but through a weakness of people to waste what they have earned. It was the devil's money, not his, and not ours.'

'That is why you refused the hundred thousand pounds?'

'Dean refused, not me. He understood the true way, the way of purity, the way of the Lord, until his brother with all his money tried to corrupt him.'

'Mavis Winters has offered all of the children of Betty Winters two million pounds. Your husband is going to accept. Did you know this? Did he phone you up to gloat? Is this when you decided to kill him?'

'He would have refused it if he had been with me.'

'Mrs Winters, I'm charging you with attempted involuntary manslaughter. You will be held in custody pending a trial. Is there anything that you want to say?'

'I did not mean to kill him. I swear on the Bible that it's the truth.'

'My client will defend herself against this charge,' Davies said.

'That is her right,' Tremayne said.

Chapter 18

Tremayne had to agree with Clare that Barbara Winters was a strange woman, with her attitude, her contradictory comments during her interview at Bemerton Road. On the one hand she was crediting her husband with refusing the hundred thousand pounds from Alan Winters, and on the other she was taking credit for her ability to convince him of right from wrong. Tremayne could not see evil in the occasional bet on the horses. And Yarwood, he knew, would regularly buy a lottery ticket, not in the belief that she would win sixty-eight million pounds but more as a diversion from the routine of life, a chance to joke if only I had, not believing that it would ever occur. It had for Alan Winters, one of the most undeserving. Tremayne had to agree with Barbara Winters on that score, but not much else. He had remained impartial during the woman's interview, so had Yarwood, and then her husband was pleading for her to be released.

Tremayne couldn't remember Dean Winters from his childhood; he would have only been ten when Mavis was sixteen, just twelve when Tremayne had finally moved away from there and rented a flat above a shop in Fisherton Street. After that one night when Mavis had turned sixteen, he had not made love to the woman since, nor had he wanted to. Tremayne had hoped at the time that no one would find out.

Mavis had been over the age of consent, but only just. She was still in school uniform during the week and looked like a child. It had been up to Constable Tremayne to set an example, to uphold the law, to be a beacon of decency, and there he had been, seducing a young woman barely past puberty. The department's superintendent, not his inspector, would have hauled him over the coals, given him a severe dressing down, probably a written warning, and if Mavis's father had found out, he could have found himself back behind the counter of his father's shop.

He'd had a nervous few days after Mavis had seduced him; not a defence, but the truth. He had had more than his fair share of beers mixed with a few shorts. All of the young policemen drank too much, although they knew how to handle their alcohol back then, not like it was now. Five pints of a night was Tremayne's maximum, and even that would give him a thick head in the morning. He knew that a woman like Barbara Winters would have driven him mad, and he'd have ended up wanting to throttle her, not that he would have. He wasn't a Dean Winters, never had been, never would be, and with Jean, they had always been equals. He wondered why it was that two people who had been so close could have drifted apart; why being a member of the police force was so important. He knew that Yarwood was falling into the same trap of the balance between the life of a police officer and that of a regular member of the public, the ability to just enjoy other people's company without trying to analyse, to figure out their backgrounds.

He knew he wasn't a Sherlock Holmes, he didn't have that attention to detail, but he had developed an ability to observe. He had studied Barbara Winters in the interview room, also at Alan Winters' funeral and wake. She was not a bad looking woman, dressed sensibly, although not unfashionably, probably appreciated the occasional humour, the usual amount of affection, yet she held views which others would have regarded as extreme. He wondered how she could go through life with such hostility towards others. Life was about getting along with your fellow citizens, not acting as if they were enemies. And then that woman, the gossip in Landford where they had arrested Barbara Winters. What was it that she said? If the local children kicked a football into her brother's garden, it would come back with a knife through it. What sort of people would do that, he thought.

Back at his house in Wilton, the local children had no fear of him. One of them had broken the window at the rear of his house with a cricket ball, almost hit him fair and square as it whizzed past him, but what had he done? Nothing. He'd given them their ball back. Even had a bowl and a few hits after one of the young children had bowled at him, pretending to let the ball get through and knock over the stumps, or in their case a few sticks propped up between two wooden boxes. The offender's parent had apologised, offered to pay for the broken window. In the end, he and the parent had gone halves on the repair, not that it cost much, and here was Barbara Winters' brother slashing footballs. For what reason? The man was probably as much as zealot as her; he needed to be interviewed.

***

Clare observed her senior in his office, mulling over the case, his eyes closed. She thought that he looked like a cuddly teddy bear, not that he would have appreciated being told so. But there he was, arms folded, leaning back, running through the case, weighing up all that they had. Even she had found benefit in the ability to sit quietly and evaluate her life, inside and out of the police force. She knew she was lonely, missing the touch of a man. She was young, and at an age when a woman thinks of children, yet she had no one, not slept with another man since Harry had died, and she wanted to, though she couldn't be a Polly or a Liz. For them, sex and love were detached. Clare knew that the women regarded the act of procreation as a means to an end. They were both attractive, yet they slept with a man, not their age, not in good condition, purely because he was wealthy and willing to spend money on them. And then there was the brother they were sleeping with as well, supposedly because he could help them. Clare would admit that Gerry, a man who could be violent, was not unattractive: muscular, a firm handshake, a pleasant manner, and willing to take her out if she agreed, not that she ever would. Harry had been her ideal man; Gerry Winters would never be. And besides, she could admit to liking Mavis and Rachel, but their DNA was not pure Winters, whereas Gerry's was.

A date with a fellow officer had been agreeable enough. He had treated her well, held the chair back at the restaurant for her to sit down, even insisted on paying, not going halves. Yet, no spark. He had attempted to kiss her at the end of the evening, went through the accepted seduction routine as if a decent meal and a bottle of wine automatically concluded with two people naked and in bed. The man who she saw on a daily basis had taken her negative response with grace, accepted a kiss on the cheek as payment for a pleasant night.

Clare had cried that night for the man she couldn't have. She wanted to forget, to get on with her life, yet Harry remained firmly implanted, almost as a ghost from the past.

'Yarwood, are you going to sit there all day?' The voice of reality, the sound of her senior, arisen from his chair.

'Waiting for you, guv.'

'There's plenty for you to be getting on with. You don't need me to hold your hand every minute, do you?'

'I didn't want to disturb you. You looked so peaceful.'

'Thinking, that's what I was doing. You thought I was asleep?'

'It crossed my mind.'

'You're becoming too quick with your comments, you know that?'

'Yes, guv.'

They both knew the routine, the harmless rubbing each other up the wrong way. To an outsider, it would have appeared disrespectful to her, abusive by him; it was neither.

'I thought we were visiting Pathology, checking on Betty Winters.'

'The mother of the family.'

'Did you know her from before?'

'Vaguely.'

'Mavis's parents?'

'Her mother was a pleasant woman, similar to the daughter. Her father, respectable, working-class, drove an old Vauxhall. He didn't say much, but he'd acknowledge you. He always seemed sad.'

170

'Any reason why?'

'Just an observation on my part. He wasn't a drinker, and most weekends he'd be washing the car, or out in his garden, not that he had much success. I can remember it being cold back then. Maybe it wasn't, but that's what I remember. We even had a white Christmas.'

'I'm driving?'

'What do you reckon, Yarwood?'

'I'll get the keys.'

Pathology was not far away. Stuart Collins, the pathologist, took one look at Tremayne as he walked in the door and sighed. 'Tremayne, the bane of my life. What do you want?'

'Purely social,' Tremayne's reply.

'What is it with this man, Sergeant? Every time I'm busy, he's here.'

'He's a taskmaster, you know that.'

'What is it?' Collins asked. The man appreciated the chance to indulge in some banter, a chance to remove himself from the gruesome task of examining dead bodies, though it didn't worry him anymore, impervious as he was to the whole process.

'Betty Winters.'

'Seventy-nine. No medical condition other than ageing. She had taken a few sleeping tablets, not enough to kill a younger person. I can't see suicide, definitely not murder. Her death will be recorded as natural. Is that sufficient?'

'Yes. We'll need a medical certificate, a release of the body.'

'You'll have the certificate today, the body tomorrow. Is that all?'

'It is.'

'Sergeant, get him out of here, will you?'

'My pleasure,' Clare said.

***

Two days passed. Clare had found out from Barbara Winters the details of her brother. He had been flying between England and Australia. Clare had sent out a request to his airline to pass on a message to him. The man presented himself at Bemerton Road Police Station at eight in the evening. Both Tremayne and Clare were in the office.

Clare went downstairs, met the man and escorted him upstairs. She had to admit to being impressed. Barbara Winters' brother, Archie Garrett, was tall with jet black hair. He was dressed in his pilot's uniform, British Airways. 'I've just arrived back. I came here straight from Heathrow. I'd like to see my sister.'

'That will be arranged. We'll need fifteen minutes to deal with the paperwork.'

'What paperwork? She's my sister, I'm entitled to see her.'

Clare sensed the change in the man's attitude.

'Where's that fool of a husband?'

'He's been here every day. We've not restricted his access.'

'And good to hear. The man's a snivelling imbecile, but Barbara seems to like him.'

Tremayne met the brother, had a brief discussion. Barbara Winters was brought to a visitor's room. The brother and sister were allowed to embrace, to sit next to each other, a police officer in one corner of the room, far enough away not to hear their conversation. Neither of the two was regarded as antagonistic to each other, hence the restrictions were relatively few.

'What happened?' Archie asked.

'It's that family. They've turned Dean.'

'You were warned about allowing tainted blood into our family.'

'What was I to do? You may be able to embrace a life of celibacy, I cannot.'

'The man was poor material.'

'He was pliable. I had controlled him for so long. If his brother had not won all that money, he would still be with me.'

'And you tried to kill him?'

'No, I didn't. I was angry. I wanted to make him pay for leaving me and joining with them again. He rejected the one true path, embraced depravity and ignorance and the way of the devil,' Barbara said.

'We have suffered for our beliefs. What hope was there for Dean? He has brothers in jail, a sister prostituting herself. And as for Alan Winters' wife, what a bitch. How I would like to deal with her. The anguish she would feel, the pain, the suffering. As for your Dean, if you are ever free of here, we will deal with him. He will not stray again.'

'How?'

'We will destroy his will to resist. Now, what do we need to do to get you out of here?'

'We need to convince them that my actions towards Dean were out of anger, not out of a desire to harm him.'

'But how?'

***

Betty Winters was not accorded the same degree of reverence that was shown to her son. This time just her coffin at the crematorium, the immediate family, a priest that Mavis knew to say a few words. Tremayne and Clare had been invited. Tremayne declined, Clare accepted as a special favour to Mavis.

The open casket, the woman's children filing past. Stan was allowed to attend, but not to drink, not that he wanted to. There had been trouble when he had arrived back at Pentonville the previous time. It had taken Tremayne a couple of phone calls to deal with the warden and to ensure that Prison Officer Marshall did not receive a warning.

Tremayne had put in a special request for Fred Winters to attend. It had been granted, although Fred would have to stay with a prison officer at all times. The man was listed as violent, whereas Stan was not. None of the other members of the Winters family was pleased to see him when he arrived.

'The man's trouble,' Mavis confided to Clare.

173

Stan Winters had spoken to his brother on his arrival, as had the others. Rachel Winters had given the man a kiss on the cheek and a hug. Bertie, her brother, had shaken his hand.

Dean Winters, dressed in a suit, sat on the front row of the chairs. There was a small pulpit to the right of the casket, now closed after everyone had filed in. Rachel stood up, took her place in the pulpit and said a few words in honour of the dead woman. Clare could hear the sincerity in her voice, the only one that day. Fred, although the eldest child, declined to say a few words, but Stan was willing to stand up. He chose to read the Bible. Clare asked Fred later why he had not followed on from Rachel. 'I couldn't, that's all.'

Dean Winters said a few words, read them straight from a piece of paper, never once looking up at the people in the small chapel. His words sounded insincere to Clare. She noticed that his wounds had healed. Bertie Winters fidgeted in his chair, a clear sign that Mavis Winters had wasted her money on trying to get the man off drugs.

Gerry and Cyril sat quietly throughout the service: some emotion on Cyril's face, none on Gerry's. Margie Winters sat impassively, the previous ability to communicate, temporary as it had been, gone. She did not utter a word, only nodded her head, not even wiping her eyes. Clare went up to her afterwards as everyone stood around drinking tea, eating cakes, attempting to talk about the dead woman who was now on her way to being prepared for cremation. Margie responded warmly when Clare put her arm around her, snuggled in close. The woman was skin and bones, in need of nourishment, but she was not even willing to eat cake. 'I hated her,' she said, the first words she had said that day.

'Today's not the day to talk ill of the dead,' Clare said.

After the ceremony, it was back to the Winters' house, now host to Dean as well. He was making the occasional trips to Southampton, but apart from that he was staying close to Barbara. Her brother had brought in their lawyer; he had argued his case for her to be released on bail. Tremayne would oppose it, but it would be up to a court hearing. The woman was unstable as

174

far as Tremayne could see, and there remained a possibility that she would strike out at her husband or another member of the Winters family. He thought that she would get bail, as the lawyer was competent.

Tremayne went to Betty Winters' wake, had a terse but polite conversation with Fred. The man was a habitual criminal, and Tremayne represented the law, even though he had helped the family when he lived nearby. 'It's nothing personal, Tremayne, you know that.'

'Fred, leave well alone. Take the money and move away when you get out,' Tremayne said, knowing full well that he was wasting his time.

'I only wish I could, but I'm committed to farming. I've got a few ideas. I've been in the prison library, learning what I need to know.'

'Mavis has done well by your family.'

'I know that. A fine woman, better than Alan deserved. I wouldn't mind her alongside me.'

Tremayne knew that trouble was coming, but it was sometime in the future. He moved away, found Stan drinking a beer. 'I thought you weren't allowed.'

'Only the one. It's a miserable atmosphere in here. I've got to do something.'

'Give me one,' Tremayne said.

'You're a good man, you know that.'

'Don't tell the criminals, will you? And don't tell my sergeant.'

'Why? What will she do?'

'A smart comment.'

'But you don't mind?'

'Don't let her know, that's all.'

'How is she? After Holchester's death?'

'She's bearing up, the same as all of us.'

'Aye, that's true. All the money in the world, and it doesn't solve anything. Life's a bitch sometimes. Look at me, all those years in jail, never married, nothing.'

'That was your decision.'

'I know that, but it's a waste.'

'You're not that old.'

'As rich as any family could be, but what do you see? A room full of long faces, and outside in the driveway, Mavis's Bentley. What for? What does it do that an old bomb doesn't? I'll tell you, nothing. I'll take my two million, buy myself a small house and invest the rest. Maybe I'll take up a hobby.'

'Not robbing banks?'

'I'm not Fred. Maybe golf, maybe fishing.'

'You'd be bored.'

'Not me. I'm not an ambitious man, the need to chase young women doesn't interest me, well, not much anyway. I'm an emotional vacuum; it must be our mother that did that. We're all emotionally stunted. That one woman destroyed our lives.'

'What about those men who abused Margie and the others?' Tremayne asked.

Stan Winters took a seat. 'It was a long time ago. Do you want to bring up the past? Think of Margie. She's had a rough time, unpleasant memories. You'll only make it worse for her.'

'What happened to them?'

'We beat them up, put them on a train, one way, that's all.'

Tremayne knew it was not the truth; he decided to say no more on the subject. As Stan had said, it was a long time ago, the men's names lost in time, the chance of proving murder or otherwise was long gone.

'Fred will cause trouble,' Tremayne said.

'I'll be around. I can control him.'

'Can you?'

'I'm the only one who has a chance. We've a lot of history between us.'

Tremayne walked over to Clare. 'I'm taking Margie home,' she said.

'How is she?'

'Not good, but she'll talk to me, not the others. Her emotions are raw. She should be in a hospital, but she'll not go.'

'Her family could get a court order.'

'They'll not do that. For all their faults, they all love her, and she won't be around for much longer.'

'Are you sure?'

'No. But the woman doesn't look after herself. She's addicted, probably not selling herself, not too often that is, but the men she'd go around with wouldn't treat her too well.'

'I'll stay for a while. I'll see what the other brothers have to say, also Mavis and her children.'

'Don't expect much from Bertie.'

'I won't.'

Chapter 19

Tremayne left the wake. It was ten in the evening, and he was sober. He phoned Clare, she was back home in her cottage. 'Margie?' he asked.

'I sat her down, made sure she had some tomato soup.'

'It's hardly a meal.'

'It was the best I could do. How about you?' Clare asked. One of her cats sat on her lap; it was purring. The television was on, and she turned down the sound.

'Fred went back to prison, so did Stan. As for the others, Dean was upstairs by the time I left, so was Bertie. Gerry and Cyril were there, didn't have much to say, only that Cyril was glad to have his house to himself again. Gerry, I think he phoned up the two women.'

'Polly and Liz.'

'What about them? They're easy with their favours, especially with Gerry.'

'What do you make of Gerry?' Clare said.

'He makes sure that Mavis is safe. I believe the man is genuinely fond of her.'

'Yet she prefers you.'

'Yarwood, don't go down that road. Don't try to be the matchmaker, and besides, I've got Jean.'

'Have you?'

'I think so. We get on well. She's not coming to live with me; I'm not going to live with her. We'll meet every few weeks, have a weekend away. Mavis realises that I could keep Fred under control, but I'm not going to babysit the family. There are enough men there as it is.'

'Dean won't be much help.'

'Not at all, and his wife's bail hearing is coming up.'

'What do you reckon?'

'She'll get bail,' Tremayne said.

'And then what?'

'She'll be quiet for a few days, so will her brother.'

'He's as devout as her.'

'Possibly worse. A few days and Dean will be in their line of fire again.'

'Violence?'

'Coercion more like. I think Barbara Winters blew it down in Quidhampton. She's held the man in check for years, and then all of a sudden, he's with his family. They're in the background egging him on, telling him to stand up for his rights.'

'He'll not continue to stand up to her.'

'Not him. He likes to be told what to do. We've always assumed that all seven have the same father.'

'The differences in their characters, is that what you mean?'

'Dean is not like Fred, although Cyril is like Alan. There are similarities between Gerry, Fred, and Stan.'

'Margie?' Clare asked, as the woman concerned her more.

'She's similar to Dean, weak personality. Another woman may have eventually shrugged off what happened to her, but she's susceptible to drugs, same as Bertie. I'd say that Alan, Cyril, and Margie, probably Dean, had the same father, although there's an age difference of eight years between Alan and Margie.'

'Is it relevant?'

'Probably not. The father or fathers are not around.'

'They're not important,' Clare said.

***

Dean Winters visited his wife, found her in an ebullient mood. 'My hearing's coming up soon. I'll make it up to you, I promise,' she said. 'It'll be like it used to be, just you and me.'

'I'm sorry,' Dean said. He knew he wanted Barbara back and if that came with her funny ways, then he would accept them, even embrace them if it was required. He remembered the early years, the early nights, the passion. Back then, she had been firm in her beliefs, had told him about her father and how he had pushed her and her brother. How he had made them stand for hours on end reciting passages from the Bible. And then, the standing on street corners, a banner in one hand, a Bible in the other, attempting to waylay the pedestrians as they walked past, most taking a wide berth, others coming in too close, only to be caught. Even in winter, they'd be there at the weekend. How her school friends had ridiculed her, not invited her to their parties, not that she would have been allowed to attend. Her father would have seen to that, and now the man did not even recognise his children.

Dean knew he had been a lonely man, lacking in confidence, even a slight stutter at the first signs of nervousness, but with Barbara he had been articulate, with her always there building him up. The change in their relationship, imperceptible at first, dramatic afterwards, had occurred the day after Alan had won the money. There he was, outside Dean's house, in a red Ferrari. He had gone out to see Alan, even driven it at one stage, and inside the house, Barbara, unwilling to come out, was condemning his brother.

Up until then, he had not seen Alan for many years. He couldn't admit to missing his family that much, apart from Margie.

Apart from his isolation from his family, the relationship with Barbara had been great and the saying of prayers at meal times, the two visits to the church on a Sunday were only minor encumbrances. Yet with the Winters' wealth, his brother's insistence on him taking some for himself, his wife had changed.

No more was she dismissive of his family, not talking about them. Instead, she would bring up the subject at every opportunity, criticising them: the lazy, the incompetent, the criminal, the prostitute. He had reacted as any man would; he had fought back. With words at first, then with threats, and then by walking out on her, but not before hitting her. Not that she didn't deserve it as she'd beaten him enough times, and he had stood there and taken it. As he sat with her in that small room, he knew

180

that the good outweighed the bad and by a large margin. He wanted to be with her, and if that meant that all the cutlery, all the plates and cups and saucers had to be in line, the food cans as well, then it was a small price to pay. And now, she was promising to go back to what she had been before.

'What about this two million pounds that Mavis has offered?' he said.

'We will accept it. We will use it for charitable purposes. At least the evil will be of some good,' Barbara said. The two of them shared a warm embrace, the policewoman in the corner of the room saying nothing, only smiling. She was a sucker for a romance book, and here, in the room, there was true love, a happy ever after. She did not see the look in Barbara Winters' eye, nor did her husband.

***

Bertie Winters had been seen around Salisbury of a night time on a few occasions, invariably minding his own business, getting drunk or drugged, although the latter was unproven. What was clear to Tremayne was the man was too sullen when sober, too vocal when drunk, not that anything could be done about it, and the fact that the subject of his vexation was his mother did not bode well for family relationships. Tremayne, sitting in the Pheasant Inn one night, had taken the man to task, attempted to tell him that he should be grateful that his mother was making an effort to look after the family's interests. All Tremayne received in reply was a comment to mind his own business. Tremayne wondered why he had become involved; Clare, when Tremayne had told her, reckoned it was a guilty conscience, in that he had seduced the man's mother when he was younger. Tremayne told her she was talking nonsense.

Barbara Winters' hearing had been a formality, with her husband having made an impassioned plea for the love of his life to be released. He'd also given an account of the dangers of infinite and immediate wealth and how it impacted otherwise decent people, his wife included.

Clare had attempted another date with the police officer that she had been out with before. The same routine: the meal, the wine, the attempt at luring her back to his place. The same result, a goodnight kiss. She had wanted to invite him in, the need for a man to make love to her, but he had not been Harry, never would be. It worried her that she was heading down the Tremayne road of relationships.

Whatever the future held, it was certain that for now it was her and her two cats, though one of them was starting to age, struggling on its back legs.

Tremayne caught up with Mavis Winters after her sister-in-law's bail hearing. 'What do you reckon?' she had asked.

'I'm against it,' Tremayne said. 'The woman and her brother have some strange ideas.'

Mavis had been surprised at his appearance: a new white shirt, a freshly-pressed suit. She made no mention of it. 'Dean's gone back to Southampton with her,' she said.

'Let's hope he's okay.'

'For a few days, but she'll have him standing to attention soon enough.'

'What is it with Dean? The other brothers stand up for themselves.'

'No idea. He was the closest in age to Margie when they were growing up. He probably saw more of what was going on in that house than anyone else, no doubt some of his mother's men were abusing him, violently probably. One thing's for sure, he rarely talks about it.'

'The two million pounds?'

'I've signed it over to Dean. The other brothers will get theirs soon enough. With Fred, I'll want some further safeguards.'

'Such as?'

'I'm not sure. That's up to the solicitor. Fred has to take the money on his release on the condition that he does not ask for more.'

'He'll agree, take no notice.'

'Then he won't get the money.'

'That's a dangerous game.'

'I know it is, but what else can I do? Believe me, this money's a curse. So far, I've a son who's out of it and a dead husband.'

Tremayne did not want to get into a conversation about having too much money. It wasn't a condition he had ever suffered from, nor would he have wanted it. He preferred the uncomplicated life, and money only complicates. The solution for the Winters was straightforward, although none of them would ever take it. It had come up in the bail hearing that one of the brothers and his wife were going to devote themselves to charitable causes, how they were going to use the money for good.

Tremayne noticed that at the hearing Barbara Winters never mentioned that the money came from evil. She was careful to keep her extremist views in check. The woman was intelligent, in that she was capable of portraying the loving housewife, the friend of little children and animals. Tremayne knew there'd be trouble, and with instant millionaire status, how long before the woman cracked? Everyone has a price; he'd heard that before, not sure if he did, but what would have happened if he had had a run of wins on the horses, the money multiplying up into the thousands, possibly hundreds of thousands? Would he have looked at his house disparagingly, sought to buy a better one?

He thought he wouldn't, but now there was a woman with two million pounds. He was sure they had not heard the last of her.

'What about Gerry? He's still with Polly and Liz,' Tremayne said. Mavis had picked him up from Bemerton Road in the Bentley. He had to admit the car was magnificent, but it wouldn't have fitted in the garage at his house. Mavis had let him drive it, although he hadn't wanted to. He never let on, but his eyes weren't as sharp as they used to be, and at night he was finding it hard to focus on the road, especially if it had been raining, and the headlights of the other cars would sometimes dazzle him. They had settled themselves at a restaurant in Harnham, not far from where Alan used to go with Polly and Liz. As he drove, more like cruised, past Alan's favourite pub, the woman in the passenger's seat had not commented. Tremayne made no mention of it either.

'If Gerry's got the money, they'll be friendly to him.'

'What's your feeling towards them?'

'Ambivalent. I was angry at first, but now I maintain a cordial relationship with Polly. I also needed to ensure my investments are sound. Alan won sixty-eight million pounds. If I cashed in now, sold the house, the furniture store, the car, and put it together with the money in the various banks, I'd be down to forty-two million, and now there are six children, including Margie, that's twelve off the total. That still leaves thirty million. It sounds a lot to us. I used to think that if I had a hundred pound in my pocket, I was rich, and now I talk in millions.'

'It is a lot,' Tremayne said.

'There's always someone hassling for a handout. You can't believe how popular you are when you give it; how despised when you refuse to give more, or none at all.'

'Some problems?'

'Alan gave a million to a charity in Africa. The man who came to the house gave a spiel about schooling the children in Liberia, though I hadn't heard of the place.'

'It's in West Africa,' Tremayne said.

'Anyway, we gave him the money, a bank transfer. I'd checked it out, it seemed above board.'

'What happened?'

'The next we heard, the man's driving around in a Jaguar, having built a few tin huts in a couple of villages. He was possibly well-intentioned, the same as us, but once the money hit the charity's account, greed took over.'

'After that?'

'I learnt my lesson, Alan didn't. Polly and Liz are a prime example.'

'They're hard workers.'

'They are, but there were other women before them. Not that I ever knew who they were. He used to go up to London with Gerry, extended visits, spend the night there, have a few drinks, watch a show.'

'Alan, a show?'

'As long as the women were scantily clad.'

The two friends laughed at Mavis's comment. Tremayne had to admit that he enjoyed her company. If she had been older, if he had been more mature all those years ago, they may have made a go of it, but now he felt comfortable with Jean, and besides, playing two women, not that he ever did, was for a younger man, not someone in his late fifties.

'Gerry, you never answered about him, not fully.'

'He's not a total fool, and he's devoted to the family. I've no interest in him either, if that's what you're asking.'

Tremayne hoped he hadn't walked into a trap.

'It was inferred that you had someone with you when Polly and Liz came visiting.'

'Not me. All I had was a hot water bottle and a rogue of a husband.'

'Why didn't you object?'

'Alan had the money. It was all in his name, the house, the cars, the bank accounts.'

'But you had money.'

'I always had plenty; he wasn't tight with me, but not total access. There was one bank account in my name, a few million pounds, but the bulk was in his name.'

'Why?'

'His solicitor, someone he'd known from his schooldays. He told him to do it.'

'Good advice?'

'I wasn't going to cheat Alan. No, it wasn't good advice, but then, this fair-weather friend charged him close to two hundred thousand to set it all up.'

'How much were they worth, his services?'

'Fifteen to twenty thousand. You see, that's what happens. Everyone wants to bleed you dry, assuming it's a pot of gold with no bottom.'

Mavis ordered fish, Tremayne ordered a steak, well done. A bottle of wine between the two of them. The place was expensive, and regardless of how much money Mavis had, he was paying. He was not going to be one of those who took advantage.

'What about you, Tremayne?' Mavis asked. It was only Jean who called him Keith.

'I'll keep working.'

'Happy?'

'Content would be a better word. I don't have your wealth, but then, what use is it to me? I can afford to buy what I want.'

'What do you want to buy?'

'Nothing.'

'That's what I thought. What about Clare?'

'You like her?'

'She's sad. I sometimes see it in her eyes, but yes, I like her very much.'

'You know her story?'

'I've always known, never mentioned it to her. Time heals, they say.'

'A lot of time in her case.'

'She needs to find someone else, move on.'

'She will, in time.'

'And you?'

'I've got Jean.'

'Serious?'

'We get on well. We meet up occasionally, glad of each other's company.'

'She's got herself a good man with you.'

'I've mellowed in my dotage,' Tremayne said.

'Dotage? You're still a difficult man. How does Clare deal with you?'

'Don't tell her, but I'm fond of her. Never let her know.'

'I won't. Now, what do you fancy for dessert, and not me. I'm off the menu.'

'I never presumed, besides…'

'No besides, you're not my type. Too old for me. I'll find myself a toy boy.'

'You can afford one,' Tremayne said, realising that Mavis was joking with him.

Chapter 20

Dean Winters sat in the corner of the kitchen. The chairs were lined up. He was sitting upright, shoulders back. 'We'll be alright,' Barbara said. Her brother stood next to her, both looking at the man who was waiting for instructions.

Dean realised that he had made a mistake in returning to Southampton.

'You will sign over the money to Archie, is that understood?'

'I thought we were going to use it for good?'

'We are, but Archie will take control. You will do what you are told. Is that understood?'

'But…'

'*Is that understood?*'

'Yes, it is understood.'

'Why did you marry this imbecile?' Archie said. He was no longer in his airline pilot's uniform but casually dressed in a tee-shirt and jeans. The brother and sister had the man where they wanted him.

'He does what he's told.'

'But he is still one of them.'

'That is why I have never bred with him, my dear brother.'

Dean looked at the pair standing next to the kitchen sink, knew what they were, knew that there was no escape. He had been happy in Salisbury in Mavis and Alan's home, he had even got drunk on a couple of occasions, and nobody had complained. But here, in this house of horrors, subjected to physical and mental abuse, there'd be no respite.

He knew about Barbara and Archie's childhood. The father who would lock them in a cupboard for days on end for the merest infraction, who'd beat them with a leather belt, who'd make them stand for hours at attention, all the while spouting fire and brimstone at them, eternal damnation for their being alive when their mother was not. Dean had sympathised with his wife, understood the pain she felt after the hold of the father had lessened. Back then, when they had met, she had been kind and gentle, at least with him, not his family, but she had changed. The father confined to a nursing home, the son taking on the mantle, subjecting his sister to abuse if she deviated from the one true course, blaming her for choosing love over righteousness, for seeking the pleasures of the flesh over abstinence.

Dean knew that he needed out and to be back in Salisbury, although if he made an attempt to move, they would restrain him, lock him in the cellar, while they sat upstairs and decided what to do with the money.

Dean knew that whatever it was, it would not be for the benefit of the deserving.

They had arrived back from Salisbury the day before. On the trip down, Barbara had spoken about a new beginning and how she was going to devote her life to her husband. Once at home, they had retreated upstairs and made love. For that night and the morning after, they had been as newly-weds, until Archie arrived at the front door with two large suitcases. He did not bother to knock, he had a key. He found the two of them embracing.

'I've taken three months' leave,' Archie had said.

'This is my house. Get out,' Dean had shouted, but to no avail. He had received a punch in the face for his impertinence.

'You're a miserable little worm. You will learn obedience. You will learn that total obedience to the Lord, to me, is the only way. I will guide you on your journey.'

'You're an evil bastard,' Dean had said, only to be thrust into a cupboard for a few hours to cool down. On his release he had found his wife and her brother in deep thought, deciding on their future, not his.

They had spoken about following the path of righteousness, of helping others, but he had not been swayed by the desire to do good. He knew that they intended to help themselves the way their father had, a businessman who had no issue about preaching goodness while doing anything and everything to increase his wealth. And now the family that they both abhorred had given them the easy way.

***

There were always two certainties in the Winters family: one, that the mother, Betty, would not die, and two, that Margie would.

The first certainty had proved to be incorrect, the second had not.

Clare was the first in the office to receive the news. Gerry phoned her. 'It's Margie.'

Clare phoned Tremayne who phoned Jim Hughes. Clare was the first at Margie's place. Upstairs, a medic as well as Mavis, Gerry, and Cyril. Rachel was on her way. Sprawled across the bed was the lifeless body of Margie Winters. Gerry and Cyril had tears on their faces, Mavis was resolute and in control. 'We just came to check on her. We hadn't heard from her for a couple of days.'

'We'll need our people to check out the room, conduct an autopsy,' Clare said, a lump in her throat. The woman had been doomed for most of her life; her death should not have come as a surprise, yet it hit home hard.

'We had always hoped,' Gerry said, 'that somehow she'd come back to us, and now, she's lying there.' Clare put her arms around him. He seemed better for her sympathy.

'Why?' Cyril asked. He was no better than Gerry, as he held a handkerchief to his eyes.

'We'll find out,' Clare said.

Tremayne entered the room, looked at the dead woman, put one of his arms around Mavis's shoulder. 'It was bound to happen one day,' he said.

'I know,' Mavis said.

Tremayne spoke to the medic. 'What's the diagnosis?'

'It's a possible drug overdose.'

'Intentional?'

'That's not for me to say.'

'Thanks,' Tremayne said. He realised that the medic would be non-committal. It was not the man's function to say what had happened; that belonged to Jim Hughes and his crime scene team, as well as Stuart Collins, the pathologist.

'It would be best if we leave the room,' Tremayne said.

At his suggestion, everyone moved to the hallway outside. Jim Hughes arrived, kitted himself up and entered the room, accompanied by Tremayne, who had also put on protective gear. 'What's the situation?' Hughes asked.

'Margie Winters, forty, drug-addict, a prostitute.'

'Is the death suspicious?'

'Not in itself but her brother was murdered. We'll need to see if this is related.'

'I'd hazard a guess that she's overdosed.'

'Any reason?'

'Don't hold me to it. There are no apparent signs of a struggle, even though the room's a mess. The woman was clearly not healthy, probably under-nourished.'

'How long do you need?'

'A few hours. My team will check it out, see who else was here. Was she actively prostituting herself?'

'We don't think so. She was looked after by her family, the best they could.'

'Not very well by the look of this place.'

'That was her decision. There was a firm offer for her to move into the Winters' home in Quidhampton, all the medical help she could ever want.'

'And?'

'She refused it all.'

'Okay. We'll do our job and then send the body to Pathology. You'll have a verbal report later today, a written one tomorrow. After that, you can check with Pathology.'

Outside, Tremayne spoke to the assembled family. Rachel had just arrived. 'Margie will be transported to Pathology in the next few hours. It appears not to be suspicious, although we'll confirm later. We'll need to take statements from those who were here. Rachel, you've arrived later, so we don't need your statement. Yarwood, can you go back to Quidhampton and deal with it?'

'Yes, DI.'

'I'll phone Stan and Fred,' Mavis said.

'I'll contact Dean,' Gerry said.

***

Tremayne sat in his car outside of Margie Winters' flat, realising that the Winters family were part of his life story. Even though there had been years when he had not seen them, he had occasionally bumped into one or another of them, always guaranteed a warm welcome, and now Margie was dead.

He had seen it before: one murder and then a string of deaths, some violent, some not. Betty Winters, the mother, dead from old age, Margie, the youngest of the seven children, died because of her mother. Tremayne hoped that no one else would die.

He turned the ignition in the car, prepared to return to the police station. His phone rang. 'Tremayne,' he answered.

'Stan Winters here. Mavis just phoned me. I want to be with the family.'

'I'll see what I can do. I'm not sure it's possible.'

'I trust you, Tremayne. If you can't, I'll understand.'

'How are you?'

'You know the answer to that question.'

'Let me see what I can do for you. No promises.'

'That's understood.'

'I'll not be able to get Fred out, not until the funeral.'

'He'll know that.'

Tremayne prepared to leave for the second time, the phone rang again. Tremayne recognised the number. 'Gerry,' he said.

'Mavis has phoned Fred. He took it bad. He'll be looking for you to arrange for him to come to the funeral.'

'I can do that. I'll try and get Stan out before. He's already phoned me.'

'We'll not forget what you've done for us.'

'I must admit to feeling upset over Margie.'

'Your sergeant's here with Mavis and Rachel. All three are in tears, especially your sergeant.'

'That's fine. She'll take the statements in due course.'

'One other thing. We can't contact Dean. I'm driving down there.'

'I'll come with you,' Tremayne said. 'I'll meet you in Guildhall Square, ten minutes. We'll use my car.' Tremayne knew that something was amiss. There was no evidence, no reason, but he felt a sense of foreboding. Whatever it was, he needed to be in Southampton at Dean and Barbara Winters' house.

Ten minutes later, Gerry arrived in Guildhall Square. He was driving the Bentley. If it were purely social, Tremayne would have gone with him, but it was not. 'We'll use my car,' he said.

Gerry parked the car, phoned for Cyril to come and pick it up. It didn't pay to leave an expensive motor car standing idle for too long. The hooligans, the envious, would see it as a target for vandalism.

'Not much of a car,' Gerry complained as they drove down to Southampton.

'We may need it.'

'You've got your suspicions?'

'About Dean's wife and her brother, yes.'

'And Dean is there. As children, he was a damn nuisance. If it were Cowboys and Indians, he'd be the Indian tied to the post.'

Tremayne phoned Yarwood. 'What's the mood there?'

'Sombre. We've not seen Bertie. Supposedly he's coming to the house.'

'Get some uniforms from Bemerton Road to find him.'

'I've already done that.'

'Mavis and Rachel?'

'Rachel's taking it badly. What about Jim Hughes?'

'It's a possible OD, probably unintentional. If it's not, I'll talk to Stuart Collins to say it was.'

'The family will understand. If it's suicide, then declare it.'

'Okay. We're nearly at Dean Winters' house. I've got a bad feeling about this.'

'The sixth sense?'

'Whatever it is, it just doesn't feel right.'

***

Tremayne drew up outside Dean and Barbara Winters' house. In the driveway, a Mercedes. 'I've not seen that car before,' Gerry said.

'Spending the money already,' Tremayne said.

The two men walked up the driveway, passed the car. Tremayne rang the doorbell, the chimes audible inside the house. No answer. He rang again. Still no response. The two men walked around to the back of the house; the lights were on, indicating that someone was at home. Tremayne knocked on the kitchen window, and then the back door. The sound of a car at the front. He rushed around the house to see the Mercedes reversing at speed from the driveway, clipping his vehicle as it went, breaking a tail light. In the driver's seat was Archie Garrett. His sister was in the passenger seat. Tremayne, realising the urgency of the situation at the house, dialled Yarwood. 'Mercedes SL350, YA16 UMS, late model, one or two years old, dark green. Put out an all-points, use Dean and Barbara Winters house as the reference. Instruct them to stop and detain two occupants: Barbara Winters and Archie Garrett.'

'What else.'

'Just do it, Yarwood. We're busy.'

Tremayne pushed up against the front door of the house with no success. Gerry assisted, the lock broke, and the two men entered the house. Inside, everything was spick and span. 'Dean,'

Gerry shouted. No response. Tremayne headed for the rear of the house, Gerry ran up the stairs.

'He's down here, Gerry,' Tremayne shouted.

In the corner of the kitchen lay Dean Winters, black and blue from a severe beating. He was naked and unconscious. Tremayne dialled the emergency services.

'Dean, Dean,' Gerry said, sitting his brother up. Tremayne found a sheet in the utility room next to the kitchen and covered the man.

'What kind of bastards are these people?' Gerry said to Tremayne, as his brother slowly came around.

Six minutes later, there was an ambulance siren and a medic came into the house. 'What's happened,' the woman asked.

'The man's taken a severe beating. Severe lacerations across his back.'

A police car from the local station arrived. Tremayne showed his badge; they held back although it was in their jurisdiction and they would need to file a report.

'Is this what you've suffered all these years?' Gerry asked his brother.

'No, not like this,' Dean said. He was weak but conscious, the medic applying ointment to the exposed wounds, administering a painkiller.

'He'll need to go to the hospital,' she said. 'No broken bones from what I can see, but he'll need to be observed for a few days.'

'Before, Archie left us alone, but with the money he became inflamed. It corrupts, it always has. It's killed Alan. And now it's almost killed me.'

'You'll be alright, Dean. We've put out an all-points for them.'

Tremayne looked at Gerry; he understood. Margie's death would be kept secret from Dean for the time being.

Chapter 21

Dean Winters' injuries were not life-threatening, although he would be in Southampton hospital for several days, and then convalescing for a few weeks. As expected, Mavis came to the rescue with the best medical care, the counselling required after such a traumatic occurrence. Also, a room was being prepared for him at the house in Quidhampton.

As for the man himself, Dean was profoundly ashamed to admit the level of abuse that he had suffered over the years, mainly mental, sometimes physical.

'What can you tell us, Dean?' Tremayne asked him. Clare was with him, having driven down from Salisbury. Outside, waiting to visit him, were Mavis, Rachel, Gerry, and Cyril. Tremayne had briefly let them in to see Dean, or at least, Mavis, the undisputed matriarch of the family now. It was a police investigation, the two absconders not seen since they had reversed out of their driveway. The car was found abandoned less than five miles away.

The two of them had vanished. Tremayne was worried. Two people with no criminal records, apart from Barbara's pending trial, had clearly flipped, and he knew that people in their state of mind were no longer responsible for their actions. Caged animals facing imminent starvation will attack another and eat it; trapped humans will react in a similar manner. They had to be regarded as very dangerous, to be approached with caution.

'It was always Archie. You don't know what their childhood was like,' Dean said.

'That's not an excuse,' Tremayne said.

'Barbara's innocent.'

Clare could see that the man, no matter what was said or done, would continue to support his wife.

'What happened?' Tremayne asked. He had been forewarned by a trauma counsellor at the hospital that asking the patient too many questions could have a deleterious effect on his well-being, not that Tremayne needed to be told. He had encountered people during his career who had been subjected to severe mental and physical abuse, some who had nearly died at the hands of another.

'I had to be disciplined, don't you see? I had sinned.'

Clare stood to one side of the bed, wondering what it was with people who felt the need to harm others, to harm themselves, to believe that life was a set of rules: break them and it was eternal damnation or the need to self-punish.

'Did they kill Alan?' Tremayne asked.

'Not Barbara. She only did what Archie told her to do.'

'Have you been beaten like this before?'

'No. It's the first time. Barbara would hit me sometimes, lock me in the cupboard for my own good, but nothing more. It's Archie, I'm telling you. He's the one who controls.'

'But why?'

'Don't you understand. Their father controlled them, blamed them for the death of their mother.'

'Why?'

'I don't know. The man was always pleasant to me, but Barbara told me things; things that no child should endure.'

'Such as?'

'Physical disciplining, psychological conditioning, a house without entertainment where all three would sit around the table reciting biblical passages. And then Barbara was not allowed to socialise: straight to school, straight home. It's a wonder she survived.'

'It doesn't sound as if she did,' Clare said.

'I was working for her father; he deemed me suitable. Sometime afterwards, Barbara and I married.'

'Deemed?'

'Oh, yes. I had to ask his permission. But I knew I wanted Barbara, still do.' Dean moved in his bed, attempting to ease the pressure on the bandages wrapped around his upper body. His face was swollen, the first signs of bruising starting to show.

'We need to find your wife and her brother. Any ideas?'

'None.'

'Do they have any money?'

'I withdrew eighty thousand pounds for them.'

'Why?'

'For their charitable work.'

'And you believed this?'

'Barbara would not lie to me.'

'But you say she's controlled by Archie. Why, Dean, why? You've had a good education, better than anyone else in your family, yet you defend your wife's actions. Didn't you enjoy your time away with Mavis? The chance to do what you want? The chance to get drunk and overeat?'

'It was sinful. I see it all so clearly.'

'Barbara will be arrested, you know that?'

'I'll not testify against her.'

'That's your right. What about her brother?'

'He was right to do what he did. I understand.'

Tremayne and Clare left the man in his private room at the hospital. Outside, Tremayne spoke to Mavis. 'He still believes in her.'

'After all he's been through?'

'Stockholm Syndrome,' Clare said.

'What's that?' Mavis asked.

'It's conditioning whereby the hostage develops a psychological allegiance to their captor. That's what has happened with Dean. They've done this to him, and he still sides with them.'

'Is it permanent?'

'Probably not, but it will take time. He can't have any association with his wife.'

'Did they kill Alan?' Mavis asked.

'It seems possible, although why?'

'Maybe they realised that Alan would never give his brothers any more money? Maybe they assumed that I would be more generous?'

'It's possible. Devious, but a risk on their part,' Tremayne said.

'Am I in danger?' Mavis asked.

'We don't know. Until we find them, we're all in danger. This pair is desperate; their actions will not be rational.'

***

Tremayne and Clare returned to Salisbury. The local police in Southampton had a full description of the missing pair, as had their counterparts in Salisbury. The possibility remained that they had killed Alan Winters. The case file for his murder would now have the name of Samuel Garrett's two children on it.

Archie Garrett, well respected, bachelor, a senior captain for British Airways, remained an enigma. The man was highly regarded for his skills, and not once, not even after psychological tests had been conducted at British Airways, had he shown anything other than a man with moderate views, calm under pressure.

Tremayne knew that he was a dangerous individual. A weak man, such as Dean Winters, would be panicking, but not Garrett. He'd been calm, ensuring that he and his sister remained hidden, planning the next move.

Superintendent Moulton, briefly in Tremayne's office on his return, was excited that another murder was about to be solved.

'A change in the man,' Clare said.

'He blows hot and cold. Not to worry; he'll be back to form soon enough. What do you reckon, Yarwood? Do we have Alan Winters' murderers?'

'I'm not ready to concede that yet.'

'The right answer,' Tremayne said. 'Granted that they would have hated Alan Winters, but it's not conclusive.'

'The plan, if it is that, is full of too many variables. How would they have known that Mavis would give the money to the brothers, and why did they refuse the first offer?'

***

After three days there was still no sign of Archie Garrett and Barbara Winters. Dean, able to be moved from his hospital bed, had relocated to Salisbury, a nurse hired to look after him. Clare met up with him after one day back, noted that he seemed fine. It was early, and he was eating a full English breakfast. Mavis was busying herself arranging Margie's funeral, Dean having been told of her death.

The pathologist had issued a report that the woman's death had been as the result of a heroin addiction and her general poor health.

Clare sat down next to Dean, the cook serving her a full English breakfast as well. She had been trying to cut back, as a few extra pounds were creeping on, but she would not refuse. 'How are you?' Clare asked. She could see that the swelling on the man's face was going down in places, still black and blue in others.

'It's impossible to say. I loved my wife, but now it's over. Whatever happens, we could never be the same again.'

Clare could sympathise. After all, she had loved Harry Holchester, and he was dead. It was difficult, always would be, but life moves on. She was, she knew, a strong personality, and that she would rise above it. Dean Winters was not; the man would suffer.

'Margie?' Clare asked, not sure if the man was up to the question.

'It's probably better for her.'

Clare thought his answer was rational. She finished her breakfast and went and spoke to Mavis. 'Barbara Winters and her brother, Alan's murderers?' Mavis said.

'Did you see what they did to Dean?'

'Sadly, yes.'

'It doesn't make sense. How did they know the money would come to them eventually?' Clare said.

'What do you mean?'

'Did you give any indication that you would be more generous to the family if Alan weren't around?'

'I suppose I may have. Alan had never experienced money, assumed it would never run out, but there were enough rogues out there wanting to take it.'

'The charity in Liberia,' Clare reminded her.

'You don't need to go to Africa to find rogues. There are plenty here. We gave fifty thousand to a committee in another village to organise food for the aged.'

'What happened?'

'They went on a fact-finding tour overseas.'

'And the aged?'

'Still hungry.'

'And with Alan alive, there'd be no attempt to deal with these people?'

'He'd get angry, but that was all. And, besides, he was occupied.'

'Polly and Liz?'

'He also needed to help out the local publicans.'

'Violent when riled?'

'Not with me.'

'And Dean? What are you going to do with him?'

'He'll not change. I've become the mother now.'

'You'll do a better job than she ever did.'

'I'll do it, but it's not a job I want. Bertie's enough for me, and now there's Dean, and Cyril will need help.'

'Why?'

'The same old problem. Before, his financial situation kept him in check, but now he's got money, and he doesn't know what to do with it.'

'The same as Alan?'

'No doubt, but I had to give the brothers a reasonable amount, otherwise if I showed favouritism to one over the other, there'd be jealousy, and me having to listen to them. If Cyril spends his share, then I'll ensure he has somewhere to live.'

'What are you going to do about Bertie?'

'I hope he'll grow out of it.'

'Will he?'

'I hope so, but I'm not optimistic.'

***

Archie Garrett knew that he had been foolish. He thought of the father, the man who had destroyed their lives. The savagery of the man who had beaten his children for the slightest infraction. And now that man was dead to the world, locked in his own mind, not conscious of those around him. And still Archie could find no sympathy in his heart, only a feeling of hatred for him and for those who had impacted his life.

He had loved his sister, the only person who knew what went on in their childhood home. He had loved her until she had tired of him and had wanted another. He remembered the first time that she had introduced Dean Winters to him. Their meeting had been uncomfortable. He had been polite but resented the man who had usurped his sister's affection, distorted her, and there they were, exchanging smiles, knowing smiles, holding hands. He knew then that she had given herself to him, the one person that he had wanted. He remembered the day their mother died. It had been cold that day, ice on the path at the rear of the house. He and Barbara, wrapped up against the cold, only ten and eight respectively. Their mother, loving as always, shouting from the kitchen to keep themselves warm, not to catch a cold.

As their mother watched, he remembered Barbara calling for her to come outside and to help them to make a tree house, although it was only two feet off the ground. And then their mother coming out of the back door, slipping on the path, cracking her head on the concrete as she fell, the blood oozing.

It had been him, the more sensible of the two children, who had rushed next door to summon help. He remembered the ambulance and then the time in the hospital waiting for news, only to be told that their mother had died.

The two of them had attended the funeral, a hundred people there, a sign of how much she had been loved. And then the grieving process, the decline in their father's stability, his need to express his anger in violence, his extreme belief in the Bible, the Old Testament in particular. In time Archie understood that their mother's death had driven the man to despair, not that anyone outside the house would notice, not from him or from his children. They were too scared to tell anyone, too young to stand up to his bullying.

And in time he understood his father, his sister's inability to give herself entirely to her father's beliefs, her need to dress in the latest fashion, the need to have friends. He had not wanted friends since then, and whereas the pretence was complete, with the hearty bravado of a night out with the boys, even the occasional woman, he did not want any of them on a permanent basis. For him, he would prefer to spend his evenings with the good book, reading it page by page, memorising it, trying to learn from it.

As he and his sister sat in a room in a hotel in Portsmouth, not far from Southampton, not far from where Charles Dickens had lived, he knew that the future would need to be an affirmation of their father's teachings, a need to show that the Garretts were a pious and honourable people. Dean Winters came from a family of sinners, even before they had won the devil's money. Archie Garrett looked over at his sister, saw that she was desperately sad. He considered their options.

Chapter 22

For two weeks there was no sign of Archie Garrett and Barbara Winters, but time enough to conduct Margie's funeral. Not this time the horse-drawn hearse, the floral bouquets; instead, a funeral held in the chapel at the crematorium. Tremayne and Clare attended, on this occasion as friends of the family. Clare was glad to be invited, sorry that it was to commemorate the life of one of the fallen. Apart from the immediate family and the two police officers, there was no one else. Mavis read from the Bible, Dean, improved but still not fully recovered, gave a eulogy, long on the good parts of her life, short on the degradation that she had experienced in later life. Even Tremayne, at the request of the family, had agreed to read a short passage from the Bible. Clare was grateful that she had not been asked. There had been too many sad moments over the last year; she was overcome with emotion, so much so that it was Mavis, the stalwart, who had comforted her.

Rachel Winters also rose and spoke about her aunt, as did Stan and Fred Winters. Stan had been released from prison three days before the funeral on strict conditions: no visiting the local pubs, no causing trouble. He adhered to them, not venturing from Mavis's house in Quidhampton other than to deal with Margie's funeral. Fred arrived ten minutes before the funeral service started, a prison officer at his side. Once the ceremony was over, he would be going back to prison. Tremayne had spoken to him on his arrival, found out that he wasn't happy about the restrictions but pleased that he was present.

At Betty Winters' funeral there had been little sadness; at Margie's it was excessive. Once the funeral had concluded, the assembled group returned to the house in Quidhampton, everyone saying their farewells to Fred, including Tremayne and Clare.

'Thanks for getting me here,' Fred said. It had been Tremayne who had supported his request to be allowed to attend.

Back at the house, the mood, sombre initially, became increasingly lively afterwards. Bertie Winters sat in another room drinking a can of beer. Clare thought that his condition had worsened. She went and sat by his side. 'Bertie, you're not joining in.'

'Not me. I don't feel like it. They're out there pretending to care, but did they?'

Clare sensed the negativity, knew that the young man was incorrect. 'What do you mean?'

'They didn't stop her, did they?'

'They tried. She was welcome in this house. There was always the best medical assistance available.'

'That's easy. Just throw enough money around, ease the conscience.'

Clare left and went back to the other room. Bertie was obviously blaming his increasing addiction to drugs on others, not himself, his negativity being directed at others as if they were responsible. It was clear that the best medical treatment would not solve his problems. Margie had had an abusive childhood; Bertie had not. It would make no difference, his genetics were inclined to addiction, his sister, Rachel's, were not.

Back in the other room, Clare helped herself to another glass of wine, spoke to Stan. She knew that he would like to take her out, knew that she would decline. Stan was not her kind of man, although he had proved to be kind, and had helped Mavis in the days leading up to the funeral, not once deviating from his task. Fred, on the occasions that Clare had spoken to him, even at the church, was a different kind of man; he'd cause trouble whatever happened. Tremayne, free of policing responsibilities for once, was indulging in two of his favourite pastimes, beer and cigarettes, having found a willing partner in Stan. In spite of his previous release from prison when Stan had violated the conditions and had got drunk, Tremayne had managed to

organise an extra day for him. Tomorrow when both he and
Tremayne were sober, Tremayne would drive him back.

Dean was not drinking. Clare went over to talk to him.
'How are you?' she asked.

'I'm fine,' the man said. It was clear that he was still
suffering trauma. He was dressed in a dark suit, the bruising on
his face barely visible.

'We're still looking.'

'We were happy in those early years. What went wrong?'

Clare could see that Bertie was not the only one in a bad
mood. 'That's life,' she said. A flippant remark, she thought. The
only one she could think of.

'It was her father. With us, it was our mother. Why is it
that the people who should love you end up destroying your
lives?'

She spent a few minutes with Dean, and then went and
spoke to Rachel. This time, the reception was more positive. 'It
was a good send-off,' Rachel said. Of all those in the family,
Rachel was the most balanced, Clare could see that. She had
inherited her mother's good sense, her positive outlook on life,
her father's good looks. Mavis, Clare had to admit, was not the
most attractive of women. She was pleasant to look at, but the
symmetry of the face and her complexion were not ideal,
whereas with Rachel they were.

'No boyfriend here?' Clare asked.

'I'm not sure about him. How about you?'

'Not at the present time.'

'But one day?' Rachel said, conscious of Clare's former
relationship.

'In time, I hope so.' Clare was genuine in her comment.
She had visited Harry's grave during the week, placed some
flowers on it, said some words to him. For the first time, she had
not cried, not even felt sad. She knew, standing at the grave, it
was time to move on, her period of mourning was over.

Tremayne leant against a pillar in the sunroom to the rear
of the house. Clare went out to talk to him, found him to be in a
good mood; Stan, a kindred spirit was keeping him company.

'What is it, Yarwood?' he said, although with a slurring of his words. She was pleased that he was taking it easy. The last few weeks had been difficult for everyone. There was still no arrest for the murder of Alan Winters, and since then two more of the Winters' family had died, one beloved, the other not, as well as the savage beating of one of the brothers.

'It's remarkable how cheerful everyone is,' she said.

'It's a wake. It's not a time to be miserable. We can reflect on Margie, but we can't allow our lives to be brought down because of it.'

Clare had wanted to discuss the case; the fact that there were still two people who had not been found. Further research into the Garrett household and the children revealed some anomalies. The man's treatment of his children was not unknown, even at the time. One of the schools they had attended had registered a complaint to the authorities after Barbara Garrett had arrived at the school with a broken arm; her brother, on another occasion, with a black eye. At one stage, both of the children had been removed from their father and placed in care, only to be back with him within a month.

Clare hoped that the rules had tightened up since then and that no child would be suffering in the present day.

Mavis was busy ensuring that everyone was fed and had a drink, even though caterers had been brought in.

'How's Dean?' Clare asked.

'He still misses her,' Mavis said. The two women had sat down, the caterers taking over.

'After all that has happened to him?'

'I know we were always unkind to her, bitch that she was, but what had happened to her as a child must have twisted her.'

'It doesn't excuse her for what she has become.'

'I suppose so. Do you believe that she and her brother murdered Alan?'

'It seems the logical conclusion.'

'And no idea where they are?'

'None. We know they were in Portsmouth, but since then, nothing. They must be desperate by now. They had cash, but they're not using credit cards or withdrawing money from an ATM. It's only a matter of time before they reappear.'

'I keep telling Rachel and Bertie to be careful, to take security, but neither takes any notice.'

'Rachel's sensible,' Clare said.

'The car that rammed her up near the hospital? Any more news as to who and why?'

'None. We've assumed it was an accident, possibly someone who had drunk too much or didn't have a licence.'

'Rachel was sure it was deliberate.'

We don't think it was Barbara or her brother.'

'Someone else?'

'We're not pursuing that line of enquiry at the present time. Our focus is on Barbara and her brother. They're both capable of violence.'

'So's Fred. Did you see him at the church?'

'I saw him. He was pleasant, at least to me.'

'Of all the Winters children, he's the only one I can't like,' Mavis said.

'Does he know about Dean and his problem?'

'Dean told him at the church.'

It was ten in the evening before Clare left, giving a drunken detective inspector a lift home, his vehicle left in Quidhampton. She knew that she'd be in the office the next morning bright and early; he wouldn't.

***

Archie Garrett and Barbara Winters sat in a small café not far from Salisbury. Archie had purchased a car in a private sale and had paid cash. He had not shaved since their rapid retreat from Barbara and Dean's house. Barbara had dyed her hair blonde, cut it short. They knew they would not be easily recognised, and apart from the police showing photos in the hotel in Portsmouth, the first day after they had left Dean unconscious, they had seen no police presence.

Archie had realised that beating Dean had been wrong, but that was what had happened to him. He knew that both he and his father had a sadistic side. In the garden at home, he had enjoyed pulling the wings off butterflies, watching them squirm before stamping on them. With his father, it was tormenting his children, hurling them across the room, not feeding them, locking them in a cupboard or in the cellar.

'What are we going to do?' Barbara said. Archie could see that she was becoming sadder. He knew that there was no hope for them. He had nurtured his career, not once having faltered in his duty. To British Airways, he was the exemplary pilot, the man who could be relied on, but outside, the uniform removed, another persona. His father had been the same. At the time he had hated him, but now he understood.

'We cannot go back,' Archie said. He looked at his sister, the one person he had loved, but she had not loved him; she had loved Dean. Maybe that was the reason he had beaten him. They had been in that house, attempting to convince him of his sins in Salisbury, attempting to bring him back the way he had been before. Barbara, he could see, had weakened during her husband's absence.

He assumed Dean's belligerent attitude, his insistence that Archie was not welcome, was because of his family. They had convinced him that he had to stand up for his rights, to take control of his wife. Archie knew that could not be allowed. His father had only consented to the marriage on condition that Dean would look after Barbara in the manner to which she was accustomed, and now he was not following that order. And when Dean had stood up to him, throwing his suitcases out onto the driveway, he had reacted and hit the man. The first time with gentle force, and then with more, taking out the belt that his father had beaten him and Barbara with. The two of the children, both naked, both cowering as the man had come at them, both holding each other, hoping for relief. Relief that never came, and now Dean was resisting him. He had literally ripped the man's clothes off him, hitting him with the belt, throwing the occasional fist. Barbara had been shouting for him to stop, not wanting to get too close, the sight of the belt frightening her, and then the doorbell rang, the sound of the police knocking on the kitchen window.

The two of them, he and Barbara, running for the front door, jumping into the Mercedes and taking off. Archie knew the situation was grim; Barbara was not able to make any decisions. He knew that if he were not there, she would weaken and offer herself to Dean, give evidence against him to the police.

Chapter 23

Clare was in the office by seven in the morning the day after the funeral. Tremayne came in forty-five minutes later. Clare had not expected him to be bright-eyed and bushy-tailed so was not surprised to see him bleary-eyed and with no tail at all.

'Aren't you taking Stan Winters back to the prison today?' Clare said.

'At 10 a.m. He'll be ready.'

'Will you?'

'If you get me a cup of tea, I will be,' Tremayne said. 'Just this once.'

The two sat in Tremayne's office. Clare was full of energy; her detective inspector was not. 'Maybe I should drive him back?' Clare said.

'Maybe you should.'

Clare spent her time dealing with paperwork, Tremayne started with it, put it to one side. He was troubled. There were two people on the loose who had been willing to indulge in violence, and so far there was no sign of them.

Although the Winters maintained some security, it was insufficient. The question lingered in Tremayne's mind as to how Archie Garrett – his sister was regarded as subservient in their relationship – managed to get Alan Winters from Polly and Liz's place up to Stonehenge. It was known that the Bentley was outside their flat and that Gerry was driving, yet his recollection of the evening had been vague. If Alan had been dropped at home, then why was he at Stonehenge? Had he gone out again and why? Still more unanswered questions.

Tremayne did not have long to dwell on the matter. Realising that he was not in the best condition from the night before, he took a walk around the police station. Superintendent Moulton was in the hallway.

'Tremayne, what's the latest?'

'We're following up on all possible lines of enquiry. It's only a matter of time.'

'That's as maybe, but these two have been on the loose for some time. Do you regard them as dangerous?'

'Not to the general public, only to the Winters.'

'It's amazing what all that money can do.'

'It is. Not that you and I will ever find out.'

'Not me,' Moulton said. 'A police pension is all I've got to look forward to.'

'The same for me.'

'Don't you ever feel like throwing in the towel?'

'Are we talking retirement here, sir?' Tremayne said.

'Not at all. All the negativity of a murder investigation, the sorrow, the anger, the senseless taking of life by another, that's all.'

'It gets to me sometimes, I'll admit to that, but I've become inured to it. The Winters are an exception in that I've known them a long time.'

Tremayne could see the subtle attempts to talk about his retirement; he had no intention of rising to the bait, and besides, he had one man to return to his prison, two suspect murderers to deal with, and Jean, his former wife, to phone. The first responsibility he saw as an obligation, the second as confusing, the third as pleasurable.

Tremayne returned to his office; Clare was waiting. 'Yarwood, time to go?'

'If you want to pick up Stan Winters at 10 a.m.'

The two walked to Clare's car. She could see the look on her senior's face. 'What is it?'

'How did they get Alan Winters to Stonehenge?'

'He was unconscious.'

'That's not what I mean. We know that he left Polly and Liz's place, with a car outside. Did he drive or did someone else? And where was Gerry?'

'Are you having doubts about the Garrett siblings?'

212

'Not in itself. They're both capable of violence, or at least, Archie is, but from what we know, his violence comes from anger.'

'And taking a man up to Stonehenge to kill him does not. It's a calculated act spread over a few hours.'

'Precisely. And there was no anger in Alan's murder.'

'We've been down this road before. We have a murdered man, two violent people. Do you need more?'

'It may be enough to ensure a conviction, especially if they can place the Garretts in the vicinity of Salisbury.'

'But how? According to Dean, Archie was overseas at the time.'

'We have proof that was the case, but it's not conclusive. He could have flown back using a different name, committed the murder and then left the country again.'

'It's not logical.'

'I know, but why kill the man? They despised him and what he represented, but why murder? And then, why accept the two million pounds, and reject the one hundred thousand? Archie Garrett is a logical man, firm in his beliefs, as is Barbara. Why did they change?'

'Seduced by the money?'

'Not them. I just don't believe it.'

'But the car in the driveway?'

'That's unclear. We know they had purchased a Mercedes. According to Dean, he had signed over sufficient money to Archie, and that he had bought the car.'

'Dean's word.'

'There's no proof that the car was the result of the Winters' money. Archie Garrett must be paid well. He may just have bought it for himself.'

'We'll need to talk to Dean and Gerry on our return.'

***

Neither Tremayne nor Stan Winters said much on the way up to Pentonville. The previous evening, the police inspector and the convicted felon had both drunk excessively. That morning, of the two, Tremayne seemed the better, although it was marginal. For the first fifty minutes of the trip, both of them slept soundly; the only noise in the vehicle was the snoring of the two men. Clare could see the humour in the situation. Her phone rang. 'There's been an incident,' Moulton said.

It was unusual for him to phone her. 'What kind of incident?'

'Rachel Winters is missing.' Clare woke Tremayne. She handed her phone over to him.

'The woman never reported for work. They phoned her mother to check. Apparently, Rachel Winters is known for her timekeeping. The mother went looking, found the daughter's car a mile from the hospital.'

'They knew our phone numbers. Why didn't they phone us?'

'They didn't think it was suspicious at the time.'

'But now?'

'They've received a phone call,' Moulton said. Tremayne looked at his phone, flat battery. 'Your phone didn't ring?' he asked Clare.

'Not mine. It's been with me all the time.'

'You'll need to come back. We've put out an all-points.'

'The phone call?'

'Ransom. One million pounds or else.'

'Understood. Archie Garrett?'

'That's for you to find out.'

'And Mavis Winters has told the police?'

'She's an astute woman. She knew that the best chance of her daughter being returned alive was to let us know.'

'I've got Stan Winters with me. He's due back in Pentonville.'

'I'll phone the relevant people. He's under your control. Just make sure he abides by the conditions of his release.'

'I trust Stan. He'll do the right thing.'

Clare turned the car around and headed back to Mavis Winters' house. Bemerton Road was not the best place, other than for setting up a search.

At the Winters' house, there was surprise at seeing Stan again, concern over Rachel's safety.

'What did this person say?' Tremayne said on seeing Mavis.

'It was a muffled voice. One million pounds, or else they'd return Rachel to us in a box.'

'Archie Garrett?' Tremayne asked.

'We don't know.'

'You've found the car,' Tremayne said. 'Any sign of violence?'

'Not that we could see. It appeared that she had pulled off the road.'

'Jim Hughes is checking the car for fingerprints,' Clare said.

'We'll assume they find nothing. Coming back to the phone call, Mavis. What else was said?'

'Only that we were to ensure the money was available by six this evening and to wait for further instructions.'

'You realise that you are not to pay this. If you do, they'll want more money.'

'They can have it all. I want Rachel back.'

'Very well. Why did you call the police, if you'll not take my advice?' Why didn't you phone us instead of Bemerton Road?'

'I was panicking. Your phone wasn't working, and I couldn't get through to Clare.'

'My phone was fine,' Clare said.

'I tried once or twice, and then I phoned the police station.'

'The person on the phone told you not to contact the police?'

'I didn't want to, but with Alan dead, I thought the person on the phone may be his killer as well. Do you think Rachel is dead?'

'We don't know,' Tremayne said. 'Next time they phone, let me talk to them.'

'With respect, guv. It would be better if I spoke to them,' Clare said.

'Are you sure about this?' Mavis said.

'If they intend to harm Rachel, they will, regardless of police involvement. They'll respond better to me than DI Tremayne.'

'You're right,' Tremayne conceded. He knew that Yarwood was more diplomatic than him, and she had a calming voice, not like his, the effect of too many cigarettes.

Jim Hughes phoned. 'We've checked the car, no fingerprints other than Rachel Winters'. We have hers on record. Also, three cars at the site. Rachel Winters' car, the Bentley, we know it from the tyres, and another vehicle. The tyres are worn.'

'Any idea as to the make of car?'

'From a tyre print? Not a chance. The best we can tell you is that it's not a new car, small in size.'

'How?'

'The size of the tyres, as well as some oil that it dripped. We're assuming the Bentley doesn't drip oil.'

'If there's no more you can tell us, thanks.'

***

The next phone call was scheduled for four in the afternoon, almost a three-hour wait. Neither of the police officers wanted to relocate back to the police station. The cook, an eager woman from a nearby village, prepared lunch for everyone. Stan was sitting in one corner of the main room, anxious for action, wanting to grab hold of the person or persons responsible. Gerry Winters was also agitated. Dean Winters was worried that his wife was involved.

Mavis Winters spent her time talking to Clare. Tremayne rested in a comfortable chair, picked up a newspaper, and started to read it. Clare could see that it was a pretence.

At six o'clock, Mavis's phone rang. Only three people remained in the room: Clare, Tremayne, and Mavis. It did not need outbursts of anger or glaring eyes if Mavis and Clare were to deal with the call.

'I want to talk to Rachel,' Mavis said.

'She's fine,' a muffled voice replied.

'Male or female?' Tremayne mouthed.

'Male,' Mavis mouthed back. The phone was on speaker. Tremayne had heard the voice as well, but he needed confirmation from the two women.

'Do you have the money?'

'I do.'

'Very well. We will phone again.'

'My daughter?'

The phone line went dead. 'What are we to do?' Mavis said.

'He'll phone back within an hour. Whoever he is, he's not very experienced,' Tremayne said.

'Why do you say that?'

'He's too quick to demand the money; you're too quick to agree.'

Fifty-eight minutes, another phone call. 'The price is now two million.' No more was said before the call cut off.

'See what I told you,' Tremayne said.

'What about Rachel? The money's not important,' Mavis said.

'Stall them this time, ask to talk to Rachel. Unless you have proof that she's fine and well, then no deal.'

Another phone call, another attempt at tracing the location. 'They're moving around,' Clare whispered to Tremayne.

Mavis looked at the two police officers to be quiet. On the other end of her phone, the voice spoke. 'Have you informed the police?'

Mavis did not answer the question. 'I want to talk to my daughter.'

'That's not possible.'

'If you've harmed her?'

'We have not. The price is two million.' Yet again the phone line went dead.

Clare briefly went into the other room where the other members of the family were waiting, Bertie included. Cyril had also arrived.

Tremayne, frustrated with the kidnapper's procrastination, walked around the room; Clare remained impassive, sitting alongside Mavis. Clare's phone rang; it was a Skype call. Clare answered; on the other end, a nervous woman. 'They know you're there,' Rachel said. 'Tell Mum that I'm fine. They've not harmed me.' Another voice took over. 'We told her mother not to contact the police. We cannot deal with dishonest people.' The Skype call ended.

'It was Rachel,' Clare said. 'They know we're here.' Tremayne came over close to her; Mavis put her face in her hands in relief.

'How?' Tremayne said.

'If it's Archie Garrett, he would have assumed that we'd be somewhere around.'

'That's unlikely.'

'It's either Dean, or they've driven past the house in the last few hours.'

Clare left the room, went and found Dean. He was sitting with the other brothers and Bertie. 'Has anyone made a phone call recently? she said, not directing her comment at anyone in particular.

'No one in here, Gerry said.'

'Dean?'

'Not me. My phone's in the other room.'

'Whoever it is, knows I'm here with Tremayne.'

'Rachel?' Stan Winters asked.

'I've spoken to her briefly.'

'Is she fine?'

'It was brief, and she sounded nervous, but she was coherent, a good sign.'

Clare had no intention of indulging in idle conversation with those not directly involved. She returned to Mavis and Tremayne. The cook had prepared sandwiches. Clare brought them back to the negotiating team.

Superintendent Moulton phoned; Tremayne's phone was on silent. He excused himself and went out through the back door of the house, lighting a cigarette.

'Yarwood's spoken to Rachel Winters,' Tremayne said.

'Do you need assistance?' Moulton asked.

'We don't know what we're looking for. It appears that they are in the area and they may have driven past the Winters' house. Apart from that, we've no idea what car they are driving. Random searches are not going to help.'

'Is the woman in danger?'

'Not sure. We know that Archie Garrett, if he's not angry, is not violent. That's the hope. Yarwood is with the mother. They'll deal with the negotiating, and now it's two million pounds.'

'Do you have the money?'

'One million. The other one will be here soon.'

'Get the woman back. The money's expendable.'

'We know that.'

Tremayne returned to Clare and Mavis. 'Any more?'

'Not yet,' Mavis said. 'She's going to be fine, isn't she?'

Tremayne could see that the woman wanted reassurance. 'Yes, she'll be fine,' he said, knowing that statistically Rachel's well-being was far from certain.

All three ate the sandwiches, supplemented with freshly-brewed coffee. It wasn't Tremayne's first hostage situation. Last time it had been an angry father denied visitation rights to his children. He had barricaded himself in his former wife's house, along with their two children. It had ended badly.

Chapter 24

Rachel sat in the back room of the old farmhouse. It was cold, and she was shivering. Her hands were tied together in front of her and secured to a wooden beam by a length of rope. She knew she could not escape. She also knew that she should be frightened, yet she remained remarkably calm. Rachel assumed it was delayed shock, or maybe it was her training in hostile situations, the dealing with grief, part of her work at Salisbury Hospital.

She had met the man once before when she was a lot younger. It had been at the wedding of her Uncle Dean. She vaguely remembered that he had not spoken much. The woman with him she knew well. Barbara Winters had given her some food and drink. 'Sorry about this, Rachel,' she had said.

Rachel could tell that she was not sorry for her, only for herself. Rachel knew some of the stories about what had happened to her uncle, yet had not been able to accept it fully. Although now, in that farmhouse, the two people, the brother and the sister, had a look about them that concerned her. The situation seemed unreal, the sort of thing that happened in the movies, not in real life. She had stopped her car when she had seen Barbara waving from the side of the road. At the time Barbara had been apologetic about what her brother had done to Dean. A trusting soul, Rachel had got out of her car, walked around and on to the pavement by Barbara's car. Unbeknown to her, Archie had been hiding in it. He had appeared behind Rachel, thrust a hessian sack over her head and tossed her into the back of the car, securing her hands with a cable tie.

Once inside, as the vehicle hurtled down the road, almost turning over at one stage, Barbara had spoken to her. 'Sorry for my brother. We're desperate, and you are our only hope.'

At the time, the woman had been conciliatory, but Rachel saw afterwards that the brother and sister vacillated between caring and malevolent. They had hit her once, would again if she tried to reason with them.

Rachel could tell that the relationship between the couple was unnatural, almost as if they were husband and wife. Archie, the elder of the siblings, caring for his sister's well-being, promising her that things would be better, they could go overseas, start their lives anew, just the two of them.

'Once your mother pays we will let you go,' Barbara said.

Archie Garrett busied himself in another room, Rachel could hear him. Whenever he approached her, she was careful about what she said. The man was unstable, spouting about the Lord's work, and what the two million pounds would do for them.

During her time at Salisbury Hospital Rachel had experienced her fair share of frightening people, but the two who held her captive took the biscuit.

She knew she was in serious trouble. A police car had moved fast down the road not more than a hundred yards away, its siren sounding. She had felt a quickening of the pulse, assuming it to be coming to her rescue, but it had passed by.

Archie came into the room where Rachel was held. He knelt down close to her. 'They've agreed. You'll soon be going home,' he said.

Rachel did not trust him. The man's expression revealed insincerity. 'Good,' she said, not wanting to say more, not knowing his reaction. She had remembered that the family had wanted to love Uncle Dean's wife, but it had not been able to. Even though she had been young, she could remember the woman's manner, her disparaging comments about her mother, Mavis. And then the years when her uncle had kept away, although he was only a thirty-minute drive away, and then it was her father, newly rich, who had made contact, taken his Ferrari around to show off to his brother.

The meeting had been acrimonious from her aunt's side, friendly from her uncle's, and then within less than twenty-four hours the car was totalled, written off in an accident with a lamppost, and now the wife was trying to be agreeable, almost obsequious. Rachel wanted to ask her why the change of heart.

Rachel looked around the room. It lacked any charm, just a basic farm cottage; the only acknowledgement of the twenty-first century was a solitary light bulb hanging up high, suspended from the ceiling by its electrical cable. It was night outside; the stars could be seen high in the sky. The sound of cars was not far away, the rustling of trees. From the other room came the voices of two people talking. She wanted to listen, to know what they planned to do with her, whether they intended to free her. Or would the two of them kill her, the same as they had killed her father? Was she to be secured to a sacred stone somewhere, offered up in a ceremony? How would it feel to have a knife thrust into her? Would it be painful, or would there be a shock? She realised that the situation was getting to her. She thought of happy times: her mother and her, not so much of her father or her brother.

And then the door in the other room slammed, and she heard the sound of her captors outside the farmhouse. She knew she had to seize the opportunity. Grabbing hold of the rope tied to the beam she pulled hard, the first time with no success, but at the second attempt it fell free. She moved over to a drawer, pulled it open. Her hands were still tied, no longer with cable ties but with rope. In the drawer, a knife. She wedged it in the top of the drawer, its serrated blade pointing upwards. Using her body to push the drawer in to clamp the knife, she secured it firmly enough. She began a sawing action, listening for those outside. They were now distant from the farmhouse, she was sure.

The rope sufficiently cut through, it released its grip on her wrists. She was free; she knew she had to make a run for it.

Opening the door on the other side of the room, she was quickly out of the cottage. She was running, the cars in the distance, their lights blazing, getting closer. She reached the gate to the road; she was shouting for one of the vehicles to stop, they were ignoring her. As she opened the gate to rush out into the road, a voice came from behind. 'No, you don't.'

She remembered the man grabbing her in a bearlike grip and dragging her back to the cottage. The rope, doubled up, cutting into her wrists, restricting the circulation to her hands. Expecting the man to laugh, and then seeing the belt.

'Don't. She's our hostage. If she's harmed, they'll not pay,' Barbara said.

And then the man's voice. She remembered that before the pain started. The belt cut her hard across the face, and then her buttocks, her breasts, her legs.

It was some time before she regained consciousness. She was lying on a bed, her feet secured to the metal frame, her hands tied in front of her, this time with a cable tie. Not that it mattered. She was in agony, initially unable to move. Barbara sat on one side of the bed, with a bowl of warm water. There was the smell of disinfectant. 'You shouldn't have got him angry,' she said.

'Do you intend to kill me?' Rachel asked.

'Of course not, but Archie's under a lot of pressure,' Barbara said. Rachel, weakened as she was, unable to move other than with care, could tell that the woman had had a lifetime of abuse and brainwashing.

Managing to lift herself from her prostrate position, putting two pillows behind her, Rachel sat up. She could see that the room, in comparison to where she had been before, was pleasant. The sheets on her bed were clean, and there were flowers in a vase on the dresser close to the window.

'Has this been your life?'

'With our father, and then with Archie.'

'And Dean?'

'I loved him. He treated me well, and we were happy.'

'You hated my family.'

'I came from hate, yet I loved Dean.'

'Do you still hate me?'

'Not you, but you are different. Please, you cannot understand. If I could be back with Dean, I would treat him differently.'

'Would you?'

'I would try.'

Rachel could see a dim spark of humanity in the woman. The door to the bedroom swung open, the face of Archie Garrett appeared. 'Sorry,' he said. 'You should not have tried to escape. We will have the money soon, and you will be free. Barbara will stay with you and make sure that you heal.' The door closed and the man left.

'He is like my father. We hated him, but he has left his legacy. Archie could kill in his anger, remember that. Don't try to escape again.'

It was clear to Rachel that she would not be capable of escape for several days, maybe for weeks. She ran her hands over her legs and arms, pushed in on her body. There appeared to be no broken bones.

'I'll get you some soup,' Barbara said. She left the room; Rachel leant back and fell asleep.

***

There was only one concern for Tremayne and Clare: the safe return of Rachel Winters. It had been nine days of on-again, off-again negotiations with her captors. A voiceprint comparison of the muffled voice and Archie Garrett's voice messaging on his mobile had confirmed the two people to be one and the same.

The money was ready, an agreement had been struck. Clare had been nominated as the person to deal with the handover of the ransom, a retrieval location for Rachel not yet determined.

Tremayne sensed a hesitancy in Archie Garrett, who knew full well that once Rachel had been handed over, then the full weight of the police forces across southern England would be mobilised. Dean paced through the house in Quidhampton, his primary concern for his wife. Mavis thought that there was no hope for him. Gerry disagreed, as he had been spending time with the man. Cyril was staying in Quidhampton for the time being, although Stan had transferred back to prison the day after the kidnapping.

Superintendent Moulton had tried his best, Tremayne knew that, but Stan Winters was a prisoner serving a jail sentence, and his continued freedom did not assist in his niece's rescue. Tremayne agreed to keep him updated on a daily basis.

Analysis of the phone calls from Archie Garrett had picked up the sound of a road close by, but none of the noises associated with a city location. It was agreed that it was somewhere in the country, although the birds chirping in the background had revealed nothing significant.

Clare and Tremayne were now based at Mavis's house, a couple of bedrooms set up for them. A neighbour had agreed to look after Clare's cats. The primary contact was Mavis's phone and now Clare's, as she had taken the lead role in the negotiations. Moulton had wanted to bring in a trained negotiator from London; Tremayne had resisted. Clare had met Barbara Winters and Archie Garrett; a professional would not have.

Tremayne knew he was putting on weight, the difference between snatched pub meals and a cook on hand keeping everyone fed.

The Bentley was outside and ready. It had been agreed that Clare would drive the car to the retrieval point; the money was to be deposited elsewhere. Clare had been adamant that no money would be handed over until Rachel was confirmed to be free and was inside the car. Archie had not liked the idea, which took up another day of negotiations.

Clare's phone rang. She was in the kitchen. She moved to the other room with Tremayne and Mavis.

'Is it?' Mavis whispered. Clare nodded her head.

'Sergeant Yarwood, the money is to be deposited in cash at a location in Southampton. I suggest you leave now.'

'And Rachel?'

'We will discuss that later.'

Tremayne looked over at Clare, gave her a clear sign to follow instructions. Clare walked out of the front door of the house and settled herself into the Bentley, her phone on hands-free, a location device fitted inside the car. She pulled out of the driveway and headed towards Southampton. There was an explicit instruction to all police vehicles to report if they saw the car, but not to hinder its progress.

Clare arrived in Southampton. Her mind was focussed on handing over the money, expendable as far as all were concerned, and taking Rachel back to her mother.

She headed for the dock area, as per the instruction received. Her phone rang. 'You will leave there and drive to Southsea. You can use the car's GPS to find the way.'

'I know the way,' Clare said. 'Is this going to continue?'

'It will until I am satisfied that you are alone.'

'We want Rachel, not you.'

It was twenty miles; the traffic was heavy. She arrived in Southsea on the Hampshire coast. She parked the car near the South Parade Pier. Her phone rang. 'Proceed to the corner of Nightingale Road and Kent Road.'

Clare followed instructions, saw a police car not far away, its number plate recognition technology picking up the Bentley. Clare knew that her phone's location, as well as the car's position, would be confirmed as one and the same. She could only imagine the situation at Mavis's house, the assembled family waiting for news. She knew that Tremayne would be smoking more than usual.

'You will see in front of you a rubbish bin. You will place the money in there and leave.'

'Rachel?'

'Until you remove that police car from the other side of the road, she will not be freed.'

Clare phoned Tremayne. 'Please keep all vehicles away from the area,' she said.

One phone call and the police car left.

'Now, put the money in the bin and leave.'

'Rachel?'

'She is here with me.'

'I need to talk to her.'

'Clare, I'm fine. Do what he says,' Rachel said in the background.

With the money placed where instructed, Clare waited. Five minutes later, an open-bed truck pulled up alongside the bin. A man got out of the driver's seat, picked up the bin and put it in the back. The truck then drove off. Clare noted the number, although she did not inform anyone of it.

'Good, I can see that you're following instructions.'

'Rachel?'

'You will drive to Buckler's Hard on the Beaulieu River.'

'That will take me nearly two hours,' Clare said. 'You have reneged on our agreement.'

'Not at all. I will wait for the truck to come to me. Once I have the money, you will have Rachel.'

Clare phoned Tremayne, told him of the situation. 'You've no option,' Tremayne said.

'What about Rachel?' Mavis asked.

'I've spoken to her,' Clare said.

'And?'

'She said she was fine. Let me carry on with what I'm doing.'

'We trust you, Clare.'

'Thanks.'

It was over thirty miles to Buckler's Hard, now a tourist attraction. In the past, it had been a busy shipbuilding community that had built ships for Horatio Nelson, the great naval hero of Trafalgar.

After an hour and twenty minutes, another phone call. 'I have the money. I will need another three hours.'

'This is not the agreement.'

'It is the only agreement if you want the young woman returned.'

'Is she unharmed?'

'She is well.'

'That's not what I asked.'

'She will be returned in one piece. Be thankful for that. And do not phone Detective Inspector Tremayne again. If your phone rings, check it is my number.'

'Your number keeps changing.'

'To stop you tracing it.'

'Then how will I know it is you?'

'The last three digits will be 346.'

Clare arrived at Buckler's Hard. It was late in the day, and the tourists had left. She found a café open and ordered two sandwiches and coffee. She had to admit the village was attractive. Her phone rang, it was Tremayne. She cancelled the phone call and sent an SMS instead.

No more contact until Rachel is free. Garrett's instructions.

Tremayne understood; Mavis did not.

After two more hours, Clare's phone rang. She checked the last three digits: 346. She pressed the answer button.

'At the top of the village, there is a park bench. Can you see it?'

'Yes.'

'Underneath the left-hand leg there is an envelope with a key. Inside you will find an address. Rachel Winters is there.'

Clare walked up to the bench, felt underneath the leg, found an envelope. She opened it and then phoned Tremayne. 'It's a five-minute walk from where I am.'

'We'll get down there as soon as possible.'

'Don't. We've played this his way so far. Let me get Rachel first.'

The road up to the farmhouse was not in good condition; it was quicker to walk, although Clare ran. At the farmhouse, rundown but still with a rustic charm, she found the main door. She inserted the key; it opened. She moved quickly through the house, checking the downstairs, then upstairs. In a bedroom at the top, she found Rachel, restrained, her mouth covered with tape. She was conscious and alive. Clare quickly removed the ropes securing her, and the tape from her mouth.

'Clare, thank you, thank you.'

Rachel had her arms around Clare; both women were in tears. Clare called Tremayne, barely able to operate the phone. 'I've got her.'

Rachel spoke to her mother who was hugging Tremayne. After five minutes, while everyone calmed down, Clare was able to talk to Rachel. 'What happened?'

'They left this morning. Barbara treated me well, especially after...'

'After what?'

'I tried to escape. Archie went mad, beat me the same way he had beaten Uncle Dean.'

'How are you now?'

'With you here, I'm fine.'

A police car from the local police station pulled up outside, as well as an ambulance. Clare spoke to them, informed them of the situation. She was taking Rachel back to her family home.

Chapter 25

Archie Garrett boarded the plane at Heathrow. He had made contacts over the years; a false passport and the necessary documentation were his. He knew that where he was going, life would be excellent, although without Barbara it would not be the same. He had given her enough to survive, and she had been guilty of no other crime than kidnapping. He knew that it would be Dean Winters who would care for her, whether she was in prison or not. The man was weak, whereas he, Archie Garrett, was not. He would never fly for British Airways again, never see England, but the one thing he regretted most of all was that he would never see his beloved sister, the only person who could understand what had happened when they were children.

Once Archie's plane had left, Barbara Winters phoned Tremayne. She was arrested the day after Rachel had returned to the family home.

***

Tremayne had not expected to hear from Barbara Winters unless it was as a result of the search for the woman, and there she was, on his phone. 'Archie's gone.'

'Gone where?'

'He's left the country. I'm willing to hand myself in.'

Not willing to take the risk, Tremayne phoned a local police station in London close to the address that the woman had given as her location. Fifteen minutes later, she was in their custody. Three hours later, she was in the back seat of Clare's car. Clare was driving, with Tremayne in the back handcuffed to Barbara Winters. 'I'll not cause you any trouble,' she had said.

Upon arrival at Bemerton Road, Dean Winters was waiting. He rushed up to his wife, threw his arms around her and kissed her. She turned away. 'I'm guilty of kidnapping Rachel.'

'I'll wait,' Dean said. Clare could see romance in the scene; Tremayne thought the man a whimpering fool.

Superintendent Moulton was delighted; a murderer in custody, waiting to be charged. Tremayne felt that the man was premature. It was clear that Barbara Winters had crimes to answer to, but homicide was still far from certain.

The scene at the Quidhampton home the previous day, when Clare had driven in with Rachel, had been jubilant. Tremayne was there, proud of his sergeant, not willing to show it other than to offer his congratulations for good policing, although wanting to give her a hug.

No such reluctance to show emotion inhibited Rachel's mother. She grabbed hold of her daughter who winced from the pain, her mother easing off, not letting her go. Once the initial tender moment was over, Mavis embraced Clare, even lifting her off the ground. 'Thank you for bringing my daughter back to me,' she said. 'Anything you want, just say the word.'

Clare wanted to say give me the Bentley. She knew she'd be back to driving a police issue car, nothing compared to the elegance of the car she had just been driving. Inside the house, Gerry and Cyril were pleased to see Rachel back, Dean was apologetic for his wife, and Bertie struggled to say anything.

A doctor was on hand to check Rachel out. 'I need a bath first,' she said. Mavis almost bounded up the stairs to run the water, Rachel sat downstairs. Tremayne wanted to ask questions but decided that could wait.

Tremayne phoned Stan and Fred Winters to update them; both men were appreciative of the call. A police commendation was due for Clare, too, for the manner in which she had dealt with the woman's rescue, a satisfactory outcome for all concerned.

Once Clare had released Rachel from the cottage, the local police established a crime scene. Jim Hughes and his crime scene investigators were dispatched to check out the cottage, reporting nothing untoward other than that three people had been there, their fingerprints all on record. A local shopkeeper remembered Archie Garrett when she was shown a photo.

***

Barbara Winters, after being formally charged with the kidnapping of Rachel Winters, had been taken to the interview room. Dean had wanted to employ a lawyer; Barbara had declined. And besides, she had no intention of denying the charge.

Outside the interview room, Dean waited. Inside, Tremayne and Clare sat on one side of the table; on the other, the charged woman.

Tremayne followed the procedure, informed Barbara Winters of her rights. Once that was over, the questioning began. 'Mrs Winters, you have been charged with the kidnapping and holding for ransom of Rachel Winters. Is there anything you want to say in your defence?'

'I am offering no defence. I'm guilty as charged.'

'Your brother, Archie Garrett, is no longer in the country, is that true?'

'I have already told you this.'

'Do you know where he has gone?'

'I do not know.'

'But you could have gone?'

'Yes.'

Clare looked at the woman, could only see someone oblivious to the seriousness of her situation. If she had been on drugs, the police sergeant would have said she was high.

'Why didn't you go?' Clare asked.

'I could not agree with what he did to Rachel.'

'Why?'

'My father had treated me that way.'

'And you were reliving it?'

'I liked Rachel. She was my friend, and I allowed her to be hurt.'

'And your brother?'

'He has become what our father was. I no longer want to be with him. I want to be with Dean.'

'You will go to jail.'

'Dean will wait,' Barbara Winters said.

'We have contacted Interpol, the overseas police agencies, to keep a watch out for your brother. We will find him in due course,' Tremayne said.

'You will not. He knows his way around the world.'

Tremayne knew that the woman was probably telling the truth, although two million soon goes, or one million five hundred thousand, as he had given his sister half a million at Heathrow. Once the man had exhausted his money staying hidden he would eventually tire of exile and would return.

'We need to know about Stonehenge. How and why you and your brother killed Alan Winters.'

'We did not kill him.'

'But you hated the man and what he represented.'

'I hated his family and the money he had stolen.'

'Gambling is perfectly legal in this country.'

'Not to my brother and myself.'

'Yet you are willing to accept two million pounds for returning Rachel?'

'It was only the money that Dean had signed over to Archie before...'

'Before we broke up your little tête-à-tête. Your brother nearly beat Dean to death for that money, and you say it was illegal money. Why did you want it when you would not accept the hundred thousand? Were you holding out in the hope of a bigger payout? Did you murder Alan Winters because you couldn't control him, assuming his wife would be more generous? I put it to you that you contrived a plan to take him up to Stonehenge, to point the blame away from you and your brother.'

'It's not true. We're innocent of his murder. That would be against God's law.'

'Isn't kidnapping?'

'Yes, but...'

'But what? Mrs Winters, you and your brother murdered Alan Winters. Who did you think to place the blame on? His wife, his children, his brothers? Mrs Winters, you and your brother killed Alan Winters solely for the sake of getting two million pounds. How do you plead?'

Clare thought that her senior had gone too far, but said nothing.

'We did not kill Alan Winters.'

'Then who did? Your brother has the anger, the ability to inflict violence, and you both had a motive. Why have you handed yourself in? Are you hoping to make a plea bargain?'

'We are innocent.'

'Then why take the two million? And don't give me that baloney that you were going to use the money for good.'

'That is what it was for. We had great plans.'

'And what happened? You and your brother saw the money, decided it was better in your pockets than in those of a starving child in a refugee camp, is that it?'

'No, yes. I'm confused,' Barbara Winters said.

'I suggest a ten-minute break,' Clare said. Tremayne took the hint.

'You were tough in there, guv,' Clare said once the two of them were outside the interview room.

'I need to break through. I need to know the truth.'

'And she's not giving it?'

'Not yet.'

'She could be telling the truth.'

'If it's not them, then who else could have killed Alan Winters?'

'Polly Bennett and Liz Maybury?'

'But why? Alan was the sugar daddy, not Mavis.'

'They've still achieved their aim.'

234

'Okay, what about the brothers? Alan's given them a hundred thousand each; they want more.'

'Stonehenge?'

'Concentrate on the murderer, not the location.'

The interview recommenced. Barbara Winters looked composed. 'I wish to make a statement.'

'Very well,' Tremayne's reply.

'I am genuinely sorry for what was inflicted on Rachel Winters. My brother, Archie, as a result of what we both suffered as children, holds sway over my life. For many years, he was not around, or at least not on a regular basis, as he was based overseas. My marriage with Dean was troubled, although I still loved him, even if I could not like his family. Rachel, I realise in the time that I spent with her in that farmhouse, is not the same as the other Winters. She is a lovely woman, who I allowed to be beaten by Archie.

'Archie, who suffered more than me as a child, has become what our father was. A man who could be charming, yet held inside him dark secrets and dark thoughts. I instructed Dean to refuse the one hundred thousand pounds initially offered; I saw it as the proceeds of gambling. Dean agreed with me, and besides, we were financially sound. The money was not vital.

'Archie returned to our lives. He became aware of the two million. He said it would be used for good, but now I know that was not the case.

'After Rachel's release, I drove Archie to Heathrow. He boarded a plane and left. There was a ticket for me in a false name; I declined the offer. I am certain that I will not hear from him again. I spent several hours deliberating my future before phoning Detective Inspector Tremayne. My brother was overseas at the time of Alan Winters' death. Neither he nor I were involved, although it is clear that we are the most likely suspects. Regardless of that fact, we are innocent. I will admit my guilt in the kidnapping of Rachel Winters; that is my only crime.'

Clare could tell that the woman had told the truth. She looked at Tremayne.

'Mrs Winters, we will conclude this interview. You will be remanded in custody pending a trial,' Tremayne said.

Outside in the hallway, Dean Winters approached the two police officers. 'My wife?'

'She is in custody,' Clare said.

'Can I see her?'

'It will be arranged.'

Stepping out of the building while Tremayne lit a cigarette, Clare asked him for his evaluation. 'They did not kill Alan Winters,' he said.

'No evidence?'

'The woman is penitent. She told the truth.'

'The family?'

'Who else? The Winters family's problems are not over yet. Two of them are guilty, and the man's death has given them sufficient motive.'

'Who's the most likely?'

'Mavis.'

Chapter 26

Tremayne knew of one way to bring the investigation to a conclusion. He'd used it before; it was brutal and people's emotions would be laid raw. Before he arranged it, he needed to talk to Mavis. He knew she was the prime suspect now, in that she had received the lion's share of the money, and if she were guilty, she would have had an accomplice.

Tremayne phoned Jim Hughes, the CSE. 'Two people at Stonehenge?' he asked.

'Two to carry the body to the Altar Stone, one to inflict the fatal wound,' Hughes's reply.

'Any possibility of cult behaviour, ritual?'

'You've read my report.'

'I'm just running ideas past you. I need to raise the heat to wrap up this case.'

'Alan Winters' death has a sense of the macabre, nothing more.'

'Someone with a dark humour?'

'Maybe. The man was the golden goose, hardly a reason to kill him though.'

'Unless others gained from his death.'

'Did some?'

'They did, but they could not have been sure beforehand.'

'The two million for each of his brothers could have been known.'

Tremayne ended the phone call, sat back in his chair. It was early in the afternoon. Clare was busy typing up a report.

'Tremayne, is that all you've got to do?' Moulton said as he walked in the door.

'What do you think I'm doing?'

'Sleeping by the look of it.'

'I'm thinking through the case, trying to get an angle on who would gain from the man's death, and why.'

'I'll grant that you and your sergeant handled the kidnapping of Rachel Winters well enough, but this murder enquiry has dragged on too long. I need it wrapped up within five days.'

'Why the deadline?'

'The usual.'

'I'll fight you on that.'

'That's why I'm letting you know. I don't want a battle on my hands. If you wrap this up, I'll make sure you're not on the list.'

'Magnanimous of you, sir.'

'Not magnanimous, just being a realist. I've got a big enough fight arguing to secure enough money to make Bemerton Road viable. I just don't want you giving me aggravation as well.'

'It won't be the same, you not dropping in every five minutes with your latest retirement offer,' Tremayne said.

'That's as maybe. Five days and then someone needs to be charged with the murder of Alan Winters.'

'We'll do our best,' Tremayne said as Moulton left.

Clare came into Tremayne's office. 'Friendly?' she said.

'We've got five days.'

'Mavis?'

'She's the only one who knew what would happen on her husband's death.'

'But you don't believe it was her?'

'I don't want to.'

'You can't let personal feelings interfere with this.'

'I'll do my duty, the same as you. You're friendly with the woman as well.'

'I admire her. She's a thoroughly decent human being. You could have done worse than her, guv.'

'Maybe,' Tremayne said.

***

Tremayne and Clare found Mavis at the house in Quidhampton. She was fussing over Rachel. Both of the women gave Clare a hug first and then Tremayne. He was a little embarrassed by the show of affection.

'How are you, Rachel?' Clare asked.

'I'm fine, thanks to you.'

'Any long-lasting effects?'

'Am I mentally scarred, is that what you are asking?'

'At least you can talk about it. And you're a strong-minded individual. Dean, unfortunately, is not,' Clare said.

'He's determined to make sure she has the best legal team on her side.'

'How do you feel about it?'

'I'm down nearly two million pounds as a result of her, what do you think?'

'I think you'll support Dean with whatever he wants.'

'You're right, I suppose.'

'Our visit is not social,' Tremayne said. He had taken a seat in the kitchen, the cook busy at the other end preparing the evening meal.

'You'll stay?' Mavis asked.

'You may not want us to,' Clare said.

'You'd better explain.'

Tremayne stood up, took the mug of coffee that the cook thrust into his hand. 'Archie Garrett and Barbara Winters did not murder Alan,' he said.

'Then who did?' Rachel asked.

'Someone in this family.'

'One of us?' Mavis said.

'There is no proof against Garrett and Dean's wife. Archie Garrett's alibi holds up, and Barbara could not have committed the murder on her own.'

'But she could have with Dean?'

'It's a possibility. Mavis, you've given two million pounds to each of the brothers?'

'That's been done, but you've known that for some time.'

'Did Alan's brothers know that you would do that if you had financial control.'

'Gerry did.'

'You had discussed the possibility with him?'

'Not in detail, but we spent a lot of time together. If I went anywhere, he'd invariably drive.'

'And you used to speak with him.'

'Just chatting mainly.'

'But he was concerned about the money that was being wasted?'

'He enjoyed spending the money, and he had no problems getting drunk with Alan, taking on his women.'

'Polly Bennett and Liz Maybury?'

'Yes.'

'Where is Bertie?'

'You don't suspect him? Mavis said. Clare could see the concern on the woman's face.

'Not entirely, but I need everyone here. We need to wrap this up.'

'It will destroy Mum,' Rachel said.

'It is not the victim who suffers in a murder, it is those who are left, and I must do my duty,' Tremayne said.

'That's why we liked you all those years ago,' Mavis said.

'You may not like me after tonight.'

'We will.'

'I want Polly and Liz here as well.'

'If it is required.'

'It is. And Bertie, what's his condition?'

'Asleep.'

'Drugs?'

'He'll be fine. When do you want everyone here?'

'One hour. That's Cyril, Gerry, and Dean as well.'

'They may not all come,' Rachel said. 'They may be busy.'

'They'll be here. I've already pre-warned Bemerton Road. Either we meet here or at the police station. We know where everyone is and they will all be picked up in a police car and brought here. Yarwood, make the phone call.'

***

It was closer to ninety minutes before everyone was in the house. Polly Bennet and Liz Maybury sat in one corner; Mavis had acknowledged their presence, a courtesy hello. On the other side of the main living room were Cyril, better dressed than usual, Gerry, surprised to see the two women in the house, and Dean, quiet, his head down.

Rachel, dressed for the occasion, instead of the dressing gown she had been wearing earlier, sat next to Clare. Mavis stood in one corner.

'Thanks for coming,' Tremayne said. 'Let me give you all a rundown of the investigation so far.'

'We know what happened,' Bertie said. Clare could see that he had been drinking.

'I need to remind everyone that this is a police investigation into the murder of Alan Winters. If I repeat myself, stating what is already known, then I will. Is that understood?' Tremayne said, directing his gaze at Bertie.

'I suppose so, but I've got to go out in thirty minutes.'

'No one is leaving this house until I've concluded. It's either here or down Bemerton Road Police Station.'

'We understand,' Mavis said.

'Very well. We know that Archie Garrett was not involved in Alan's murder. Not because he would not be capable, but his alibi is watertight. During the hours when the murder was committed, he was at thirty-five thousand feet.'

'Barbara?' Dean said.

'Not on her own, which would mean that you were involved. Were you?'

'I'd not kill my own brother.'

'But one of his brothers did.'

Cyril stood up. 'Not me, not my own brother.' Gerry felt the need to press his innocence as well.

'Don't look at me,' Bertie said.

Tremayne ignored the previous comment. 'The motive is money; the significance of Stonehenge is unclear.'

'Get to the point,' Gerry Winters said. He was trying to avoid looking at Polly and Liz, not successfully.

'Alan, for all his generosity, did not know how to handle the sixty-eight million pounds that he had won. It's not unusual for people with no experience of vast amounts of money to lose it within a short period of time. If Alan had continued the way he was, the money would have all gone in five to ten years. At that time, the Winters family would be back living in a council house and scratching by on a meagre wage. Some of you would be concerned about that; others would not.'

'We'd all be upset if there was no money,' Cyril said.

'The issue is not whether you would be concerned in five to ten years. The issue is whether you understood the situation and were willing to do something about it before that time.'

'What do you mean?'

'Mavis is clearly more financially competent than Alan. With her, the family fortune is safe. All of you would recognise that fact. Since she has gained control of the money, she has given each of the brothers two million pounds, something that Alan had not. The most he had given was one hundred thousand each, on Mavis's urging. As far as Alan was concerned, he'd won the money fair and square; it was up to him who he gave it to.'

'Why are we here?' Polly Bennett asked.

'I'm coming to that,' Tremayne said. 'Mavis had told Gerry that she would give a substantial amount of money to each of the brothers. He probably told Cyril, possibly Stan. Stan, as we know, is in prison so he could not have been involved in the murder, as is the case with Fred. Cyril is too laid back, similar to Alan. He'd wait until the money ran out before complaining, and he was quite happy to live in his council house as long as he had sufficient money to live on. Dean was in Southampton under Barbara's control. Which means there are two possibilities. It was either Dean and Barbara who killed Alan, or else it was Gerry and one other.'

Dean was quick to protest his innocence; Gerry was not.

'Which of you two killed Alan Winters?' Tremayne asked.

'I didn't,' Dean said. 'Barbara may have had her faults, but murder was not one of them.'

'Yet she allowed her brother to beat you, almost killed you, and then there is what happened to Rachel.'

'The woman was kind,' Rachel said.

'Maybe she was, but she does what her brother tells her. Maybe Dean knew about the possibility of the two million, told his wife, who then told her brother. Archie could have been the driving force up at Stonehenge, Dean doing what he was told, but there's another complication.'

'And what is it?' Mavis asked.

'The reason Polly and Liz are here,' Tremayne said.

'What have we got to do with this?' Liz Maybury said.

'You were screwing him, you and Polly,' Mavis said. Up till then, she had been polite to the women. Tremayne was pleased. Everyone was starting to get a little tense.

Tremayne continued. 'On the night of the murder, Alan was with Polly and Liz. Outside, according to the two women, was the Bentley. Who was in that car? It would normally be Gerry.'

'Not that night. Alan was driving the car.'

'That's the first time that anyone's admitted to that, and why didn't Alan tell the women that he was driving? And how did the three get to their place?'

'I drove them, and then I left the car and took a taxi home.'

'And now you are sleeping with Polly and Liz?'

'You know that, and so what?'

'The two women had not been responsive to you when you had no money, but once Alan was dead, you were in their bed. Is that correct?'

'Not for some time.'

'Not until you told them about the two million. And even before you had the money, they were sleeping with you. Let me evaluate Polly and Liz.'

Clare looked over at the two women. 'DI Tremayne will not be diplomatic. Please say nothing,' she said.

'Thanks, Yarwood. Polly Bennett and Liz Maybury are ambitious women. They are not afraid of hard work, as can be seen by the furniture store that they convinced Alan to buy for them. He did not, however, give them a clear title. They knew this, and it's possible he was tired of them. Both of the women are bisexual by their own admission. They are willing to use their bodies to get what they want, and Alan was the vessel through which they channelled their efforts. They are also intelligent and able to formulate the way forward. They could see that Alan was a hopeless cause, whereas Gerry was not, and if he had two million, then they would have had no trouble transferring their affections to him. Also, he was able to convince Mavis, or she had figured it out, that the furniture store remained a significant asset, and that it would be better to let the two women stay there until the business could be sold. After the altercation between Liz and Mavis, the relationship between Mavis and the two women has been tenuous but workable.'

'It's purely business,' Mavis said.

'Cyril, I'm discounting you from our enquiry,' Tremayne said.

'Thank you.'

'Don't thank me. It's only because you have no drive and no ambition. It's hardly a ringing endorsement. Dean, you were not involved. Not because Archie would not have been capable, but he wasn't there, and his violence comes from anger. It needed a clear head to take Alan up to Stonehenge, someone with the ability to think ahead. Stonehenge was a diversion in that it would shift the blame onto other individuals who had been wronged by Alan, who had failed to give them money when they had asked. It needed Polly and Liz to set it up.'

'We did not kill him,' Liz said. She was on her feet and ready to come forward at Tremayne. Clare interceded and put her back in her seat, roughly pushing on the woman's shoulder.

'Gerry Winters,' Tremayne said, 'you'll be taken to Bemerton Road Police Station for further questioning, as will

Polly Bennett and Liz Maybury. We will find a case against you and the two women for the murder of Alan Winters, your brother.'

'It was Polly's idea,' Liz said.

'You bitch,' Polly said. 'You thought it up, but it was me with Gerry at Stonehenge. And I'm not taking the blame for killing him, that was Gerry.'

'Will you sign a statement to that effect.'

'Yes.'

'You two bitches,' Gerry said. 'If only you had kept quiet. Couldn't you see what Tremayne was trying to do? He had no proof.'

'Gerry, why?' Mavis asked.

'You don't get it, do you? I saw how he treated you; the money he wasted. Someone needed to do something, and you would not have killed him. It was up to me to save the family.'

'At what cost?'

Clare went and sat down next to Rachel, who was in tears. She put her arm around the young woman. Cyril sat still, stunned by the revelation; Dean looked down at the floor. Polly Bennett and Liz Maybury said nothing, both sitting apart.

'Yarwood, ask the two uniforms to come in,' Tremayne said.

Gerry attempted to make a run for it; he had the keys to the Bentley. Outside, the driveway was blocked by a police car. A brief tussle, the handcuffs applied, and he was driven to Bemerton Road. Polly Bennett and Liz Maybury, handcuffed by the two uniforms who had come into the house, were led away.

'I'm sorry about this, Mavis,' Tremayne said.

'It's not your fault. It's the damn money.'

'Maybe Alan wasn't so lucky after all.'

'There was no luck there. It cursed our life, I know that now.'

The End.

ALSO BY THE AUTHOR

Death and the Assassin's Blade – A DI Tremayne Thriller

It was meant to be high drama, not murder, but someone's switched the daggers. The man's death took place in plain view of two serving police officers.

He was not meant to die; the daggers were only theatrical props, plastic and harmless. A summer's night, a production of Julius Caesar amongst the ruins of an Anglo-Saxon fort. Detective Inspector Tremayne is there with his sergeant, Clare Yarwood. In the assassination scene, Caesar collapses to the ground. Brutus defends his actions; Mark Antony rebukes him.

They're a disparate group, the amateur actors. One's an estate agent, another an accountant. And then there is the teenage school student, the gay man, the funeral director. And what about the women? They could be involved.

They've each got a secret, but which of those on the stage wanted Gordon Mason, the actor who had portrayed Caesar, dead?

Murder is the Only Option – A DCI Cook Thriller

A man, thought to be long dead, returns to exact revenge against those who had blighted his life. His only concern is to protect his wife and daughter. He will stop at nothing to achieve his aim.

'Big Greg, I never expected to see you around here at this time of night.'

'I've told you enough times.'

'I've no idea what you're talking about,' Robertson replied. He looked up at the man, only to see a metal pole coming down at him. Robertson fell down, cracking his head against a concrete kerb.

The two vagrants, no more than twenty feet away, did not stir and did not even look in the direction of the noise. If they had, they would have seen a dead body, another man walking away.

Death Unholy – A DI Tremayne Thriller

All that remained were the man's two legs and a chair full of greasy and fetid ash. Little did DI Keith Tremayne know that it was the beginning of a journey into the murky world of paganism and its ancient rituals. And it was going to get very dangerous.

'Do you believe in spontaneous human combustion?' Detective Inspector Keith Tremayne asked.

'Not me. I've read about it. Who hasn't?' Sergeant Clare Yarwood answered.

I haven't,' Tremayne replied, which did not surprise his young sergeant. In the months they had been working together, she had come to realise that he was a man who had little interest in the world. When he had a cigarette in his mouth, a beer in his hand, and a murder to solve he was about the happiest she ever saw him. He could hardly be regarded as one of life's sociable people. And as for reading? The most he managed was an occasional police report or an early morning newspaper, turning first to the back pages for the racing results.

Murder in Little Venice – A DCI Cook Thriller

A dismembered corpse floats in the canal in Little Venice, an upmarket tourist haven in London. Its identity is unknown, but what is its significance?

DCI Isaac Cook is baffled about why it's there. Is it gang-related, or is it something more?

Whatever the reason, it's clearly a warning, and Isaac and his team are sure it's not the last body that they'll have to deal with.

Murder is only a Number – A DCI Cook Thriller

Before she left she carved a number in blood on his chest. But why the number 2, if this was her first murder?

The woman prowls the streets of London. Her targets are men who have wronged her. Or have they? And why is she keeping count?

DCI Cook and his team finally know who she is, but not before she's murdered four men. The whole team are looking for her, but the woman keeps disappearing in plain sight. The pressure's on to stop her, but she's always one step ahead.

And this time, DCS Goddard can't protect his protégé, Isaac Cook, from the wrath of the new commissioner at the Met.

Murder House – A DCI Cook Thriller

A corpse in the fireplace of an old house. It's been there for thirty years, but who is it?

It's clearly murder, but who is the victim and what connection does the body have to the previous owners of the house. What is the motive? And why is the body in a fireplace? It was bound to be discovered eventually but was that what the murderer wanted?

The main suspects are all old and dying, or already dead.

Isaac Cook and his team have their work cut out trying to put the pieces together. Those who know are not talking because of an old-fashioned belief that a family's dirty laundry should not be aired in public, and certainly not to a policeman – even if that means the murderer is never brought to justice!

Murder is a Tricky Business – A DCI Cook Thriller

A television actress is missing, and DCI Isaac Cook, the Senior Investigation Officer of the Murder Investigation Team at Challis Street Police Station in London, is searching for her.

Why has he been taken away from more important crimes to search for the woman? It's not the first time she's gone missing, so why does everyone assume she's been murdered?

There's a secret, that much is certain, but who knows it? The missing woman? The executive producer? His eavesdropping assistant? Or the actor who portrayed her fictional brother in the TV soap opera?

Murder Without Reason – A DCI Cook Thriller

DCI Cook faces his greatest challenge. The Islamic State is waging war in England, and they are winning.

Not only does Isaac Cook have to contend with finding the perpetrators, but he is also being forced to commit actions contrary to his mandate as a police officer.

And then there is Anne Argento, the prime minister's deputy. The prime minister has shown himself to be a pacifist and is not up to the task. She needs to take his job if the country is to fight back against the Islamists.

Vane and Martin have provided the solution. Will DCI Cook and Anne Argento be willing to follow it through? Are they able to act for the good of England, knowing that a criminal and murderous action is about to take place? Do they have any option?

The Haberman Virus

A remote and isolated village in the Hindu Kush mountain range in North Eastern Afghanistan is wiped out by a virus unlike any seen before.

A mysterious visitor clad in a space suit checks his handiwork, a female American doctor succumbs to the disease, and the woman sent to trap the person responsible falls in love with him – the man who would cause the deaths of millions.

Hostage of Islam

Three are to die at the Mission in Nigeria: the pastor and his wife in a blazing chapel; another gunned down while trying to defend them from the Islamist fighters.

Kate McDonald, an American, grieving over her boyfriend's death and Helen Campbell, whose life had been troubled by drugs and prostitution, are taken by the attackers.

Kate is sold to a slave trader who intends to sell her virginity to an Arab Prince. Helen, to ensure their survival, gives herself to the murderer of her friends.

Malika's Revenge

Malika, a drug-addicted prostitute, waits in a smugglers' village for the next Afghan tribesman or Tajik gangster to pay her price, a few scraps of heroin.

Yusup Baroyev, a drug lord, enjoys a lifestyle many would envy. An Afghan warlord sees the resurgence of the Taliban. A Russian white-collar criminal portrays himself as a good and honest citizen in Moscow.

All of them are linked in an audacious plan to increase the quantity of heroin shipped out of Afghanistan and into Russia and ultimately the West.

Some will succeed, some will die, some will be rescued from their plight and others will rue the day they became involved.

ABOUT THE AUTHOR

Phillip Strang was born in England in the late forties, during the post-war baby boom. He had a comfortable middle-class upbringing, spending his childhood years in a small town seventy miles west of London.

His childhood and the formative years were a time of innocence. There were relatively few rules, and as a teenager he had complete freedom, thanks to a bicycle – a three-speed Raleigh. It was in the days before mobile phones, the internet, terrorism and wanton violence. He was an avid reader of science fiction in his teenage years: Isaac Asimov, Frank Herbert, the masters of the genre. Much of what they and others mentioned has now become a reality. Science fiction has now become science fact. Still an avid reader, the author now mainly reads thrillers.

In his early twenties, the author, with a degree in electronics engineering and a desire to see the world, left the cold, damp climes of England for Sydney, Australia – his first semi-circulation of the globe. Now, forty years later, he still resides in Australia, although many intervening years were spent in a myriad of countries, some calm and safe, others no more than war zones.